I0660238

# Let's Talk...
# Love Therapy

------

## LB TAYLOR

Let's talk… Love Therapy
Copyright © 2018 by (LB Taylor)

All rights reserved. No part of this book may be reproduced or transmitted in any form or by any means without written permission from the author.

This is a work of fiction. Names, characters, places, and incidents either are the product of the author's imagination or are used fictitiously.

ISBN 978-1-7327818-0-1

Front and Back cover photo by Freddi Brown Photography
Book design by LB Taylor

Printed in USA by CreateSpace (www.createspace.com)

# *Table of Contents*

# *Acknowledgments*

First and foremost, I give all praise and thanks to God, it is because of Him I was able to start and finish this book. I thank God daily for my many blessings and struggles. It took me years to understand that my struggles were a part of the blessing. Writing this book has not only been a blessing, but also turned out to be very therapeutic. The more I wrote, the more I saw some of my own life experiences as I developed Gia's character. It is nearly impossible to write about dating as a single woman and not reflect on your own dating experiences. Seeing parts of yourself through someone else's eyes can be a scary thing, but very enlightening at the same time. This book was not developed overnight; it has taken me over three years to complete. I still to this day don't know if I would call it writer's block or just me being afraid to embark on this thing called writing. There are so many people I want to acknowledge. However, I am unable to name everyone.

To my daughters, Gabrielle and Madison: Thank you for your love and support throughout this entire process. None of this would have been possible without your daily words of encouragement, which meant so much to me. You continued to push me whenever I talked about being tired or uncertain that I could do this. Your love and strength held me down and kept me going. You helped me make important decisions when it came to my book, the cover, and so much more. Gabrielle, when I said to you, I needed a manager, you stepped up and took the lead with no questions asked. I remember sending you an event I wanted to attend and you told me "No Mom, that is not a good use of your time!" LOL. I knew at that moment you were on top of your management game and the only manager for me! Madison, for you to be so young, you are wise beyond your years. You have given me some of the best advice during this process. In between classes, homework, and just your normal college student responsibilities, you still managed to send your mom the best input I could have ever gotten—and for free. I am so thankful for you both, you guys made being a single mom the best job ever! I thank God every day for you

1

and pray that you know that every book I write, every decision I make, everything I do, I do for the two of you. I am so extremely proud of you both! But most importantly, I am so grateful that God chose me to be your mom! I love you more than life itself. xoxo 😲😲

To my mom, Billie: Thank you for your continuous love and support! You have been here for me from the very beginning, no matter the need. I was not always the easiest child to raise with this mouth of mine; but you allowed me to grow through your guidance and support. I could not have asked for a better role model for myself and my daughters. You are not only an amazing mom, but an even more amazing grandmother to all of your grandchildren. It is because of you that I am the strong, confident woman I am today. However, no matter how old I get, I will continue to look to you for all the answers. You have no idea the joy you bring to my life. You are always there to listen and to give advice as needed. You encourage me to be the best me I can possibly be and to never give up on my dreams. Whenever I need you, I always know you are just a phone call away. Thank you for being the best mom and friend a girl could ever ask for. You are my ROCK and I love you so much! xoxo

To my bonus son, Jeremy: Thank you for being the special young man you are. Thank you for all the love and support you've shown me throughout this process. I appreciate all the advice and encouraging words you provided me with. There was never a hesitation when asked to help out with my book signings, podcast shows, or anything pertaining to this process. You are the best bonus son ever! Love ya! xoxo

To my BFF, Freddi: Thank you for just being you! I cannot express enough how much your friendship means to me. The level of love, respect, trust, and honesty we have for one another is the reason my daughters view our friendship as "friendship goals." I could not have gotten through all the countless days and nights of crying and laughter if it were not for you being there. I also appreciate the fact that you know when to listen and when to give advice without ever passing judgment. We have gone through so much together over our 30+ years of friendship. Whenever I needed to vent I could count on you to be a listening ear. I will never forget that one time I called you in tears because writing this book was starting to get to me, and you told me

"Don'tt stop writing, turn your pain into paper!" I turned that quote into one of my daily affirmations. I look forward to thirty more years. Let's keep showing 'em what real "friendship goals" look like! Love ya! xoxo

To Jade and Wilnona (The And I Thought Ladies): Thank you for encouraging me to continue with my writing. Because of you, I turned my first book into a novel. It's funny how God will place certain people in your life. I was just a complete stranger on a redeye flight back to the city. However, you shared so much, and gave me some great advice, including the idea to start my own podcast show. I will forever be grateful. Much love! xoxo

To my editing team, Iolande V. Argent and Myra Burke: Thank you for being the best thing to happen to me while writing this book. Iolande, as my main editor from start to finish not only did you push me; but as my first book you made the process painless and enjoyable by sharing all your knowledge. You taught me a lot about editing and writing a book, without ever making me feel uncomfortable or unknowledgeable. You gave clear deadlines and timeframes to help keep me on course. Myra, without hesitation, you came in near the middle as a second set of eyes but became so much more. You gave me some amazing feedback. You took me back to school with your "RED mark-ups" but I am thankful because it forced me to reread my manuscript each time. Your editing skills and suggestions were much appreciated. I would not have been able to complete this book if it were not for the two of you. Behind every great writer is a bomb-ass editor! You ladies were such a blessing. Much love! xoxo

To my "A" Team, LaKesha and Darah: Thank you so very much for being the best team a girl could ask for. When I came to the two of you and asked if you would be "readers" for my manuscript, you guys agreed without hesitation and did an amazing job with your feedback and suggestions. You became readers and editors all-in-one. I am so blessed to have the two of you in my corner! Until the next book... Love ya! xoxo

To my cover design team, Billie, Freddi, Velvet, Marla, Darah and LaKesha: Thank you for being a huge part of that process. I created so many designs but you all were troopers and never complained. To my website designer, Darah, thank you for spending your lunch breaks and time after work to put together one amazing website. Much love! xoxo

To my girl-gang, Regina D, Staci, Maelena, Crystal W, Danica, Toni W, Karma, Jacqui, Velvet, Toni B, Monica, Kia, Angela, Dawn, Brandi, Kendra, Debbie B, Nikki, Bridget, Patt, Darcia, and my sisterhood-cousins: Thank you for all the love and support you have shown me while writing this book. What I love most about my girl-gang is that it consists of family and friends. I am blessed to be surrounded by a core group of women. You guys make life fun and our "Girls Night" lit! I would like to give a special thanks to everyone who has participated on my podcast show (Love/Sex/andLies...Let's Talk). Again, I am unable to name everyone, but know that I am thankful for the role each of you play in my life. Your love and support is unmeasurable. Love ya! Xoxo

Special thank you to Travers Johnson: writer, editor, and content strategist with more than twelve years of experience in print publishing, digital media, and communications. I don't know what I would have done without your sharp eye and great editing skills. I appreciate you for taking on this project. You're the BEST! xoxo

# *Introduction*

I am a member of the tiny team, standing at five fabulous feet and two cute inches. I have curves in all the right places. My complexion could be considered creamy caramel with freckles that make my face pop. My long dark curly hair beautifully accents my African American features. I'm an established entrepreneur who also works a full time job everyday as a Business Analyst for a premier contracting firm in my area.

My pulse quickens a bit as I sit here in the waiting area for my first bi-weekly counseling session with Dr. Edwards. I'm rather nervous because although I was referred to him by one of my girlfriends, when I first called to make the appointment I wanted to be sure that Dr. Edwards would be the best fit for me. My main concern was that I did not want someone who would simply pacify me; I expressed to him that I was not looking for a "yes doctor". A person like me needs someone who is perceptive enough to not only notice when I'm bullshitting but also have the fortitude and willingness to call me out on it. Once he assured me that he's been in the business for more than 10 years and has a proven track record of calling a spade a spade, I could see why my girlfriend thought that we would be a good fit. He goes on to ask if there were any areas in my life that I wanted to discuss. Well, being an extremely private person makes it really hard for me, however, I do recognize that I need help when it comes to my private life, and being guarded.

Although I knew I came to talk about certain things in my life, hearing Dr. Edwards be so direct about it caught me off guard. All of my memories just began to flood back into my head, vivid remembrances of my experiences. I took a deep breath and reassured myself that this is an opportunity for me to lean on someone else about the things going on in my life and receive honest and unbiased feedback.

As I take my first few trepid steps into Dr. Edwards' office, I remember our initial telephone conversation where he asked if there were any specific areas of my life that I wanted to focus our discussion around. Of course, I start with the Big 3: Control – I consider myself a huge control-freak; Privacy – I am over-the-top private; and finally, to call myself Guarded would be the understatement of the year!

I'm inside Dr. Edwards' office, which is located on the campus of one of the local universities. It is not what you would expect; it is small and old looking, as if the university has not done any upgrades since its existence. And on top of that, the air conditioner barely works. Dr. Edwards is a lot younger than I expected, I was looking for a man well into his fifties. He looks to be in his [insert age] and is probably 5'8, has a brown complexion, and wears eyeglasses. He is not flashy with his style of dress (unless you consider khaki pants with a pullover sweater flashy). Dr. Edwards makes me feel comfortable immediately. He started the conversation off with basic questions about me, my age, birthday, my life, and my kids.

I am a single mom of two amazing daughters. My oldest daughter recently graduated from a top university and my youngest daughter is a freshman at one of the top boarding schools in the States. "Wow! You must be proud of them both," he said. "Absolutely," I replied. "They made being a single mom easy for the most part. My oldest, Peyton, has no problem verbalizing her view on my freakish controlling ways and how I take being private to another level."

He jumped straight into the nitty gritty of my purpose for wanting therapy. "Ms. Williams, over the phone you mentioned that you were a control freak. Let's go into more detail as to what a control freak means to you and how we can get to the core of it. Can you give me an example of a particular instance?"

"No, not really, because it's in all areas of my life! Personal, work, relationships and friendships! However, I will say this, my daughter (Peyton) doesn't like when I give them the "eye" whenever we are in the middle of a conversation with anyone outside of us. She said it's weird because I won't even share what would be considered normal girl talk. (I'm laughing)

"Well is that true," he inquired.

"Yeah. It's very hard for me to share because I don't trust anyone," I replied. "I believe the only way for something not to be repeated is by not telling it to begin with. I'm not saying this is the best way to handle things but it works for me."

"Okay, we need to figure out what's got you so protective of any and everything having to do with your personal life," he said.

"Yeah, I know but if it helps, I've been this way since high school. The privacy part comes from experiencing secrets being told by previous friends. It taught me at a young age to protect the things I don't want repeated. Now, I may have taken that to another level." (We both are laughing now).

Dr. Edwards then proceeds to tell me that he believes it is deeper than that. "Deeper than what,", I question. "Deeper than high school friends telling secrets. I am not saying that this wasn't a true experience for you and caused you to close up some, but I think that if you took a very introspective look at your life and who you are, there lies the real answer to really why you are so private and guarded. I want you to take the next week or so and just meditate on who you are and what causes you to be private. Think of a moment you've had where you have felt the need to not open up when appropriate and what stops you. Whatever that 'what' is will help you get to the root of things."

I thought to myself, "Dang, he really is diving right into it. I just met you sir, geez." But, as I said before I needed someone to be direct with me.

Dr. Edwards and I go on to discuss some other personal issues and before I know it my hour is up.

I schedule my next two-week appointment with him because I like his style. I think this therapy thing may work out for me after all.

Now let me take you all on this journey as I share my experiences on dating. The struggles are real when it comes to my dating life. The love, sex, and lies, on top of all my ups and downs will keep you wanting more. My strength, along with my flaws, are immeasurable.

# 1

## Girl Talk
## ***Friends with Benefits vs Booty Call***

It is the weekend and it's time for some Girl Talk. Ladies, I first have to ask, is there a difference between "friends with benefits (FWB)" and a "booty call (BC);" or are they one and the same?

This is one of those topics that could be debated for days. However, for me, there is a difference. When I think of FWB, I think of someone that I have a friendship with, and it is not just about the sex. Again, this is just me and my take on the difference. At this point in my life, I have had three FWB relationships; two of which lasted for three or more years; and those first two FWBs were years prior to me meeting FWB number three.

Now for FWB number three, his name is Rashad and I cannot speak about him in the past tense because he's still very much a part of my life. This man is many things to me, and it's funny, because he came into my life at a point when I had not only decided to practice celibacy, but also had already been celibate for two years. I still to this day cannot explain how this man was able to get me into bed after making a promise to myself that I would ONLY DATE with NO SEX.

Rashad is that guy that we all meet in our lifetime, where the usual rules of our life just don't apply. He can send all your rules and inhibitions flying out the window. You know he is not the man you want to be in a relationship with, but you cannot not have him in your life. Yes, he is that guy.

After it was all said and done, I knew that I wanted Rashad in my life. This man allowed me to feel free right away, and that scared the hell out of me. The main reason FWB relationships work so well for me is that I am so guarded. I figure, why not get the best of both worlds without having to let down my guard. FWB number three was not exactly like the other two. He was/still is a challenge but a challenge that I will gladly take on. I never thought I would meet someone just as guarded as me, and often question why God would ever place someone like that in my life. I ask myself all the time why it is that this Friends with Benefits relationship with this very guarded man works so well for me, but the answer is simple…it just does. This man is easy to talk to, but more importantly, he satisfies me sexually on every level, which is not an easy thing to do.

Therefore, all three relationships were exactly what I needed at that particular point in my life. They each provided me with the consistency that I love, but without the commitment I did not want. For me, it wasn't/isn't about titles or being monogamous, it was/is all about consistency. I love having that one Friend with Benefits that I can depend on when I am horny, wanna go out, or just needed to vent. On so many levels, those relationships allowed me to feel free. As far as I was concerned, I had and still have the best of both worlds. I had some amazing male friends that I could talk to about anything, spend my time with, and have great sex while doing so. Hell, what more could a girl ask for in an uncommitted relationship? Not only do we respect one another's boundaries, but more importantly, neither of my FWBs ever make me feel like I was a part of any type of rotation. When we were together, it was just us spending quality, fun, free time together without all of the hardship that comes in some relationships where a title has been attached. When we are not together, it's cool and we respect each other. Not that the other person isn't thought about, but I'm living my life and he's living his.

So men, take note: if you're going to enter into a Friends with Benefits situation with multiple females, just be mindful not to make them ever feel as though they're a part of a rotation. Especially if you are not able to give them what they need sexually, because you are out here spreading yourself too thin.

I am not interested in having missionary style 15-20 minute quickies with my FWB. I expect more. I want to be turned out each and every time (well, at least most of the time). It's called a sexual relationship for a reason. So men, we want to get turned out and have sex on a regular basis, (at least I know I do....LOL).

Now ladies, you have to be careful of whom you choose to be in these types of relationships with. Just as not every female is cut out for this type of relationship, not every man is cut out for this either. You also have to be careful of who you share this information with. Not each friend will just be happy that you're "gettin' it in" or understand that this is simply where you are right here right now and it's working for you, which at the end of the day is all that matters for real.

Your so-called friends, especially some of the married ones, will be the first to pass judgment. Those friends tend to forget that they were once single and had multiple sex partners, and I am not talking long term Friends with Benefits (them chicks were straight booty calls). It amazes me how certain friends have selective memory about their past once they got married and/or in a committed relationship. Nonetheless, you have to always be secure and confident with your life choices. As for me, I was very happy doing me. Although the "over the top super private" me, learned a long time ago to just keep shit to myself... Well, that was until now.

You may be thinking how can one have sex, go out on dates for years and not get emotionally involved. Well, if you take someone like myself it was easy because I was, well, still am very guarded and over the top private.

I know you must be reading this thinking to yourself; this is some B.S., there is no way you are able to have a long-term sexual relationship and not get emotionally involved. Really? Not only can it be done but also it has been done. I am not saying this is the case for everyone but it is possible. However, if you and your Friend with Benefits fall into something more, that's great. But if not, that's fine too. Granted, it takes a unique personality in order to have this, make it work, and still maintain a friendship once it is over.

Firstly, both parties have to be on the same page. I cannot stress that enough. Some people enter a FWB relationship with the hopes or the goal in mind that this will lead to something greater. This creates a problem if one person is content with keeping you as a FWB, and the other person is trying to take things to another level. It creates a constant cycle of disappointment, feelings of rejection, and hurt from the person that wants more and you don't want your friend to feel like that. So, it creates even more problems than an actual relationship, in my opinion. But when both parties are in agreement that we are only FWB and nothing more, then it can be a beautiful thing, my friends.

Now when I think of a Booty Call, I think of someone that is simply there for late night last minute sex, or better yet "a good fuck." This is who you call when your Friends with Benefits aren't available, or better yet, you do not have a Friend with Benefits in your life. Nevertheless, keep in mind guys & gals if you decide to travel down this road there's no turning back once you've crossed that line. Thus, the two of you may never have a committed relationship if you start as just a "Booty Call." I was always told growing up "once a booty call always a booty call." Therefore, go into this type of arrangement with a full understanding of all the rules associated with being a booty call. You also need to be careful of who you enter this type of arrangement with; this is not something you do with someone you already care about, someone you've been in a previous relationship with, or someone you're emotionally tied to on any level. You must be real with who you are as an individual, because not everyone is capable of handling this type of setup. First, you have to be the type that is able to compartmentalize, because that is the only way this will work successfully.

The booty call owes you nothing and vice versa. Unlike the FWB, you are not friends. This person typically does not care about your well-being no more than the normal concern for humankind. I know it sounds harsh, but it is the truth and I think this reality needs to resonate so you won't allow yourself to get hurt. If you currently are in a booty call situation and the thought of this person not caring for you hurts your feelings, then you may need to check yourself and ask have you developed feelings for your booty call. If that is the case, it's best to end the situation now before it develops further and you end up heartbroken.

You cannot allow your emotions to get involved and the best way to avoid this from happening is by always remembering the following: you never ever kiss, because kissing exceeds the intimacy level for someone you are just fucking. I am not at all saying you cannot enjoy kissing on an oral level with your booty call because you want to get as much enjoyment as you possibly can from this hookup. However, always be selective when it comes to oral sex because that is not something you want to do with everyone! However, it is necessary that you avoid any tongue action, thus keeping your lips away from your partner's mouth. Never allow yourself to get so comfortable with your booty call that you stop using protection. He is not your man; you guys aren't in a monogamous relationship, so he shouldn't reap the benefits of one. Therefore, condoms are your best friend, so ladies don't get caught up on him telling you how he can't feel it when he's wearing a condom, and fellas, don't allow her to tell you how she's on the pill. Understand that even in this day and time, women lie about being on the pill and men just lie…PERIOD.

Bottom line, and I cannot stress this enough: condoms are your best friend and must be worn every time. Again, this holds true across the board, be it a Friend with Benefits or a Booty Call, go into this smart and use protection EVERY TIME. At no point should either of you ever flip the script by trying to turn this into something more. It is called a "booty call" for a reason. In the end, it really does not matter whether you believe there is a difference between the two or if you see them as one and the same. I just want single men and women to know that there is nothing wrong with having a Friend with Benefits and/or being a Booty Call if that's what you so desire.

You have to enter them both with a clear understanding, with absolutely no agenda, and be in control of your emotions at all times. Men, if you are going to have multiple women, make sure you can handle them all adequately. Keep in mind that this is a sexual relationship, so if you are going to put them in a rotation, you have to maintain your part. This means giving the bomb sex to each of your female sex partners. Women, if you are going to take on this challenge you have to stay in control of your emotions. You are both adults, so if you are grown enough to enter into this agreement, then be grown enough to deal with the outcome. If you know going in that "more" is the ONLY thing you are in search of, then clearly this type of arrangement is not for you. In addition, knowing this will prevent anyone from getting hurt in the end.

# 2

# The Carpenter

*Now with that said; let's get into it! Allow me to introduce you to my main man Rashad. He and I were Friends with Benefits and doing it well!*

Let's talk…. I started seeing this guy, Rashad, about a year or so ago. Now I've known Rashad for years, but never saw him as someone I was interested in dating. No particular reason just didn't.

It was late December 2013, my girl Jasmine and I were on our way to a Christmas party happy hour in the city. It was the Thursday evening right before Christmas and two of our girlfriends were hosting the event.

I rode to the lounge with Jasmine; it's a 25-minute ride from where we live. Jasmine got the music jamming in the car trying to get us pumped because normally we would be home in our PJs. It was a cold winter night, but we didn't let that stop us; gotta show support to our girlfriends.

I was wearing this cute black leather jacket, big wrap scarf, jeans, and leopard print booties. Jasmine was rocking jeans, black leather jacket, and cute pumps.

The happy hour was free before 9pm, so we made sure to arrive before there was a cover charge. It was in the city, so parking was limited and the area was a little sketchy. We walked up to the building. It reminds you of a brownstone.

There were two men at the door checking IDs. They directed us to go upstairs. Jasmine and I found seats at one of the tall bistro tables near the front of the lounge.

I walked around to say my hellos; gave hugs and kisses to my two girlfriends who were hosting, then went to the bar to get my normal drink: Malibu rum and pineapple juice). Shortly after being there, Rashad walked up to our table.

"Hey, what's up?" he said.

"Hey Rashad," we answered. "We're drinking and listening to music, having ourselves a good time."

He and Jasmine play catch up while I just sit there listening, joining in from time to time. At one point, I remember thinking to myself how fine Rashad was, I then found myself checking him out.

He was tall, about 6'2", with this beautifully perfect brown complexion. He was slim and bald, with light brown eyes and a full beard. He was fine as shit. It's crazy because I'm somewhat attracted to him and now seeing him in ways I've never seen before.

He was wearing jeans with this bad black leather jacket.

Jasmine says "That's a bad leather jacket, Rashad!"

Rashad responds, "Thanks, I got it from this little shop in Miami a year ago."

"Let me take y'all's picture."

"Okay," we say, and then pose."

We both asked to see the picture and then we asked him to text it to us. I knew Rashad didn't have my number, but I asked anyway.

"Hey, do you have my number?" I asked.

"Nah, I don't think I do," he answered.

"Okay, well take my number so you can send me the pic," I said, knowing I didn't really care about the pic— I just wanted to give him my number.

Rashad started talking about work.

"I'm working overtime tonight," he said.

"What time do you have to go into work?" I asked.

"10"

"Oh wow, you do know it's 9:15; are you gonna make it there in time?"

"Yes, it's right down the street. It will only take 5 to 10 minutes to get there."

"Oh okay, if you say so."

Thirty minutes later Rashad leaves for work. As he walks away I lean my head over and think to myself, damn he has a sexy ass walk. "Breathe, Gia. He's your girl Alanna's BFF and you know how they tell each other everything. You are too private for this to be worth it, you don't want folks in your business," I say to myself. But I take another quick peek anyway.

Ten minutes later, my cell rings. I don't recognize the number, but answer anyway.

"Hello?"

"Hey, I told you I would make it in time." The semi-familiar voice on the other end said.

"Rashad?" I asked, barely able to hear him over the music.

"Yes, I'm at work," he answered.

"Oh, okay! That was fast, I didn't realize how close Union Station was to us."

"Yeah, I told you it was right down the street."

" Well, I'm glad you made it there on time."

"I'll talk to ya later."

"Okay, bye!" I hung up. "Jasmine that was Rashad. He's at work."

"Oh, he called you?" She looked puzzled.

" Yeah, to let us know he made it to work." I said.

" Okay..." Her voice trailed off.

It was funny to me that Jasmine was trying to insinuate something else but I didn't say anything. I'm personally over here pondering the quick call myself. I'm thinking to myself how I was so glad that he called me but I played it cool, and he definitely could not pick it up in my tone.

Fast forward to New Year's Day and I receive a text from Rashad.

"Happy New Year Gia!!! ☺"

"Happy New Year!!" I replied.

A couple days later I receive another text from him, but this time the text is really random and doesn't make much sense.

Rashad: Check out my photo on Tango http://tango.net/q/pic

Gia: What's tango?

Rashad: Video chat... I f$*%ed up by sending that text to my entire contact list! Smdh LOL

Gia: LOL.. So u didn't mean for that text to go out??

Rashad: Sure didn't. I hit the wrong send option. Lls

Gia: Is that like online dating but thru video?

Rashad: No! Lls. Rofl. It's like Skype & IG

Gia: Oh...Lmao. You wouldn't do online dating?? I can't stop laughing....

Rashad: I am on pof... lls

Gia: What's pof? I'm not in the loop. I don't do online dating. Oh Jasmine said it's plenty of fish...lol


My cell phone then rings. It's Rashad.

"Hello!" I'm in my car with Jasmine. Rashad is on speaker.

"Hey, what's up?"

"Nothing much, just hanging out with Jasmine. What you doing?"

"I'm just out right now but gotta go back to work later this evening. Y'all should come down and meet me for drinks."

"Oh, really? Are you still at Union Station?"

"Yep, so we could meet up at Fat Tuesday's."

Jasmine jumps into the conversation. "What's up Rashad? How you been, and how was your New Year?"

"It was good," he quipped.

"Oh okay so what'd you do? Did you go out?" she asked.

"Nah, I went to church with a friend," he replied.

"Oh, okay that's cool. So what's going on with you and your other female friend? Are y'all not seeing each other anymore?"

"Nah, that's over."

"Okay, I noticed that I hadn't seen any pics of the two of you lately on Facebook. So what else you been up to?"

"Nothing, just working. Oh, and I just bought this little car to drive back and forth to work so I can stop driving my truck every day."

"That was smart. Well take care, and here's Gia," Jasmine said and handed me the phone.

"Hey, so whatcha gonna do for the rest of the day?" I asked.

"I'm gonna run a few errands and then try to take a nap before I go back to work."

"Oh, okay. So what time do you have to be back at work?" I asked.

"9."

"It must be good to have all that extra over-time."

"Yeah, it's been great! Well enjoy the rest of your day and I'll let you know about coming to have drinks."

"Okay cool, talk to you later."

"Okay bye."

Later that evening I sent Rashad a text.

Gia: Hey, did you make it into work?

Rashad: Hey, I did but what is this text really about because you don't care if I made it to work. Lol

Gia: lol, I do care, I'm just trying to be a good friend.

Rashad: What you doing? Do you wanna come see me, I can take a break when you get here.

Gia: You want me to come all the way to DC?

Rashad: Yeah, if you're not doing anything. We can talk.

I think for a second, because normally I wouldn't do this. But I'm trying to do things a little differently this time, and like I said—Rashad is that guy that you will do the abnormal for.

Gia: Ok sure, I'll come see you. Let me slip on some clothes. I'll call you when I get close.

Rashad: Okay! That will work.

I called Rashad because I was a little lost so he can walk me through how to get to exactly where he is. I picked him up out front of Union Station. We go park my car. It's cold out so I put the heated seats on and leave the car running. Rashad and I have a nice one-on-one conversation about life, dating and so on.

The following week, Rashad and I met for dinner and drinks. It was nice to spend time with him. We talked, laughed, and got to know each other better. Rashad was not shy by any means. He had questions— very personal questions at that. I was caught off guard by his directness, but still answered his inquiries.

"When was the last time you had sex?" Rashad asked.

"Well that's not too personal at all!" I said, sarcastically. "Well, if you must know, it's been a little over 2 years!"

"Really?" Rashad said, surprised. .

"Yes, really!" I replied. "So if all you are looking for is someone to hookup with, you need to keep looking because I ain't her!"

Rashad laughed then said, "Nah, it's not like that at all. I was just asking."

We continued on with dinner and conversation. I just started feeling at ease with him. It was good to have someone to just vibe out with, and since I wasn't looking for a relationship at the moment, this was an ideal setup.

The two of us decided to keep our relationship private and with no commitments. This was great; until it wasn't.

Things were going great; Rashad and I were going with the flow. It was now late January and Rashad invited me over his house to chill. At this point we had been talking for about a month. I got there and he had his hookah machine out and we watched a movie.

"Have you ever smoked hookah?" he asked.

"Yes, once but I didn't know what I was doing because I don't smoke," I replied.


"It's nothing to it! Come on and try it. I'll show you and I'll switch out the shisha for you," he said.

"Okay," I said.

So now we're smoking, talking, and watching a movie. I'm having a great time and for the first time in years, I felt completely FREE! And it was an amazing feeling. An hour or so goes by and Rashad asks me for a hug. I think to myself, "LORD...I know where this is about to go."

Keep in mind that I have been practicing celibacy for the past 2+ years. Though I had been dating this one other person for about a year, he never made me feel like I wanted to break my celibacy; I never even kissed him. Now I am sitting here with this fine ass man thinking to myself, "What are you gonna do if this man tries to take this to the next level?"

I go over to him and we hug. Then he started to caress my body and we started kissing. Yasss! He knows how to kiss.

Rashad started kissing my neck, then my breasts and then back to my lips. We end our makeout session and smoke more hookah. Before I know it, we were in his room and he has me on the bed. I'm not sure he's the one, I'm not sure I'm ready; it's been over 2 years.

"Wait, we can't do this," I say to him.

He pauses and looks me in the face and says, "Why?"

"Because, I'm not ready. You know it's been 2 years since I've done this."

"You ready!" he said, as he continued to kiss my lips, neck, and my breasts! Before I knew it, Rashad was trying to figure out how to get my jeans off because they had a side-zipper. But once that was all figured out, my clothes were coming off! And I was past ready!

Rashad was in total control, I mean in ways I had NEVER experienced before sexually!

The next day I call my BFF, Cookie.

"Hello?" she answered.

"Cookie, so I went to see Rashad last night," I said excitedly.

"Really? Okay, did you enjoy yourself?"

"OMG…It was cool. We talked, smoked a lil hookah, and we kissed a little," I laughed.

"Wait…did y'all 'just kiss?'" (I laughed). "Gia, did y'all have sex?!" she asked.

"YESSS…"

"OMG...you gave up your celibacy? So was it worth it?"

"OMG YESSS…It was amazing. One of the best sex partners I've ever had. I just loved how in control he was. His level of confidence is a huge turn-on for me. I love that type of shit. I love a man who knows what he wants and how to get it. I love that I never know what position I'm gonna be in next without any words being conveyed."

"I can't believe you did it, you actually gave up your 2+ years of celibacy. But I'm happy for you!" she said.

"Yeah, it's a nice change. There's something about him that makes me feel FREE! I can't really explain it, but it's been 10 years since I've felt this free with anyone. I love knowing that I can be conservative me or freaky me. I love the freedom he has provided me. I never feel like he wants to put me in a box."

"That's awesome," she said.

"Yeah, there's no pressure. We're just going with the flow, and it's refreshing!"

The following week Rashad called and we meet up for drinks after work. A few days later I went over to his house to chill. Before the night was over we were covered in each other's juices and spent from an intense lovemaking session. It's always an adventure whenever we get together, and tonight was no different. From the numerous positions to the costumes and toys, we really— I mean really— enjoyed each other's bodies that night. Foreplay with this man is just as intense as the act itself. I have never been the girl that loved giving head, but when the man you are sleeping with loves it and doesn't mind giving it in return, it makes for one crazy night of fuckin'. He is not afraid to push me to my limits ever! There is no holding back when I am with him and I love that shit so much!

After two months of dating Rashad, he went MIA… no calls, no returned texts, nothing. After a week of reaching out to him with no response, I was over it.

You see, Rashad is one of the sweetest men I know but that is Rashad "with feelings!" Now Rashad "without feelings" that dude is a motherfucker! There is an absolute clear difference between the two!

I'm no longer seeing Rashad and I'm good with it, even though I don't really understand what took place.

Now I go to my counseling appointments with Dr. Edwards. I'm sharing with him how I haven't heard from Rashad. He has basically gone MIA.

Dr. Edwards asked, "Why do you think he has decided to cut things off without any type of warning or communication?"

"I have no clue. I thought we were cool and everything was going well. I would ask him but he's not responding to any of my texts.

Honestly, Dr. Edwards I am done reaching out to him. You said to let down my guard and look at what happened. I'm not about to be pressed and keep being the one reaching out. The crazy part is that our mutual friend Alanna's birthday happy hour is next week and I know he's gonna be there."

"Okay, so how do you plan to handle seeing him again?" he asked.

"I don't know, but I'm not going to not go because he's gonna be there."

"Well, whatever you decide to do, just be sure to remain calm and speak."

"Oh, I'll speak but that's it. I'm not about to trip off of him!"

It was the last Thursday in February 2014. Today is Alanna's birthday happy hour. So that I didn't go alone, I took my oldest daughter Peyton.

You already know I looked super cute… I was wearing a pair of distressed blue jeans, a black fitted leather jacket as my top and a pair of tall boots made of leather & fur! Oh, and I'm rocking my gold name necklace with a pair of large gold hoop earrings.

Happy Hour was at Takoma Station Nightclub located in DC. Peyton and I arrived and gave hugs to the birthday girl and a few of my other girlfriends. Music is pumping, it's pretty packed inside and there's no sign of Rashad. I'm relieved, but know it was only a matter of time before he arrived. Thirty minutes pass and Peyton and I have ordered drinks and appetizers. I order my norm (Malibu with pineapple juice) and Peyton orders a Long Island Iced Tea. I get up to go to the restroom and when I come back, I see him. Rashad has arrived. We don't speak, we barely make eye contact. As the night goes on, we both do our own thing, dancing to the music while enjoying our girlfriend's birthday.

The next day I called Cookie to tell her all about my night. She asked if I thought that Rashad would reach out to me after seeing me at the party. I wasn't sure. I doubted it because he didn't seem to care one way or the other. And I wasn't about to chase after him. He got the wrong one because Gia with no feelings is just as matter of fact as Rashad with no feelings. I'm not ugly and I don't need to put up with his shit!

Fast-forward two months, I run into Rashad at a mutual friend's house. We haven't seen one another since Alanna's happy hour. This time we speak but don't have much to say. Later that evening on my ride home I stopped at the 7-Eleven and right as I parked my car I receive a text.

"Hey, do you want to see each other, but without making it a big deal?" the text read.

I don't recognize the phone number so I go through previous text to see who it is. It's Rashad!

"Hey, sure we can talk about it. Give me a call," I respond. I don't hear from him until the next day via text.

"Hey, sorry I was knocked out when you texted me back last night," he said

A couple of days later Rashad and I meet for drinks and dinner. He and I had a very interesting conversation. We both agreed to continue the relationship as FWBs.

Therefore, Rashad & I went into this second round with the understanding that we were both free to date other people. Again, I made it clear to him how important it was for him not to say a word to our other friends. I am beyond private and I don't like people knowing who I'm dating, let alone fucking! Rashad reassured me that I had nothing to worry about because apparently he had promised Alanna he wouldn't date any more of her friends. He told me about most, if not all, of Alanna's friends he had been with. Some he dated, others he just had sex with.

I told Rashad that was fine, but I was not about to be sneaking around. He said, "I don't want us to sneak around; I just wanted you to know what I agreed to with Alanna."

Okay, Rashad.

With that said; I had an idea Rashad had other women he was seeing/having sex with. However, even though Rashad was the only man I was seeing, this setup was totally cool with me. And there are multiple reasons I was ok with this.

First, I do well in this type of relationship. I honestly prefer them because I feel protected when I'm not giving too much of myself.

Second, Rashad never talked about the other women he was seeing and/or having sex with; I guess you can say he did a great job at protecting me from that part of his life. I could appreciate that to some degree; nonetheless, I still knew they existed. Though he would never come right out and say he was fucking other women, I knew. I knew because there sat on his nightstand a large box of condoms. You know the size box you can find at your local Costco Store.

The boxes would last him several months, which let me know he wasn't getting it in as often as I had assumed. Knowing he was using condoms put me at ease especially since the two of us had decided to no longer use condoms at this point. On some level I was relieved to know that Rashad was at least protecting us.

# Chapter 2: The Carpenter

At this point we are six or seven months into our second round. Therefore, this new arrangement didn't bother me initially because I was aware of our non-committal relationship. The two of us had our share of ups and downs. Although I loved how our friendship was growing and developing, it still was not without issues. I can't tell you how many times I called it quits; or should I say "called myself calling it quits." Whenever I felt that Rashad wasn't giving me what I needed from this setup I would say "I can't do this anymore." Rashad would wait me out, let me calm down by giving us some space; this would usually last a day or sometimes two days depending on how mad I was with him.

It was a Friday night and the phone rang. I answered.

"Hello?"

"Yeah Gia, what you doing?"

"Hey Rashad, what's going on?"

"Do you wanna come over, I'm on my way home and you can meet me there?"

Rashad would call me up as if nothing ever happened asking to see me. Just two days prior I had cursed him out for not showing me the attention I needed from this FWB relationship of ours.

I had the hardest time telling this man no. I enjoyed spending time with him, he tries to act tough but he has a loving spirit. Though Rashad drives me crazy from time to time. He makes me happy! I appreciate the fact that he is trying to work through my issues. I'm not the easiest person to date but I'm loyal to those I give my time to.

With that said, I'm still a little salty when it comes to Rashad. So I get another call from him.

"Hey! What's going on?"

"Nothing, what's going on with you Rashad?"

"I'm calling to see if you wanna talk. I wanna know if you want to come meet me so we can talk."

"Okay, what time do you want to meet? I'm working overtime, so I'll call you when I get off."

"Okay."

We met and Rashad says to me, "I know you think I'm fucking a lot of other women, but I'm not. It is not at all what you're thinking. I don't know why you keep going off like you do."

"Listen, I don't want you taking my options away. I need you to always be upfront with me, tell me what it is and let me make the decision to stay or not."

"Okay." He gets on his phone and pulls up these funny videos from social media, we laugh and all is good with us. I go home and move on with my evening plans.

It was Tuesday night; I met Rashad at his house. He was just getting out of the shower; we have basic conversation as he lotions up but watching the muscles flex in his arms as he rubs lotion on each of his body parts is torturous for me. It's late but we call ourselves gonna watch a movie and that lasted for about an hour before my body started throbbing. Needless to say we spent the rest of my visit entangled between his sheets— licking, sucking, rubbing, touching, and just loving on each other while the movie watched us. Rashad is the perfect partner for me because we both have a high sex drive. I have never had a man take me to so many different levels sexually. Experiencing sex with someone who is capable of taking you on highs, lows, and so much more is unreal!

Rashad and I continued with our open relationship while building what I thought was a strong friendship. The two of us spent time together. Rashad and I saw each other 2-3 times a week. We had good conversations, and did normal FWB relationship type things, even though it wasn't a "relationship" in the normal sense. I was crazy about this man and would do anything for him. I had his back and was there for him whenever he needed me to be. Things were great, or so it appeared.

We had decided to keep this relationship private. That was a huge deal for me from day one! I am super private, therefore, I didn't want the group all in my business. No one needed to know intimate details of our relationship. Well we each told our best friends about the relationship but aside from them, we kept it private, because we both agreed our privacy was for the best.

Now, as far as I was concerned, being private didn't mean that we would never go out or do things together; It only meant that we would keep our most intimate details private and wouldn't announce to the world that we were seeing one another. But if someone saw us out, then oh well. I decided to just go with the flow because at this point I was enjoying our time together and our sex life. I mean, this man turned me out sexually, but more importantly, I enjoyed the friendship we had developed. The two of us had a very complex situation going on.

As the months went on, I started hearing things about Rashad from other people because they had no idea of our relationship. Things about him and other women, along with the women he was meeting on a dating website. I heard he'd been taking them out, meeting up for coffee, drinks, and dinner. However, I can't say a word because of how I found out, but there's always a way around everything. It's not like I don't know he has a profile on the Plenty Of Fish dating site. So I found ways to bring his page up because I too was on that same website.

I joined POF to prove to Dr. Edwards and myself that I could do it. But, I never went on a date with anyone. It wasn't me; the online dating thing is just weird to me. Moreover, I did a little experiment while on the site. I changed my race from "African American" to "Mixed" but didn't change any of my pics or any of my information and I got way more hits as a "Mixed" female then I ever got as a "Black" female. Crazy right? All the men sent the same type of messages to me. "Hello beautiful," or "Hello, sexy. When can we get together?" No real conversation ever. Needless to say, I didn't last on that website very long.

I went to my bi-weekly appointment with Dr. Edwards. We talked about how things were going for me on the website and why I don't date "strangers" if you will. I know it's strange to hear anyone say how they've never dated a stranger, but I have never dated a man that wasn't already in my life in some way, shape, or form. Every boyfriend or friend I dated, I already knew him. He was either a friend of the family, a friend of a friend, or someone I went to school with.

I told Dr. Edwards how I'd tried to be open to dating men I met on the street. I would accept their numbers and I'd even given out mine more times than I can count. However, when they call I don't answer, and if I took their number, I would never call. I'm not sure why I like to date in my own comfort zone. I think for me it's because of my control issues. I seem to meet men all the time, and every time, I say to myself, "ok the next time I won't lie and say I'm in a relationship; instead I'm gonna accept their phone number and actually go through with calling." But it never happens. I always go straight to my go-to line: "Sorry but I'm in a relationship."

"Dr. Edwards, what am I gonna do, because dating the guys I'm familiar with doesn't seem to be working out for me? I cannot even blame it all on the men, because over the years I have dated some amazing men. whenever they try to get close to me, I push them away. I do things to sabotage the relationships; if I feel like I'm getting too close or start to feel feelings in any way I do shit to push them away. I am not going to allow anyone to ever hurt me again and that is my mindset."

The funny part is that I call them FWB's (Friends with Benefits) but in real life, I am just dating them because I stay in these types of relationships for years. It's not like I'm out here sleeping around. Since the devastating breakup with Frank (which I will get into later). I've had two FWB type relationships. The first lasted 4 years and the second lasted 3 years. During each of those relationships, I was only intimate with the one person, even though we were not in any type of committed relationship.

"Why is that? Gia, why do you think you commit without owning it is a commitment to them?" Dr. Edwards asked.

"I don't know! That's why I'm here for you to help me figure it out. But I can honestly say that I have never had sex with more than one guy in the same year, month, or week. If I'm seeing someone, I stick to only dating whoever that particular man was at that time."

I guess it's safe to say that I love being in these non-committed/committed type of relationships (as I laugh).

"So can you honestly say you never had any feelings for either of them?"

"No, I'm not saying I never caught feelings because of course I cared about them both, but I never allowed myself to fall in love; is what I am saying. When I felt things were getting too close, I pushed them away. I have become great at protecting my my heart. I am not saying it's a good or bad thing. I am just saying it is something I learned to master."

"Gia, is it possible your breakup with Frank played a role in why you now only have FWB type relationships? You referred to your breakup with him as devastating. I know it was 10 years ago but you'd be surprised at how past relationships play a role in your future relationships."

Let's talk a little about what took place between you and Frank because we can't move forward to the why without talking about where it all stemmed from. So that I'm clear, Frank is not the father of your two daughters, correct?" he asked.

Correct! Frank was my very first adult relationship after my 12 year long relationship with my girls' dad ended. I refer to him as my first "adult relationship" because I was 31 when I started dating him. For the first time I was able to experience what it felt like to truly be in love with someone. Frank was indeed my very first love. I had been single for a year when he and I started dating. He taught me it was okay to trust and what it meant to be in an unconditional loving relationship. He and I had such an amazing friendship that developed into love. I trusted him, but 5 years into the relationship I learned that he had started cheating with his coworker. To say I was shocked would have been an understatement. That relationship taught me that even the so-called "good guys" cheat. So after I got over the hurt and pain his betrayal inflicted on my life, I made a promise to myself that I would never allow another man to get close enough to hurt me on that level ever again. I knew I couldn't allow what I had gone through with Frank to prevent me from loving again. But moving forward I would do things differently. I wasn't really sure what 'that' looked like but I knew something had to give. So I guess on some level I went into protective mode."

"Wow!" Dr. Edwards exclaimed. "Gia, I don't know if you realize it or not but you just said why you've chosen to have a FWB versus a more committed type of relationship. You are so afraid of getting hurt that you have built this wall in hopes of protecting your heart. You trusted Frank and he hurt you, so now you keep everyone at bay."

"I guess you are correct but I'm not sure."

"You are what I call a 'runner!'" he said.

"What do you mean?" I asked.

"Whenever you feel yourself catching feelings for the other person, you run. You assume they will hurt you but before you give them a chance. You would rather walk away first. At some point, you are going to have to allow yourself to be vulnerable. You are going to have to allow your guard to come down and give someone a chance," he responded.

"It is about CONTROL and not giving up that power!" I countered. The control freak in me won't allow myself to just go with the flow, even though I tell myself otherwise. Maybe it's a combination of them all. Who knows...Nevertheless, Dr. Edwards, I honestly feel like as guarded as I am, when the right man comes along, he will find a way to break through whatever barriers I am putting out there," I sighed.

"Yes, that can be true to some degree. You are correct; the right man will not be intimidated by your strong personality and will not back down when you start to push him away. I know the thought of letting go of control is a scary feeling but how do you move away from this place of being stuck if you do not take a chance. More importantly, with taking a chance comes transparency," Dr. Edwards said.

He continued: "You can start with Rashad. You said yourself that you felt free when you are with him. Try giving him a chance. You have to learn how to communicate your wants, needs and even your fears. You have to allow yourself to be completely transparent. As scary as that may sound, at some point you are going to move out of your own way. You think you are protecting yourself but you are not."

"I know, but after getting hurt in my last relationship 10 years ago with Frank, I made a decision to never allow another man to ever hurt me like that again. Therefore, the only way to protect my feelings has been to not allow myself to fall so deep that I am devastated should it not work out."

"I understand, but you cannot always control love or how you feel about a person. Love sometimes sneaks up on you and, unfortunately, sometimes we get hurt. For your homework next visit, I want you to think about how you can let go of some of your control issues. I also want you to ask Peyton, Cookie, and Jasmine if they are willing to write an example on how your ultra-controlling ways have had an impact on them and/or your friendship."

"Okay, I can do that."

Two weeks later I am back for my therapy session with Dr. Edwards and I have my homework completed.

*My oldest daughter did not hold back with her examples. Neither did Cookie or Jasmine.*

## *Peyton's letter of examples:*

### Mom's HW

Controlling in all areas of life

Control starts at a 5 (1-10 scale)

Each area of life is on different levels

## Privacy= level 10

### Ex1: lvl 10

Telling Aunt Katy (her blood sister) about her nickname which is Felicia

*even though mom sent a mass/group text to friends telling them about the nickname I GAVE HER.

-she didn't give me, the 23 yr old originator of the nickname "permission" to tell anyone

-she got really upset/annoyed

- gave me her evil eye

**Evil eye:** a look Gia gives a person who shares what she considers "too much information"

### Ex.2: lvl 8

Sales Associate): hey I went shopping at Blue Mountain

Tonya (mom friend): Oh, Gia was just saying how she loved shopping at Blue Mountain

Gia: evil eye to Tonya ʘʘʘʘʘʘʘʘ

Small things that people consider normal to share in a casual conversation can be like treading on ice if you say something that mom for whatever reason does not want to be shared.

However, you do not know if you can share anything because you cannot read her mind. It takes YEARS to figure out her weirdness when it comes to sharing. In addition, even I still get the evil eye for stupid stuff.

**Ex.3: lvl 7/8**

Mom is at the house with friends.

I say: "Oh mom we gotta get insurance today."

Mom: evil eye followed by annoyed voice of ok. (To shut you up)

Her girlfriends do not know what I mean. I live with my mom so I could be talking about her helping ME get insurance. ON THE OTHER HAND, one of them might have a good suggestion of a cheap insurance company.

**Ex.4: level 5 control**

Cleaning up a room because you may put something in a place she does not think it should be.

## *Cookie's letter of examples:*

When you first asked me to assist with the homework assignment, I immediately went to our relationship – meaning, in what ways do you control me or have control over our relationship. I struggled with this one because I could not find many or any examples. I had to look up the definition of controlling to determine if it was more controlling behavior or just being direct.

According to Webster's Dictionary, I found that controlling is having a need to control other people's behavior or having the power to control how something is managed or done.

Staying true to the aforementioned definition, I would say that you are controlling in the following ways:

### Controlling a conversation

When you are done with a conversation, you state YOUR opinion and then end the conversation very matter of fact. This, in turn, makes the other person feel like "OKAY; nothing else needs to be said."

### Planning a group event/activity

Sometimes, versus going with the flow with the group or suggested activity, if you are not feeling the event or activity, you will shoot it down because it may be something that you may not necessarily want to do. Then it is hard or difficult to suggest something else.

**Relationships with men**

You will guard your heart and feelings to "control" the outcome of the relationship. You state up front what you want or think that you want so that if the relationship works out the way that you "really" wanted it to go, you are "okay". But, I think that you are not. You end up feeling hurt in the end.

## *Jasmine's letter of examples:*

The situation that comes to my mind on our girls' weekends. Please see below:

- When we were in Miami, Nikki and I wanted to go get something to eat and you got up out of your bed and asked us why we were hungry and stated we just ate.

- Miami: When a stranger on the street spoke to me, but you thought that I had not spoken back.

- Then there was the trip to New York and you were adamant that we were going back to H&M when I think Sherri had referenced something else.

Additionally, I think you control those things you are protective of, like yourself. So you are firm in your convictions and what your position is. So I would say yes you're controlling but I now understand why.

OK that is it for now, I still love you in and out of season. That's what friends are for.

One night, I guess it was around 9:30pm or so, I was over at Rashad's house when I noticed that the condoms that he usually keeps on his dresser were disappearing. Not to say that they had just started disappearing, but this is just the first time that I noticed how it made me feel. For the first time, I was really bothered by seeing this. I was startled, because no matter how hard I tried, I just could not shake this weird feeling. When the sun arose the next morning as I lay in Rashad's bed, the realization hit me that I now love this man!

Oh shit! How in the hell did I allow this to happen? The first thing I do as soon as I leave his place and I'm in the privacy of my car is call Cookie.

"Hey girl, what's up?" I began. "So, last night I was with Rashad at his place, and you know how I've been telling you about how open he was and how he keeps the condoms out? You know, not trying to hide things because we're just friends? WELL, for the first time, seeing that the condoms are gradually disappearing really bothered me."

"Really?" Cookie replied. "Why do you think you felt that way, and more importantly, what are you going to do about it?"

"GIRL, I really do not know," I said. "You know me a lot better than most people and you know how guarded I have always been. I know that I do not make it easy for men to get close to me, and I like to think that I've been doing a really good job of protecting my feelings. Now this can definitely become a problem. I'm not sure how to continue on the way we have been without being bothered by the other women, and the disappearing of the condoms?"

"I don't profess to be an expert on this particular subject," Cookie cautioned, "but I do know this: you're going to have to figure it out soon, and having a conversation with Rashad would probably be a good first step in the process."

"I just don't know," I said, "but I feel like I can't say anything to him because there's no commitment between us. That's what we both agreed to when we first started seeing each other and I don't even know if a commitment is what I want. I'm so confused!"

"Well Gia, what are you going to do? And know that whatever you decide, I've got your back," she said.

"Thanks, Cookie. I know you're always down for me but I don't think I'm going to do anything, for now," I replied.

You can only imagine how hard moving forward in this friendship must have been for me, but I stayed in control of my feelings. Never asked Rashad for a commitment, nor did I ever ask him to stop fucking the other women. I did, however, eventually share with him that I wasn't staying in this just for the sex; I stay because I care about him so much.

It's fall, and Rashad and I have been on a good roll. We still see each other at least 2-3 times a week, and life is great! I am loving him so much, even though I cannot and will not ever tell him. But he knows. Though we still are not in a fully committed relationship, I can tell that Rashad's feelings for me have grown since the start of this FWB relationship. He is more open to discussing my issues, whereas before, he would end the entire relationship. Thursday night, Rashad and I are at dinner. I bring up our relationship and why we are not able to move forward in more of a commitment.

"Now you know the only reason we cannot is because I promised Alanna that I would not date another one of her girlfriends," Rashad said.

"This is some BS, because you said she did not have a problem with you dating Angie," I countered. "I am confused— are you not a grown ass man? Are you telling me that Alanna controls whom you date or do not date?"

"She is my BFF," he said. "I am not going to go against her, and you know that is the only reason."

"Whatever, Rashad!" I replied, annoyed.

Let us not forget that Rashad has dated several of Alanna's other friends. I know because he told me so! Again, what is it about me that made Alanna not want him to date me? Hell that is still the million-dollar question. This becomes a problem for the two of us, a constant conversation. Rashad has always shown me that he cares for me a lot but at the same time, he is equally as guarded as I am. Very careful not to allow himself to fall too hard. He is content with the way things are but for me, not so much. The two of us continue with our relationship, we continue to build an amazing friendship.

Rashad and I are doing great. We continue to see each other several times a week, and not just for sex. We enjoy spending time together and the sex is just an added bonus. With that said, he and I are still just FWBs but we're good.

One evening, I receive a call from Rashad. He wants to know what I'm doing because he wants to come over. He asks if the girls are home because I'm weird about my girls being around men I'm just dating. I let him know that Peyton was but he can still come over. He then says to me "how about I come over and you come outside so we can break-in the car? We haven't done that yet." You know I'm down for anything outside the normal having sex in the bed. So I say "okay" let me know when you're out-front. Thirty minutes later Rashad calls and he's outside, parked in one of the parking spaces in front of my neighbors house. At this time I was living in a townhome development, so needless to say, there were a lot of homes and a lot of parking spaces underneath bright lights.

# Chapter 2: The Carpenter

Again, this type of stuff turns me on so I'm down for whatever. I slip on a flowy sundress and head out to the car. Rashad gets out the front and gets into the backseat. I also got into the backseat. Yes, the windows are tinted but we are still in the middle of my parking lot. We talk briefly before I start to massage his dick, then pull it out and start to perform oral sex on him. This was our foreplay and he loves it. Once I'm done Rashad takes off his pants, pulls up my dress and sticks it in. I start off on my back as he grinds, and before you know it, I'm riding him so hard. I don't want it to end, I absolutely love having sex with this man. While I'm fuckin' him good, Rashad say to me "Why you fuck me so good?" I smile and kiss him because it feels good to know how much he enjoys having me.

After we finish having sex, we're talking and Rashad tells me "Damn you got some good ass pussy." I give a slight smile and say "You're being sweet" (because what do you say to that). "No I'm not just being sweet," he said, "and I know I can't be the first dude to ever tell you that." We finish the conversation with a kiss and end the night. I love this side of him, he pushes me sexually and it is such a turn on for me. This man and his skill-set takes me to another level and I don't want it to ever end! And not because we had sex in the car because of course that's nothing new. It is something about the way he controls the act itself that turns me on. I love that neither of us gave a damn about the possibility of getting caught by one of my neighbors. It is one thing to have sex in a car, but it's something different to have sex while surrounded by so many houses and cars. There's not a box when it comes to our sex life.

It's still early fall 2014. Rashad is feeling himself but I am not feeling it. We made plans for him to spend the night at my house. I am at the gym with my daughter Peyton and when I get in the car there is a text from Rashad.

Rashad: "Hey, I am not sure if I am coming over because I am tired."

45

Gia: "Wait…What do you mean you are not coming over? I am so tired of the games you have been playing lately. If this is no longer what you want, then leave me alone. I do not know how many times I must tell you that I am not in this just for some dick! I am not ugly, so getting dick is the fucking easy part. Do you think you are the only one who can fuck? I am so sick of this shit, I am sick of you thinking you are going to go days without seeing me. I am not some fucking hookup and if that is all you want, then go get that shit from the other bitches you fuckin' with. Because what you're not going to do is put me in any type of rotation. I told you the moment I start to feel like I am a part of a fucking rotation, we have a problem. I'm so fucking done right now. So if you're not coming, fine, don't come because I'm so fucking over this shit right now! Enjoy your fucking night!"

Rashad: "What the fuck are you talking about? I just said I was tired; this is not about no other female."

Gia: "Whatever, Rashad. I am done."

I get home, shower and get myself ready for bed. The phone rings, and it's Rashad.

"Yeah, so whatcha doing?" Rashad asks after I answer.
"Nothing, just got out the shower," I reply.
"Well, I am about to come over since you got me upset and now I can't sleep."
"Ok, Rashad," I said.

An hour later, Rashad gets to my house. We go upstairs to my bedroom. He puts his work clothes up and we get in bed. It is late at this point, 11:30ish. We are talking.

"Look, you gotta stop going off whenever I say I can't see you," Rashad said. "I was tired; you know I have been working overtime. You always think I am with some female, when I am not."

Just as he says this, his phone rings. I look up at him. "REALLY?" I say, somewhat annoyed.

"What? I cannot control who calls me or what time they call," he retorts. "Gia, you think I am out here just fuckin' everybody whenever I am not with you. I am telling you I am not out here getting as much pussy as you think I am. I am with you several days a week, so stop tripping over other females because it is nothing like what you think."

"Yeah, Ok Rashad," I respond.

We kiss, and I start giving him oral sex because it is his favorite form of foreplay. This man's sexual skills take me to another level and I just love him so much!

It's Thursday night in September and I just got to Half Notes Lounge for our girlfriend Angie's birthday celebrations. All my girlfriends are in the house along with Angie's other friends. I am sitting next to Jasmine as usual, and we are drinking and having a good time. I noticed Rashad was not there yet, so I texted him.

Gia: Hey, are you coming to Angie's party?
Rashad: Yeah, I am pulling up.
Gia: Great because I wanna see that handsome face of yours.
Rashad: It will be nice to see you too.

Rashad walks in looking fine as ever. We play it cool as always; remember, none of our friends know about our relationship. He is mingling, orders himself a drink, and having random conversations with everyone at the party. I am off to the side still sitting with Jasmine at the other table. I need to go to the restroom, so I ask Jasmine to walk with me. We gotta pass by Rashad.

"Hey Rashad!" Jasmine said, and gives him a hug.
"Hey Jasmine!" he replied, and then looked at me.
"Hey," I said, and give a wave.

"Oh, so I don't get a hug?" he said, playfully. We hug and I continue making my way to the restroom.

As the night goes on the live band is performing, we are dancing and taking shots. At this point, Angie the birthday girl is LIT! Angie has a seat and tells Alanna she needs to go to her car to get her flats, but Alanna insists that she  not go by herself. Rashad is standing there and offers to go get her shoes out of the car. He comes back and now Alanna is trying to figure out who is going to follow behind Angie to make sure she gets home safe. So Alanna asked Rashad if he could follow Angie because it's on his way home. Of course, Rashad said he would and I did not have an issue with it at all. However, I was expecting to hear from him after he made sure Angie got home ok. Nothing, not a call or text from him. Now, my mind is running with all kinds of thoughts about what he is doing and wondering if he is still at Angie's place. You already know the next morning I sent him a nasty text.

Gia: Good morning! Why didn't I hear from you last night? Did you decide to stay at Angie's house and give her a little birthday dick? Let me tell you, if I find out you fucked her, we are going to have a problem. Because that shit is not fucking ok on any level…

Rashad: What are you talking about? I didn't stay at her house and I didn't fuck her, Gia! Since it was so late, I went straight to the yard and slept in my car. I told you I haven't fucked that girl in 2 years. After we ended things, that was it! I was on the phone with Alanna the entire ride to Angie's house, and even after I left her house.

Gia: Whatever the fuck Rashad. So you want me to believe that you slept in your damn car instead of taking your ass home?

Rashad: Yeah, because it was already 2 a.m., and you know I gotta be at work at 6 a.m. I didn't wanna go home and chance oversleeping after all that drinking I did. Gia, I'm telling you I didn't fuck her.

Gia: Ok, Rashad! You better not be lying to me because I'm not ok with you still fucking her. It's one thing for you to be out here fuckin' bitches I do not know or know about. But I'm NEVER going to be okay with you fuckin' her, especially now that she and I are friends. That shit is not cool, and I am not fucking having it.

Rashad: You don't have to worry about that because I didn't and we don't need to keep going back and forth about it.

Gia: Okay!

Rashad and I continued seeing each other on a regular basis. What we have developed is so different from where we started. Things are good, we stay consistent, and we try to go out to dinner and not just meet up for sex.

Today is the day of all days: my birthday! As usual, my girlfriends and I made plans to celebrate another year of fabulousness. This year we decided to do Sunday brunch. First things first, I've got to go shopping because you know I want to look super cute on my special day. I head straight to the mall where I find the cutest little sheer top and leather jeans, which happen to go perfectly with the sexy heels I plan to wear for Rashad later. Once the girls and I wrap up our brunch, my main motivation is to get to Rashad and spend a quiet evening with him. As soon as I walk in, he removes my jacket and leads me through the living room. He then hands me a glass of my favorite wine. I'm a little excited and looking forward to what's to come. He has a tray of chocolate covered strawberries and commences feeding me. After I take the first bite, we have the hottest make-out session that ends with my new sheer blouse tossed across the room. Then Rashad tells me, "it's your special day, so it's all about you tonight babe," and he makes passionate love to me for hours. It started with the best oral sex ever, or maybe it just felt like the best because it was my birthday. Lol. This man has never disappointed me sexually! Rashad is skillful at putting me in whatever position he wants me in without ever asking me to "change positions." I swear that's one of the things I love most about him; there's nothing like a man who knows how to express himself sexually.

The following weekend I spent the night at Rashad's house, as I regularly do. We wake up and I go get us breakfast and pick up a few things for my car because Rashad is going to fix something I broke and wash our cars. I ask Rashad what he wants to do for his birthday, because it'll be here before we know it!

I'm not sure. I haven't really thought about it," he said. "I would like to go away somewhere for the weekend."

"Okay, so let's plan something," I replied. "Do you wanna go to Miami?"

"Nah, not really," he said casually.

"So where?" I asked.

"I don't know; maybe Vegas," he replied.

"Ok, I love Vegas. I'll look into it," I said "How long do you wanna go, because you know you don't have the same type of leave I have?"

"Let's just do the weekend; Friday - Sunday.

I planned everything and treated him to an all-expenses paid Vegas getaway for his birthday present. However, weeks leading up to his birthday I started to get extremely sick. I mean dropping weight like crazy, can't keep anything down, dehydrated type of sick. My doctor diagnoses me with an upper respiratory infection and a stomach virus. I took the antibiotics he prescribed me and kept it moving. Nevertheless, as the weeks go on, I'm still not feeling any better. At this point, I've already scheduled a social event at my home that was too late to cancel. The following Sunday, I had already scheduled my

Chapter 2: The Carpenter

Annual Reception for my daughter Alex's high school for African American students interested in attending boarding school. Sunday morning, I'm too weak to set up for the reception. So my oldest daughter Peyton and her boyfriend Michael set everything up for me. I somehow find the strength to get showered and dressed before my 30+ guest arrive. By the end of the event, I was so weak I had to literally crawl up the stairs in my home. A parent of one of the current students was at the event and offered to give Alex a ride back to campus for me.

After the last guest left, Peyton took me to the hospital because there was no way I could go another day feeling as bad as I did. Keep in mind, it was the Sunday before I'm supposed to leave for Vegas with Rashad. When we get to Georgetown University Hospital ER, I sign in and we wait for me to be called to the back.

"Gia!" the first nurse called, ushering me to the back to get my vital signs. Well my heart rate was so freaking high I never went back to the waiting room. The nurse asked if I could feel my heart beating as fast as it was.
I told her no but that I was on medication for my thyroid. The nurse took me to a room and the doctor came in immediately, asking me questions and listening to my heart.

"Gia, you're severely dehydrated and your blood pressure is dangerously high," the doctor said, concerned. "Have you been diagnosed with Graves' disease?"

"No," I replied. "They said my numbers were just a little higher than normal and that they were going to watch it."

"We are going to start you on an IV to get you hydrated and give you some medication to get your blood pressure back to normal," the doctor said.

"There's no reason for your heart rate to be this high while you're just lying in the bed, and that's a major concern for me. I'm going to monitor you for a little and then go from there."

Meanwhile, I told the nurse how excited I was to be leaving for Vegas on Friday, and thus, needed to be healthy. An hour or so and two bags of fluid later, the doctor came back in. "I'm sorry, but you're not going home," he began. "We are going to have to keep you. Your blood pressure is still high and we need to figure out why you're not keeping anything down."

"Ok, I understand. But it's only overnight, right?" I asked, trying to hide my concern.

"I don't know, because we need to run some tests on you," he replied. "So as soon as they have a bed ready for you, we will have you admitted to the hospital."

I literally spend the next four days in the hospital. I want to get to the root of what's going on with me, but I also have a trip that I've paid for and want to attend. Thank God, I was released Thursday morning in just enough time to get myself ready for my trip.

Now, during my stay at the hospital Cookie and Jasmine came to visit. I was telling them how I had already paid for my youngest daughter Alex to attend a "field hockey tournament" with her team this weekend. That was my story, and I was sticking to it. So as far as all my girlfriends were concerned (except for Cookie, who knows about my relationship with Rashad, that's where I was going to be.

It's Friday and Rashad is working a half day. So Thursday night I spend the night at his house, get up and take him to work, go home to get dressed and to grab my bags. I go pick him up from work and we head to the airport. When we arrive in Vegas, I'm still not 100% and

## Chapter 2: The Carpenter

I'm on restrictions. I still can't do anything extra that will elevate my heart rate, but I'm just excited to be out of the hospital and on a mini vacation with my main man Rashad.

I booked us a room at The Aria, the newest hotel on the strip . We check in, get relaxed, and unpack. On the plane ride earlier, Rashad asked me to put his iPad inside my purse because he was listening to music from my iPad.

We're back at the hotel and Rashad asks for his iPad but when I go to get it out of my purse we see that it's been cracked. I feel horrible; I can tell he's mad and rightfully so, but Rashad tries real hard not to show it. Nonetheless, I still feel bad and tell him when we get back home I'm going to take it to have the screen fixed. He's cool and we continue on and change the subject. Rashad and I had a great vacation! He did his late night thing at the casinos and because I was still kind of sick, I went back to the room early both nights. So there was no wild and crazy fuckn' going on because I was still a little weak. We actually hung out, shopped, but only had sex the morning right before we were about to leave. I love that our friendship has evolved and isn't just about us having sex. We thoroughly enjoyed our time away from everyone. We had great conversations about any and everything. Well worth it in the end, until our drive back from the airport when he's texting back and forth with someone. So I get an instant attitude.

"Who are you texting?" I inquired.
"It's just a friend," he replied.

"Why are you texting a friend while you're with me?" I ask, annoyed.

"I'm just responding; it's not that serious, Gia!"
"Whatever, Rashad. You're so full of shit."

"What do you want from me Gia? I told you because of my promise to Alanna we can't be in a full blown relationship. You and I we're good!" he said, trying to reassure me.

"What? No, you just wanna keep an out by using your promise to Alanna," I retort. "You're a grown ass man, so I don't wanna keep hearing how we are good because of some fucking promise to your BFF. You're quick to say how we aren't in a 'committed' relationship because you don't wanna be held accountable for your actions. But what we have IS a fucking relationship, regardless of whether or not it's 'committed.' If you wanna text other women while you're with me and be out here seeing a bunch a different women; then just leave me alone because that's not what the fuck I signed up for!"

The next 30 minutes were spent in silence, and instead of me staying the night, I dropped his ass off at home and kept it moving.

I didn't call or text him. Rashad knew I was pissed so he gave me my space like he always does when I'm mad at him. Later that week, Rashad called because he has two extra tickets to the Wizards game and wants to know if Alex and I wanna go. I say "sure" because Alex loves basketball and it's Rashad's way of making up with me. We met him at the game. Now this will be his first time meeting my youngest daughter Alex (because again, everyone knows how weird I am about bringing men around my daughters). He actually was the first man to sort of meet them, because I still didn't tell her that he's someone I'm dating, but that he's just a friend who happened to have two extra tickets. Everything goes well at the game, there are no awkward moments like I had anticipated considering the last time I saw him we did not part on necessarily good terms. My daughter was
with me so I really didn't have the energy for any drama, nor did he. We all wanted to have a good time and enjoyed the game. It ended up being a great night.

Christmas comes around and things couldn't be better between us. We've been going strong and decided to exchange Christmas gifts! Everything is great, I'm feeling stronger and our sex life has been back and popping. Since we now have so much history, the intimacy has just gotten better and better. With all the fights and silent treatments we've given each other, you would think the sex would have gotten dry but that couldn't be farther from the truth. I enjoy his body, and he enjoys mine.

However, days after Christmas, Rashad starts acting brand new again; he isn't texting or calling as much. I was a little taken aback by his behavior, questioning where it's coming from. Rashad was acting distant but not sharing with me why. This all started the last few weeks in December of 2014. I finally talk to him and the two of us have very heated conversations regarding the other women in his life, and how Rashad has been treating me. Rashad continues to maintain that he isn't getting as much other sex as I think.

Then there was New Year's Eve! Yep the infamous New Year's Eve and I had not heard a word from Rashad since two days prior. At this point I had already noticed the shadiness in Rashad as I had begun to recognize the signs when he would drift away. However, not hearing from him for two days leading to New Year's Eve was a red flag because we were at a point in our relationship where we had been talking daily. So naturally, I'm livid.. It's now 3 p.m. New Year's Day, and still not a word from Rashad. I tell myself "this is it! I'm not doing this anymore." I deserve better, but more importantly, he doesn't deserve me. The nerve of him, not even a fucking Happy New Year text?

Oh hell no! And the fact that he obviously thinks this is okay is an even bigger problem. It doesn't matter that we don't have a "title/commitment;" we are still involved and have been for a year. Damn, does that not mean anything to him? Therefore, I did what any pissed off woman would do: I sent him a nasty text after calling and not getting an answer. Hours later, he responds by saying "you're all wrong, I don't know what you think I did New Year's Eve, but as usual, you're 100% wrong with what you're thinking."

"Okay, explain to me which part I'm 100% wrong about, Rashad?" I replied. He couldn't explain.

The next text was Rashad being nasty and rude, but that's what you do when you know you're not telling the truth. This falling out between the two of us was huge! He and I had NEVER fought like this before.

Gia: I don't want to do this anymore. Just leave me the fuck alone and do you, since I'm not important enough to see you on New Year's Eve and not even worthy of a fucking text. Fuck this shit right here. I keep telling your ass I'm not as pressed as you think I am. So Happy Fucking New Year!

Rashad: Like I said, it's not at all what you think and you're 100% wrong but if you think you're going to talk to me like that, then fuck it and Happy Fucking New Year to you too!

Though I was the one to say I didn't want the relationship anymore, I really missed him as time went on. We had never gone this long without making up before. A few weeks went by and I reached out to him, but now he's so angry that he won't take my calls. Rashad has flipped the script on my ass. I've never seen him this mad or that distant towards me before… Naturally, I assume he must be seeing someone new.

Another few weeks go by and I try to reach out to him again. This time he answers his phone.

"Yeah?" he answered.

"Hey. Why haven't you been taking my calls?" I inquire.

"I'm not ready to talk to you yet, and you can't force me" he replied, indignantly.

"I'm not trying to force you to do anything," I said. "I just wanted to talk to you about what happened."

"Well, I'm not ready," he retorted, "but I'll call you when I'm ready to talk."

"Okay, Rashad," I said, exhausted.

Another week or so goes by and I receive a call from Rashad asking if we could meet to talk. I agree, and we meet at a low-key restaurant near his neighborhood. We talk about everything that has happened between us over the past month. Rashad explained his feelings and told me that he wants us to continue seeing each other, but only if I'm able to go with the flow. He went on to say how people don't ask the question "do you wanna be my girlfriend" anymore because we're not kids. You just fall into the relationship.

"So are you able to move forward and go with the flow?" he asked. "And if we fall into something more than we do, but I can't go through what we just went through again."

"Okay Rashad. I don't have a problem with going with the flow because I can't go through what we just went through again either," I replied. "I do wanna ask you a question, though: Did you start seeing anyone else during our time apart? And were you with a female back in Dec when I didn't hear from you on New Year's Eve?"

"No! How many times do I have to tell you it wasn't what you thought it was?" he shot back. "You assumed I was with a female, but I was with my cousins!"

"Yeah, Okay Rashad! So you haven't been seeing any women from the POF website?"

"Nah! I have friends, but that doesn't mean I'm fuckin' them all."

"Okay," I responded, "but you really need to stop acting like what we have isn't a relationship just because we don't have a title. Understand, title or not, what we have is a relationship."

"I hear whatcha saying. Are we going to do this or what?" he said.

"Yes, I'm good!"

We work things out and I'm happy to have my lover and friend back in my life. However, remember during this talk I asked Rashad about the other women from the dating website and I also asked if he had been seeing someone new? Rashad told me he's not fuckin' every female he meets online, and no he's not seeing anyone new.

Okay, it's time to rewind. While on vacation with Rashad, remember I cracked his iPad, therefore I offered to have the iPad screen repaired. Fast forward; prior to making the appointment I asked Rashad if he wanted to go with me because his iPad has a passcode. Rashad was like "nah, I can just remove the password before you take it." Two months after we returned from our trip I made the appointment, I get to Rashad's house to pick up the iPad and asked if he removed the passcode. Rashad plays dumb as if this is his first time hearing that he needed to either remove the passcode or give the passcode to me. He asks why they need his passcode if all they're doing is replacing the screen. I'm annoyed because this isn't new information, but I try not to let it show. I simply respond by saying let me call them again and ask if it's needed. The call was made and I was told yes they will need the passcode in order to ensure that his Wi-Fi is properly working after the repairs are complete. So I text Rashad to convey this information to him but he's still giving me a hard time about this passcode. I'm leaving the gym and we're going back and forth about this damn password. I'm thinking to myself, "this nigga can get his own damn screen fixed."

## Chapter 2: The Carpenter

I don't understand what the big deal is; I'm just dropping off the iPad at the repair shop and then returning it back to Rashad.

Needless to say, I send Rashad yet another text explaining to him why his password is needed. I go on to say, if it's a trust issue, then I can bring the iPad back to you and you can take it and pay to have it repaired yourself because I don't have time for this. Two minutes later the passcode comes through text. Again, at this point I'm super annoyed but continue on with the repair appointment. I get the iPad fixed and return it to Rashad Sunday night. However, Monday afternoon I receive a text from Rashad stating that his iPad isn't working properly. Therefore, I call the company and they tell me to bring it in. Again, I go pick up the iPad from Rashad Monday night so that I can take it back to be fixed Tuesday morning. But I can't shake the fact that I'm now suspicious as to why Rashad was tripping over this iPad like he has something to hide. So this time before dropping off the iPad, I did the unthinkable. Yes, I went through his iPad.

That's right: I, Gia, went through Rashad's iPad and read all of his IM messages along with his online dating conversations. Oh my, is all I can say. I will admit that some of what I read are things I would NEVER repeat. Have you ever seen something that wasn't meant for you to see, therefore, it is not your place to repeat? Well, that is how I felt after going through Rashad's iPad. It was bad enough I had gone through his iPad, there was no way I would ever share what I read. Don't get me wrong, it wasn't anything horrible, just personal for his eyes only. With that being said, you know that old saying "if you go looking, you shall find?" Well, I searched and found way more than I was prepared for. I really felt some kinda way, but what can I do with the information? Not a damn thing because we're in an open relationship, so technically Rashad is free to fuck whomever he pleases, right? I will admit that a lot of the conversations were really old, like years before Rashad and I ever met. However, there were still a few that were recent and the conversations between him and the women were very explicit. Now I will say this: he told the truth as far as him not fuckin' every female he has a conversation with. However, there were still a few which made it hard for me to pretend as if I didn't see anything. Especially because he had constantly tried to reassure me that it wasn't as many women as I thought.

# 3

# GIRL TALK
## ***How Many Is Too Many?***

So I call Cookie and ask the question: how many women/men are too many? Is this a matter of opinion, is it based on each individual, and where do we draw the line even if what we're in is considered an open relationship? Should Rashad have been more honest about HOW MANY women he was actually having sex with? Did Rashad take away my options by not disclosing this information? Had I known about the women would I have opted out of being in an open relationship with Rashad? Who knows, just maybe my comfort level was only 1-2 other women. Neither Rashad nor I will ever know the answer to this question because I was never given the opportunity to make that decision; it was made for me by Rashad.

However, in Rashad's defense, not all the women were current. Many of the conversations were older. Plus, he could have been thinking there was no need in disclosing how many women because he told me there were others. If you're going to be out here having multiple sex partners, should both parties be completely honest about how many people they're having sex with? It's never fair to the individual who's going into this agreement with an idea of it being one thing, when in all actuality it's something totally different. Here I am now angry by what I've read and don't know how or if I can get past it. Should I approach Rashad with what I saw? Especially since the only reason I know this information to begin with is because I went through his personal IM account. I am starting out in this conversation dead ass wrong.

"OMG, are you serious!" Cookie shrieked. "Gia I don't think you should say anything to him because he's going to know you went through his iPad. You know Rashad, and he is going to be mad. Are you ready to deal with the outcome of you confronting him with this? You already know he's going to try and use the fact that you all aren't in a committed relationship as his out. But we both know you're going to do whatever you already have your mind set on doing. I'm still shocked you actually went through his iPad."

"You're shocked?? Shit! I'm beyond shocked," I replied. "But I'm also hurt and angry because I feel so betrayed."

"I know, and I'm so sorry you're going through this," she said. "I wish I could do something to take the pain away. Just think about it before you react."

Ladies, let's get into this tea. I know where Cookie and I stand on this topic, but I am positive some would disagree with my view. Oftentimes, I have heard that you should not ask your partner "how many?" Therefore, everyone is walking around the streets pretending they don't care about his/her number. Please do not get me wrong: I do not care about his past number at all. We all have a past and how many women my man has had in his past is not of importance to me. However, as I stated before, I do want to know if the man I am having sex with is out here being all wild and crazy within his sex life. I understand when dating multiple people comes with the possibility of him/her having multiple sex partners. To each their own as long as you disclose to your partner how many.

I also want to know how many, if any, you are having unprotected sex with. We as women have got to stop being afraid to ask the men we date the tough questions. This is what I mean by holding our men accountable for their actions. At the end of the day, there is no real straight forward answer to my question. It all comes down to a matter of preference. My comfort level may only be one or two others but Mary Jo around the corner may not care how many. Therefore, the moral of this story is for everyone to do what is best for you and your relationships.

# 4

# The Carpenter II

**W**hether or not I should or shouldn't, isn't even a question because we all know with my strong ass personality I went straight to Rashad with what I saw. How could I not, given how angry I was by what I read.

It's now February 2015, and after calling Rashad out on all the shit I found on his iPad, he is pissed because I went through his IM and he feels violated—and rightfully so. But he doesn't feel that he owes me an apology, or even an explanation, for that matter. Now I'm not just hurt, I'm pissed. So I log into his online dating account and change his message to the following:

"Hello, I'm a lying cheating hoe and I'm not looking for any type of relationship. I'm just on this site to see how many women I can fuck. If you're interested in just hooking up, then I'm your man."

I know, I am petty and had no business changing his message like that. It is too late now!

Next, I responded to this little young girl he had been going back and forth with.

"Little girl, you not even ready for a man like me. Stop playing games. If you're not trying to fuck, stop wasting my time. You wanna talk big girl shit but you ain't about that life for real!"

This made Rashad call me up. It's February 14, 2015, early Saturday morning. I answer the phone. It's Rashad on the other end going off and threatening to call the police because I still had his iPad.

"Gia, if you don't give me my fucking iPad I'm going to call the police and tell them you stole it and press charges against you!" he shouted.

Naturally his tone sent me over the edge and I started yelling at him. "Are you fucking kidding me? Fuck you Rashad; you have a lot of fucking nerve telling me you're going to call the police on me. Call them; I don't give a fuck because you and I both know that shit ain't true. You're a motherfucker and I hate you right now. You're so un-fucking-grateful; you think I'm going to let you keep taking me for granted. Do you really think you can just play me? You got me all the way fucked up. I can careless if you never speak to me again because I don't have shit else to say to your ass. So don't fucking call me again and when I'm ready to give you back the iPad I'll call you. Fuck you, Rashad!" I then hung up.

An hour goes by. My phone rings. It's Rashad and his voice is a lot calmer from earlier.

"Listen, I don't want to fight with you," he began. "You have no idea how going through my iPad made me feel. I felt violated and for a man this is a big deal, the worst thing you can do to a man is to violate him. You told me that I could trust you with my password, and I had nothing to worry about. But you are no different from every other female, you went through my shit. I feel so betrayed and don't know if I can get past it."

I am taken aback because this was the first time he expressed his feelings about this situation on that level. All I could do was listen; I felt as though I owed him that much because I knew I was wrong for going through his personal messages.

"I would have never done anything like this to you," he said.

"Rashad, you are not the only one hurt by this," I said. "I understand how you feel, and I'm sorry, but I'm working and can't really talk right now."

"Gia, that's all I called to say. I'll talk to you later. Bye," and he hung up.

About ten  minutes go by and Rashad calls again.

"Two things: First, I do appreciate you," he began "Second, Happy Valentine's Day."

"Thank you!" I said, smiling. "Bye."

We had finally taken a step toward healing and forgiving one another. You see, in Rashad's eyes he can't get past the fact that I went through his iPad. Therefore, the trust we once had has now been broken. But this broken trust is two fold, because the trust I once had has also been compromised. How do Rashad and I get past this breach of trust that has now taken place in our FWB relationship? How do two people come back from something like this? The fact remains, Rashad is screwing other women I knew nothing about, and I violated his personal space. Rashad doesn't feel that he should say sorry or feel bad because I shouldn't have gone searching and because we're not in a "committed relationship."

I meet up with Cookie for drinks because I just need to vent. So I ask the question: does a title, or lack thereof, give a person an automatic out whenever something foul goes down? Especially if the two weren't just hooking up as in a booty call, but we were going out on dates, took a trip, had long conversations, shared space, exchanged Christmas and birthday gifts? Are we really going to say that what we had wasn't a relationship regardless of the fact there wasn't a title?

I'm sorry but title or not it doesn't negate the fact that what he and I had was a relationship! Feelings were involved even though neither of us would  fully own them to one another. It was very clear we had feelings for each other on some level, and anyone who saw the way we looked at each other knew we were more than just "friends." You can't hide that type of chemistry; not even on a good day. Wouldn't you think title or not we should still be held accountable for our actions? Even more so, when two people care for one another, aren't they supposed to have a mutual respect for each other?

At the end of the day, if you're going to have a lot of women/men, just be as transparent as possible because your partner has the right to know what they are  getting themselves into. I understand that how many partners one chooses to have is his or her own choice, but once you're doing more than just fucking your current partner and you add dating, gifts and time spent, then you owe that individual the complete and honest truth. You should NEVER make that decision for them; your partner should always be given the option to continue or to walk away. Rashad didn't give me that option, and now, not only do we both feel betrayed by the other,  but we aren't speaking because we both feel angry and hurt by what has transpired between us.

A week goes by and I get a call from Cookie. "Gia, have you returned the iPad yet?" she inquires.

"Nope," I say, "and I blocked Rashad from calling and texting. And I can see that he's still online talking to women. Will this pain ever end?"

"Rashad has caused you so much pain, but do you think that what you did to him has him feeling equally hurt right now?" Cookie proposes. "When do you plan on giving him back his iPad? You know the longer you keep it the harder it's going to be for the two of you to come back from this."

"I know, and I plan to take it to him sometime within the next couple of days," I said.

"I know you don't like when I keep checking up on you and sending you texts, but I really hate seeing you hurt and sad," Cookie replied. "I'm not going to say the pain will get better in time, because you already know that. Just know that I'm here!"

"Thank you, and yes, I hate when people say 'it'll be better in time'. I know the pain won't last forever, but the shit hurts right here, right now," I replied

"I know. So are you going to unblock him so that the two of you can talk?"

"Yeah," I said, 'but who knows, he may have me blocked too. We both laugh.

The next day Rashad shutdown his IM and his online accounts, so I could no longer view either. At this point, Rashad is angry so he tells me that we can never have a committed relationship for many reasons, thus, what we have is all we will ever have. Could you imagine being me and having to hear the man I now have feelings for, the man I thought was my friend, the man I would do anything for, tell me that we can never have more?

I'm feeling mixed emotions right now, because on one hand, yes I love him. But on the other hand, I don't know if he's my forever love. I mean, is he even capable of being faithful?

I wish I knew the answer to all the questions rolling around inside my damn head. But I knew going through his iPad I was taking a huge risk with our friendship. How do two people get past this level of betrayal? There's so much pain between the two of us, and at this point I still haven't returned the iPad because I'm not ready to see Rashad. I struggle with all the things I read and saw. How do I get past this level of pain I'm feeling? Rashad is good because he has always had other women. None of this is making me feel any better.

I'm at my bi-weekly appointment with Dr. Edwards. I'm telling him how it's all his fault that I'm going through this pain because he is the one who convinced me that I need to open my heart and let down my guard just a little. How I can't be afraid of getting hurt because it can't be avoided. For the first time in any of my appointments, I can't seem to hold back from crying in my session. I'm telling Dr. Edwards how for years I have always been able to protect my heart by staying guarded, and the one time I let my guard down it's for a man that isn't even deserving of me. But none of this stops me from trying to justify Rashad's behavior.

"In Rashad's defense, maybe he simply doesn't feel that I'm the one? He clearly doesn't need me for sex. He's a very handsome man that can have any woman he wants and we already know he has plenty of options. So why stay in this thing with me for two years when it doesn't take that long to figure out if a person is the one," I say to Dr. Edwards.

However, in my mind I am telling myself "Gia, you are a damn good woman and amazing in bed. He stays because of the friendship you have provided and because he loves fuckin' you, girl."

The following day, I decided to meet my best guy friend Mike for drinks and a little adult conversation at our favorite happy hour spot, McCormick & Schmick's. I tell him all about what has happened between Rashad and me. Mike tells me I need to get it together and to not give Rashad so much power.

"Here you are crying and hurt over this man, but dude hasn't given you a second thought. He doesn't even care enough about you to talk things out," he scolded. "What is it going to take for you to see that this man is doing him? He's still having sex with other women, taking them out, giving them his time. So stop the crying and talking about not going to any event dude is going to be at. He isn't allowing this to stop him from moving forward. You shut down your Facebook, you can't eat, and you can't sleep, but dude at home getting fucked and sleeping like a baby. Come on Gia, don't do this to yourself, you're a beautiful young woman that can get any man you want."

He continued: "I know it's hard right now because he's the one you gave your heart to, but Gia, sometimes you have to look at the blessing that came from the hurt. There is a reason you decided to look at his iPad that second day and there's a reason God had his shit not working properly. Giving you complete access to his iPad a second time allowed you to see the type of man you were giving your heart to. Yes on one hand you fucked up and we can't negate the fact that by going through his iPad was a whole different level of betraying his trust. However, on the other hand he also betrayed your trust by not being honest with you. This man, if that's what we're calling him, doesn't give a damn about you. No man would be so unconcerned about your feelings if he cared anything for you. It wouldn't matter how many other females he's fucking, the minute he realized you read his messages and knew how hurt you were; at that point, if he cared anything about you, he would've done whatever it took to ease your pain. The fact that he has not reached out to you without you reaching out to him, tells you this man's true feelings. I know this isn't what you want to hear, but Gia you gotta get dude out your head."

It's Monday, cold with snow on the ground and it's time to take Rashad his iPad along with all the other stuff he has left over my house, and a few extras. My plan was to ensure he wasn't home so I

71

could drop the box off at his door because I wasn't ready to see that handsome face of his. I knew I would just melt if I saw him. The call is made but Rashad decided to change the drop off location because he's not going straight home. I'm feeling nervous because I hadn't prepared myself to see him. Keep in mind I still love this man, so this isn't going to be easy for me. Needless to say, I went on and met him at his cousin's house. He texted me the address. I call him when I get out front the house. When Rashad comes to the car I try not to fully look into his face because I wasn't sure how seeing him would make me feel. I kept my car running, got out the car and grabbed the box I had packed for him. He was looking so damn cute with that sexy ass walk of his, those pretty brown eyes. Rashad is surprisingly nice to me, and greets me with a smile on his face, we even make small talk. As nervous as I was about seeing him, I put my big girl boots on, made a little small talk, dropped off that box, and kept it moving.

Inside the box was a letter I wrote to Rashad apologizing for what I had done and explaining to him how the things I read made me feel because for me, this wasn't just about what I did to Rashad. It was also about the devastating pain Rashad had inflicted on my life. A few days pass and Rashad has yet to acknowledge my letter to him, so I give him a call and we talk briefly. However, no good came from our conversation. Another two weeks pass and during that time I have only spoken to him once or twice more. I start to feel bold and miss my friend so I shoot him a quick text inviting him out for drinks. Rashad isn't sure I'm ready to continue with our relationship because I just couldn't handle things. I explain that I'm not trying to continue with the sex just the friendship. I'm still hurt over what was seen on the iPad and I am not interested in being a part of any type of rotation. All I care about is rebuilding our friendship because I still had feelings for Rashad.

He agreed to meet me for drinks and we actually had a great time. We did a lot of talking and even managed to sneak a laugh or two in there.

# Chapter 4: The Carpenter II

Rashad and I continue communicating via text, but we have not seen each other since we met for drinks. Days go by and nothing, not a word from Rashad, and then out of the blue I receive a random late night text from him.

Rashad: Hi
Gia: Hi.

In the midst of us not talking, our friends Alanna & Nia are planning their joint birthday happy hour.

### *What happens next would forever change our lives, or does it?*

Two days later, I received another text from Rashad that read "Call me."

Rashad sounds nervous but he goes on to say that he, of course, was invited to Alanna & Nia's birthday party taking place on Friday, and that our friend Alanna said she wanted to invite one of Rashad's female friends, Taylor. I am confused, so I asked, "do you mean like a date? Wait...and did you say okay knowing I'm going to be there? So are you dating this female? Are you in a relationship with her?" I'm so fucking confused right now. Rashad said she's a friend and Alanna said she wanted to invite either her or my other female friend named Kelly, because Kelly is who Alanna really wants me to be in a relationship with. At this point I'm screaming at Rashad, telling him how he is a heartless motherfucker and how could he do this to me so soon after we ended things. Hell, it's only been a month, so how the fuck could you do this shit to me? I went on to say "I can't believe you didn't tell Alanna "no" you don't want either of your female friends there because you knew I would be there as well. I can't believe you would hurt me this way. You know damn well I'm not ready to see you with another female. How could you do this to me?" Rashad said Alanna was going to invite her either way, so I said if I gotta pick one I'd rather him bring Taylor not Kelly because Kelly doesn't know anyone and would really be all over me.

He went on to say how he is not heartless, because if he was, he wouldn't have told me anything. "I would have allowed you to walk into that situation blindly but I did not want to take your option away this time," he said.

I am still screaming at him for causing this new pain in my life, and I tell him I am no longer going to the party. I then hang up.

I call my BFF Cookie in tears and share with her what Rashad has done. Cookie is upset because it hurts her to see me in so much pain. Cookie asks, "Why would he do this to you? It's only been a couple of weeks since you guys stopped seeing each other! Why couldn't he tell Alanna no to inviting Taylor." Cookie wants to text him but I said don't because he wasn't mean nor did he say it to be nasty or hurtful. Even though these words were coming out of my mouth, I wasn't sure if I truly believed what I was sharing with Cookie. We got off the phone.

Rashad & I spoke a few more times that day because I desperately wanted some clarity from him. However, all I ended up with were more questions. None of this is making sense to me. I can't believe this is my life right now. My head is spinning from all the thoughts and previous conversations between the two of us. I am a very skillful thinker. An hour or so later I'm calm but feel like Rashad is out to hurt me because of the recent events with the iPad. I am questioning why Alanna is so pressed for Rashad to bring an old friend that he only fucked from time to time (his words, not mine)... None of this is adding up in my mind. This means I need to get to the bottom of all the lies being told to me.

So I send Rashad a text and he responds:

Gia: Are u sure Alanna doesn't already know about us? Are u sure u didn't tell her that you've been seeing me? I guess I am supposed to thank u for not allowing me to walk into that situation in the blind because I would have been devastated. U have no idea how hurt I'm feeling but it's all good. This too shall pass.

Chapter 4: The Carpenter II

Rashad: I never told Alanna anything about us! I promised her after Angie that I wouldn't talk to any more of her friends & that's why I told you that we can't have anything more. Alanna & I have been friends since 1995. She's been there during some bad times. She's not a person that likes to see people hurting.

Gia: It's whatever Rashad! You've made your decision, and I'm tired of crying.

After a few hours of crying, I decided to tell Rashad I was not going to the party. I went as far to ask him for his tickets to the game. I mean, he's not going to be using them since he'll be at the party, right? Rashad said he had already listed them to be sold, but if no one buys them, I can have the tickets.

For the next couple of days I am feeling hurt, I cannot stop crying. I am in complete disbelief, I cannot seem to make sense of what Rashad has done to me. How could he ever think bringing some random female friend is okay? Just because he tells me that she's someone that he has known longer than he has known me and had been still fucking her from time to time? Is hearing this supposed to make me feel better about the situation? Are you kidding me right now? Honestly, is that little known fact supposed to make me feel less hurt?

It's Friday and I decided to attend the party after all because I needed to show Rashad that he hasn't won. It will be good for me! I walked into the Lounge looking super cute with my face beat! I wore my black Chanel leather booties, my blue Free People distressed jeans, and my black lace Free People top that showed the girls off! I walked in like I owned the joint with my badass long white coat on. I made sure not to arrive until after Rashad. Needed to make an entrance. Rashad looked surprised to see me because I told him I wasn't coming.

Now even after seeing Rashad and his female friend together, I still managed to keep it together. Neither Rashad nor I spoke to one another. I was having myself a great time and Cookie and Jasmine were both there for support. We start drinking and taking pics. At one point Cookie and I were trying to take a selfie and out of nowhere Rashad walks up and says, "Give me your phone. I'll take y'all's pic for you." Cookie and I pose for the pic and move on to our other girlfriends' group pics.

Everything was all good until I started hearing people say how nice Rashad's new girlfriend is. Oh, now I am really confused by everything I am hearing because he can't possibly be introducing her to everyone as his new girlfriend. No wait, because Rashad sat on the phone with me explaining that this woman was just an old friend (he said this in his most sincere voice)! That motherfucker! Oh wow! It was all a lie; even the part about it being Alanna who wanted her there. This is crazy, not only did he lie and tell me it was Alanna who wanted her there, but spent an hour on the phone with me prior to this party trying to convince me it was nothing—and for what?

I'll tell you why: he needed to make his story sound truthful so that I would believe all the lies about who Taylor really was and how long he has really known her. Understand that I am no fool. The moment I saw his interaction with Taylor, I knew Rashad had lied to me. It was clear this female was not just an old friend that he used to fuck from time to time. The way Rashad and Taylor interacted with one another made it very clear to me that this was something new. He was very intimate with her. He was giving her a lot of public affection.

Everything he said on the phone had been a lie. He was not bringing her because Alanna was going to invite her regardless. It was so obvious that Alanna was just meeting Taylor for the first time, just as all the other friends there were meeting her for the first time. I kept a smile on my face throughout the rest of the evening, even though I was fuming deep down inside. Okay so I get it now: the new girl Taylor (looking like she used to be a dude) gets to be with Rashad who is all of a sudden full of public affection around our friends. While I got to be with Rashad who only showed public affection when we weren't around our friends. WTF? Wow! I was an amazing friend and lover to Rashad; in return, he is giving me his ass to kiss by bringing her here. Now you see why even though I am still smiling and pretending to be having fun, deep down I am dying inside from heartbreak. "How in the hell could this be happening in my life?" I keep asking myself.

Why would he lie to me about his relationship with Taylor? But more importantly, if she's his new girlfriend, he had to have been developing this relationship while he was still seeing me. This was like another slap in the face and made it even more painful for me. I feel so betrayed by Rashad; I can't even put into words how hurt I am feeling right now. This also meant that Rashad was already with her when he asked to meet me to talk and continue. How could the man who was supposed to care about me do this? How could this man devastate my life this way? Even if he had moved on, did he need to introduce her that night and so soon after he and I ended things?

It's Saturday morning, the night after Rashad introduced Taylor to everyone at happy hour. Even though I put on a brave front at the club, I'm so hurt by his actions and lack of respect for me. I didn't sleep at all last night and I cried all night, but now it's 8am and time for me to work. I have to pull it together, so that my clients aren't asking me if I am okay. I let my clients in and we get started. Now I look the part but everything around me is a blur. This particular morning I have Ashley and Jay at my place. We are making small talk as we do every Saturday morning. At some point during the conversation, I was in such a daze it took Ashley to say "Gia, are you okay" before I realized tears were rolling down my face. Then Jay says "OMG, is everything okay?" I simply reply "I'm fine, just give me a minute" and I go into the restroom to get myself together.

A few minutes later, I return and apologize to the ladies but they aren't having it. They both reassure me that everything is going to be okay. Then Pam said let's pray and they grabbed my hands and prayed for me and for whatever it was I was going through. I will forever be grateful for that prayer. But most importantly, for their love and support at a time when I thought hell couldn't get any worse. I appreciate them both for never asking what it was I was going through and for respecting the fact that I'm such a private person.

Now I can't eat, can't stop crying, and haven't slept in two days. I want so bad to understand why? I go into my prayer closet for hours praying that God will give me the strength to get through this devastation and betrayal. It's Sunday and one would think that I would take solace in knowing that what he has with Taylor appears to be just for show, because he is not faithful to her. Not only is he still on the dating website, but just a week ago he was entertaining continuing a sexual relationship with me again. A man like Rashad don't just cut off all the women he's been fuckin' just like that. But knowing all of these things does not make the pain any less painful for me because I still have feelings for this man, and turning those feelings off isn't as easy as it may seem. I pray I find peace real soon because I'm now on day 3 of no sleep and barely eating. Lord knows this is not healthy for me but it is a process.

I'm contemplating asking Rashad for a meeting because I need some type of closure, but I don't feel I can get it without speaking to him directly. Monday comes and I work from home, so I text Rashad and ask to meet up with him. I feel like not only does he owe me an explanation but I deserve that shit. He agreed to meet me after work. Around 3:30pm I received a text from Rashad letting me know I can come over to his place at 4:30pm to talk.

I get to Rashad's house; I park my car and wait for him to come outside. Rashad gets in the car just as calm as if he did not just show up to the party with Taylor. It is so hard to stay mad at him, but I am not going to allow his cute face to distract me. We exchange pleasantries, and then Rashad gets straight to the point.

"You said we needed to talk, so what's on your mind," he asked.

"What in the hell was that whole thing about on Friday?" I began. "Why did you lie about who your friend was? It was clear, Rashad, that she is more than just a friend. That is so fucked up that you didn't come clean with me. How do you call yourself my friend, then turn around and bring her around us so soon. I've known you for years and I have NEVER seen you with a female at an event, but all of a sudden, you had to bring her. I feel like you did this to hurt me."

"I did not do anything to hurt you. She is just my friend. If or when we decide to make it more, I will be sure to tell you," he said.

"Whatever, Rashad," I said. "You're so full of shit. You made it seem as though she was someone who has been around for years, someone Alanna already knew. But that was not the case at all. It was very clear that everyone was meeting her for the first time."

"Believe what you want, but I have known her for a long time," he said. "I'm not saying you have not known her, but I am saying that Alanna and the others did not already know her. So don't try and play me."

"Why did you bring her to the party?" I pressed him. "Out of all the events, why the party and why so soon after you and I stopped seeing each other? Why would you do this to me, if you're not still mad at me for what I did?"

"Gia, it was not about you. We are not seeing each other anymore, so I can see whomever I want," he said.

"Yes, you can but why bring her around if you are not trying to prove a point?" I retorted. "You thought because she was mixed with curly hair that you were doing something? No one cares about that because she's a bamma with hard ass features and she looks like she used to be a man!"

"You are funny but you are not going to keep saying that about her," he said, barely holding back laughter.

I wasn't in a joking mood. "You can't tell me what I can or cannot say out my mouth. This is my opinion, you don't have to agree. You and I both know what you did is messed up!"

"You are not the only one mad," he said in a somewhat conciliatory manner. "Another female friend of mine said to me, 'you can be in a relationship with Taylor, but not with me.'"

"Do you think telling me this is supposed to make me feel better?" I asked, annoyed. "So I am confused as to why she would give two fucks about who you are in a relationship with. What am I missing?"

"You're not missing anything," he said. "I'm just letting you know you're not the only one mad."

"Whatever, Rashad. You are so full of shit."

"I don't know what you want from me. I already told you that I didn't bring Taylor to hurt you. Why would I do that?" he asked. We sat silently for a few seconds. "I'm hungry. Can you drive me to McDonalds?"

"Are you serious right now?" I shriek, taken aback. "You're just going to ask for McDonalds in the middle of our conversation?"

"Yes, I am hungry. I have been working all day," he said

# Chapter 4: The Carpenter II

I agreed to take him to McDonald's and we continue our conversation there and back. I drop Rashad back off at home and we say our goodbyes and that's that. Or is it?

About a week goes by and I receive a call from Rashad. It is kinda late on Friday night but I answer the phone anyway. He wants to come by my house.

"Why do you want to come over, Rashad? Aren't you seeing Taylor? I'm not playing these games with you," I said.

"I'm not playing games. I wanna see you," he said. If I come over, will you come outside?"

"Come outside for what, Rashad? Why do you want to see me? Why do you think you get to hold on to some part of me?"

"Please can you come outside if I drive over there? I just want to see you. So tell me, are you going to come out or what?"

"Rashad, are you drunk? Because clearly I can tell from your tone that you've been drinking. I don't want you driving to my house when I know for a fact that you're tipsy."

"I'm fine!" he said, unconvincingly. "I'm in my car and I'm on my way."

"No!" I yell. "Okay, listen; I'll come to you because clearly you've been drinking."

"Okay, are you on your way now?"

"Yes! Just tell me where you are," I said.

"I just pulled up to my house but I'm not going to go inside because I might fall asleep and not hear the door," he explained. "So I'm going to wait for you inside my car."

"Okay, I'm going to slip on some clothes and be on my way," I told him. I get dressed and head over to Rashad's house. I pull onto Rashad's street and there he is with his headlights on, car running, leaned back in his seat and waiting on me. I swear he drives me crazy. He is parked in the opposite direction so I bust a U-turn and park behind his car.

"Rashad, what's going on?" I asked as I got in his car. "Why did you need to see me and why did you think I would allow you to drive to me knowing you've been drinking?"

"I'm good," he slurred. "Can I get a hug?"

"Really, Rashad?"

"Yeah, man, give me a hug."

I lean over to hug him and we start kissing. The next thing I know, I'm sitting on top of Rashad in the front seat of his car, in front of his neighbor's house. We are kissing and I'm just wearing a little maxi dress, no panties (it's not unusual for me to go without panties because I never wear panties). I also have on a jean shirt that I just slipped on real quick.

Rashad is going in with the kissing. Clearly he is feeling nice because then he starts kissing my breasts and grabbing my ass. We are grinding in the front seat behind the steering wheel of his car. Minutes later, Rashad has his pants down with my dress up and we are having hair pulling, ass grabbing, breast sucking, passionate, and raw sex in front of the neighbor's house. Windows are steamy and I am banging my knee up against the gearshift but I don't care because the sex is amazing and I missed the feeling of him. I ride Rashad for a good 20 minutes and it was one of our best quickies ever! After we are done, I give Rashad a soft kiss on the lips, get myself together, and I'm out! I drive myself back home.

A week goes by before I hear from Rashad again. It's a Friday night again around 11 p.m., but I was still up because earlier that night I had hosted a Lookbook showing for all of my close girlfriends. Keep in mind I worked hard on putting that book together as a birthday gift for Rashad but because of timing, Rashad never got the book. So I dedicated the book to "The One I Love" (which is I). I had food, drinks, and I showed everyone how I came up with my poses and my outfits for each picture. The girls and I had a great evening.

So now it's 11 p.m. and Rashad is on my phone. He wants to come over.. (I have the hardest time telling this man "NO" but I'm home alone). So I allow him to come over, and I don't even ask why he want to see me nor do I ask about Taylor because I can really care less about her!

I let Rashad in, we are in the living room where the display table of all my pictures and the book is located. Rashad asked what's up with all the pictures. I remind him this was the book I initially put together as a birthday gift for him but by the time it was complete, he and I were no more. He looks at the book and the individual pictures I had blown up and tells me how nice they all are. We go upstairs to my bedroom, I turn on the TV, and we get ready for bed.

Now you know Rashad and I had sex, and what I love about him is his ability to go a long time because I have a high sex drive! Therefore, our foreplay alone usually lasts 15 minutes. I love the way he man handles me, I love being tossed around, and more than anything, I love that he never asks me can we switch positions because whatever position he wants me in, is where he is going to put me with no questions asked. DAMN...his dick is addictive, no lie! I can't get enough and there is nothing, absolutely nothing off limits when we are having sex. Rashad can have me however, wherever, whenever. I can honestly say I have never performed oral sex on any man as much I did with him. That night he had my ass up in the air and climbing the damn wall. Drunk sex is the best when your partner knows how to eat the pussy then take you to every climax level possible. I swear Rashad is the only man I have ever had multiple orgasms with and on a consistent basis! Shit, we could have ended shit sooner had I known the sex would get even better. Imagine that.

The next morning we have to get up early because I have a parent/teacher conference at my daughter's school. I take my oldest daughter Peyton's car because she needed to use my car. I get to the school to start my parent/teacher conference and a few hours later I receive a call from Peyton.

"Mom, your car won't start," she said.
"What? What do you mean because I just drove it yesterday and had no issues with it."
"Well, it's not starting at all! It sounds like it wanna crank over but nothing."

"Fuck! I have no idea what it could be. Okay, I'm almost done here and I'll be home soon," I tell her.

I get home and sure enough, my car won't start. It is Saturday afternoon so there is nothing I can do about it until Monday. In the meantime, I text my mechanic Mike to let him know that my car won't start and that I am going to have it towed to his shop first thing Monday morning. Mike texts back and gives me the okay. It's Monday, I have the car towed and Mike calls to let me know he has it. He needs a couple of days to look over it because he has other cars ahead of mine.

It's now Wednesday and I receive a call from Mike at the shop.

"Hey! Your car had me puzzled for the past couple of days but I now know what is wrong with it," Mike said. But first, let me ask you, did you see any white powdery type stuff on or near your car's gas tank?

"Uh, no," I replied, confused. "Why?'

"Well because someone put sugar in your gas tank!" Mike explained.

"Wait! What did you just say?"

"Yeah, someone put sugar inside your gas tank and now we have to replace your entire gas system."

"Who would put sugar in my tank, that is crazy!" I said. "I am not on bad terms with anyone. I have never had anything like this happen to me. I am in shock right now. But more importantly, what is this going to cost me?"

"Well because of the type of car you drive, it is expensive to replace the parts. With parts and labor you are looking at $2600," Mike said.

"Are you serious right now?"

"Yes, it could have been worse."

"Okay. I mean, I guess I don't have much of a choice. Just let me know how long it will take to fix and I will figure out the money in the meantime. Thanks, Mike!"

I get off the phone with Mike and I am pissed because who would want to put sugar in my gas tank? I call Peyton to tell her what Mike just told me. She is just as shocked and we cannot think of anyone who would do something so childish.

Next, I call Cookie and give her the tea. "You are lying!" she shouted. "Who would do something like that?"

"I don't know, but I do know that's some shit a female would do. I honestly think Taylor followed Rashad to my house."

"Really, you think so?" Cookie asked.

"Hell yeah, I don't believe in coincidences," I told her. "You are not going to convince me the night Rashad stays the night at my house, someone put sugar in my gas tank. He is the only man I have been seeing even though we are supposed to be over."

"How would she know which car was yours?" Cookie inquired.

"Are you kidding me, as much as my car used to be parked outside his house with Alex's big ass school logo magnet on the back? If you think for one second her young ass has never done a drive-by, you are crazy."

"Oh, I didn't think about that," she said.

"Yeah, and if it wasn't her, it is someone attached to his ass. But why would someone he 'just fuckin' do that? They wouldn't, that is the type of shit a female with feelings would do not just a fuck buddy. Nah!"

"So what are you going to do?" she asked. "Are you going to say anything to Rashad about it?"

"Hell yeah! I'll keep you posted."

Later that evening, I called Rashad to let him know about my car. I'm calm and try to keep the conversation very friendly.

"Hey, the mechanic called me today because he finally figured out what was wrong with my car. Apparently, someone put sugar in my gas tank last Friday night. Is there any way possible that Taylor could have followed you to my house?"

Nah, she wouldn't do no shit like that," Rashad said. "I was on the phone with her right before I left home to come to your house and house and she was home. Plus, how would she know which car was yours?"

"Are you kidding me right now? So because you were on the phone with her and she said that she was home, means she was actually at home. Come on now, you called her cell so she could have been sitting right outside your damn house. You are not going to convince me that you called her mother's house phone at 11 o'clock at night. Which means her ass could have been outside your damn house like I said."

"It doesn't matter because she still would not know your damn car," he said.

"If you think for one second that females don't do drive-bys, you're dumb as hell. Listen, I only just learned about her a couple of weeks ago, but who in the hell knows how long you have actually been messing with that girl. As much time as I spend over your house with my car parked out front that has my daughter's school logo magnet on the back? That is how she would know because I am sure she has done other drive-bys before, she is a lot younger than you. If it was not her, it was someone you are fuckin' because this is the type of shit a female with feelings would do. You are the only man I am seeing sexually and the night you stay at my house, someone puts sugar in my tank and you want me to believe there is no way your little girlfriend could have done it? Whatever! All I know is that you had better tell that bitch she is fucking with the wrong one! I had better not find out she did it or there will be hell to pay. I now gotta put out $2600 to fix some shit one of your bitches done did. Tell them bitches next time they are mad with you to put that shit in your damn car."

"Listen, I'm not going to tell you again it was not her because I was on the phone with her and she would not do that," he retorted. "So you can go ahead with all that bullshit you're talking. I am done with this conversation and don't fucking call me anymore!"

"Be done! Fuck you and your little bitch ass girlfriend too! Oh, and I don't call you. I have not once asked to see you since the split— that was you calling me asking to still see me. So do not get the shit twisted. We do not ever have to speak again and I will be good. You got me all the way fucked up if you think I am going to let you say whatever the hell you want to me! Fuck you too and I'm done with this fucking conversation," I shouted and hung up.

Needless to say, that conversation did not go over well at all. A few weeks went by and I received a text from Alanna inviting everyone to her house for a fight party. So I accept, but knowing I would have to see Rashad and probably Taylor. I have to mentally prepare myself for this because I know that bitch is the one who put the sugar in my tank. I invite my good girlfriend Mia to go with me and I fill her in on all the drama around me seeing the two of them for the first time since the car incident. Mia says to me "you are not going to fight the girl are you?" I wish I could punch that bitch in her face but I won't for two reasons. First, I'm too old for that! Second, I would never disrespect Alanna's house like that.

Mia agrees to come with me to the fight party. At this point, Cookie is no longer the only friend in that group that knows about Rashad and me. I decided to tell Jasmine back in February when all that shit was going on between Rashad and I over his iPad. Therefore, Jasmine also knows that I suspect Taylor as the person responsible.

It's Fight Night and I'm looking super cute! I slick my long hair back into a low ponytail with a side-part. I wear my light blue Free People distressed jeans, a white knit type pullover top with the back open, and my pointed-toe leopard print heels that strap around my ankles. Mia and I get to the party and all is good, no sign of Rashad or Taylor. So I start drinking to calm my nerves because I am not sure how seeing them is going to make me react. Twenty minutes later, in walks Rashad and Taylor. Rashad has his hookah machine with him and after sitting it down he makes his way around the room saying his hellos and giving hugs. So that it is not obvious we are not speaking he taps my shoulder then says "hey!" I give a half-smile and continue my drink. Taylor stands there and never says "hello" to the room but Alanna and Nia went up to her and spoke. Now all the men were hanging out in the basement, which is where Rashad would normally be as well. Not this night, he sat at the table to babysit Taylor because that bitch knew that the car she fucked up belonged to someone at that party because there was no way she didn't see it when they drove up. The entire night she didn't say more than two words, and it is not like this was her first time meeting the girls.

I am 5 or so drinks in at this point, therefore, I start talking to Mia about Taylor without realizing how very loud I was speaking. So Jasmine and Mia dump my last drink out because I am cursing at this point and ain't no telling what I am going to do next. So Mia and Jasmine start telling me that I am loud and need to drink some water. Jasmine goes on to say that after tonight, she is convinced that Taylor had something to do with the sugar in my tank just based off how she was acting the entire night. Afraid to let Rashad out of her site and not engaging at all. Taylor didn't say two words the entire night even though she was surrounded by a group of women she had already met. I told Jasmine I did not need confirmation because my gut told me it was her as soon as I learned what was done to my car. She can trick Rashad but not me because I am not having sex with her like Rashad. We pack up to leave and I go get my car and pull into Alanna's driveway so that Taylor could see who it belong to. I don't ever think it was about me personally because I don't believe she knew who the female was driving the car. I believe she has done more than one drive-by and my car was always there.

A few days later Rashad kept with his story that it could not have been Taylor because she never said anything to him about it and she would have been mad with him. I also maintain my thoughts on why she did and would never admit to putting the sugar in my gas tank. First of all, if she were to say anything about my car Rashad would instantly know that she is nothing but a young crazy ass bitch! Therefore, she is not going to risk losing him, so Taylor did what any other crazy bitch would do. She kept her man and kept her secret!

Three months go by and I have not heard from Rashad nor have I seen him. As far as I know he is still dating Taylor. It is the end of August and I realize that in a few weeks I will come face to face with Rashad at Angie's birthday party. I have this bright idea to reach out to him and break the ice. I send Rashad a straight to the point but yet simple text. To my surprise he responds pretty quickly.

Gia: Hey Rashad! What's going on witcha? How have you been?

Rashad: Hey! I'm good. Did you hear I was in an accident on my bike?

Gia: Yeah, I heard. So are you okay and back to work?

Rashad: Nah, not yet but I will be back in a few weeks.

Gia: Cool, well take care. I am glad we can be cordial. It is important to me.

Rashad: We good.

A few weeks later, Cookie and I go to Angie's birthday party. We see Rashad so Cookie speaks, he speaks and gives her a hug. I'm walking behind Cookie, so I speak but Rashad throws shade and completely ignores me. I am taken by surprise because the last time we spoke we were in a good space, not sure what the cold shoulder is all about. I don't say a word and go on and enjoy myself.

The next day, I send Rashad a text: "Hey, what's up? Why the cold-shoulder last night? I thought you and I were cool?" He didn't respond.

Two weeks go by and I reach out to Rashad because I need a fire stick. I shoot him a quick text, he lets me know that he has one,  and we decide that this evening would be a good time for me to pick it up.

# Chapter 4: The Carpenter II

I go over to his house around 7 p.m. However, while I am there Rashad hit me with the "I know you told Alanna and the other girls about you and I."

"Ohhhhhh…...so now I know why you were throwing me shade at Angie's party."

"I just don't understand why," he said. "I mean I get it you were in your feelings."

"Nah, I wasn't 'in my feelings' I was hurt!" I said. "You act like I told her all the ins and outs of our relationship, but that was not the case at all. As a matter of fact, I never came and told Alanna anything concrete about you and I. Yes, I alluded to the fact that it was you and Taylor I was talking about but never came out and told her. I only told Jasmine and Ashley."

"Well, they told Alanna because Mia and all the girls know. They have had conversations about what went down with the sugar in your tank. Alanna came to me and said she knew and why didn't I tell her."

"Is that right?" I said. "So Alanna could come to you but she could not come to the person who gave her the damn clues. Y'all funny, every last one of y'all. I love how that group stay having side-bar conversations. They only know because I wanted them to know because you already know I don't slip up and tell shit. I think it is fucked up how she can come to you but not me!"

"What you expect, Alanna my best friend," he said.

"I don't give a fuck because she and I are friends too. Therefore, she should not be out here picking sides without hearing from me."

"Man, none of that matters!" he shouted. "You weren't in this by yourself and you should not have told anyone anything without discussing it with me first."

"You're right! I should not have said anything to any of them because I already knew that they can't hold water. But, I wanted to see you pay!"

"But I didn't pay Gia, because they sided with me," Rashad said.

"Of course they did, but it's whatever Rashad, I'm over all the bullshit," I said. "Gia with feelings gave a fuck, but I don't really give a fuck now."

We finished our conversation which was very enlightening. Rashad and I cleared the air, we are now hopeful that this is a step in him and I becoming friends without the benefits. I got my fire stick and took my ass home.

The next day I called Cookie to tell her how Jasmine had been sharing information about Rashad and I even after I asked her not to share anything I told her. Cookie is in shock, but not really! We can't believe Alanna went to Rashad but ain't say two words to me about what she knew. Especially since nobody would know shit if it was not for me. I share with Cookie that I am mostly hurt by Jasmine sharing because I am closer to her; she is my sister-friend. So I feel betrayed and I'm not sure how to move forward with this new piece of information. I am truly hurt and angry by this news and if Jasmine was any other friend I would be ending our friendship right now. I do not play the trust game, you can't call yourself my friend when I can't even trust you with a simple secret. At this point it is not that she shared, because we already know I don't share shit I don't want repeated. I am hurt because I wanted to believe that I could trust her. I struggled with not telling her about Rashad and I sooner, because she is more than just another girlfriend. Jasmine is more like a sister to me. And that is why I am so angry about all of this. As far as Alanna goes, I expected her to side with Rashad, he is her best friend. I learned a long time ago not everyone knows what it means to be a friend because let me tell you how if this was Cookie, I would not just take her side because she is my best friend. Nah, I am on the side of fair and truth! PERIOD!

I went home, prayed on this new information as far as what to do about it. Decided not to do or say anything to anyone because I did not want to throw Rashad under the bus. But I distance myself from the group, including Jasmine. I know she felt something was different because she too kept her distance as well.

Days after finding out all this disappointing information, it's my birthday weekend and I invite everyone over to my house for happy hour. Yes, even Jasmine but she couldn't make it. It's a small get together; not everyone could make it but it was cool because I had Cookie, Nikki, Ashley, Alanna, Renee, and my daughter Peyton. It was fun and weird at the same time because we all know the secret but no one knows that the other knows. Crazy, right? That's my crazy life right now. A few days later it's my actual birthday and I receive a text from everyone in the group including Jasmine.

As more time goes by I still haven't spoken to Jasmine, it's clear we are not on good terms and when you have two very strong personalities going head to head nothing gets accomplished. But importantly, I just don't know how to get past the betrayal I'm feeling right now. I have a conversation with Cookie, and of course she remains neutral because she's a bomb ass best friend. Cookie encourages me to reach out and have a conversation with Jasmine. She maintains that what I'm going through with Jasmine is not "friendship ending worthy!" I decided I am not reaching out to her because she went ghost during my birthday and she had side-bar conversations about very sensitive information I had shared with her. I have never shared any private information about her that she asked me not to repeat. Hell, I have not shared private information even if she didn't ask me not to repeat, because as a friend, some things just go without saying! Jasmine didn't just recently meet me, therefore, she knew I would be mad if I found out she and the others were discussing me or my personal life.

A month goes by; it's mid-November and I agreed to meet my girlfriend Renee for dinner. She lives far, so we decide on a restaurant that's halfway between us both. During dinner, I decided to share with her about Rashad and I because at this point, I figured she had already heard anyway. To my surprise, she had no idea, and if she did, she played it off extremely well. Dinner was great, we went to this BBQ restaurant and the ribs were delicious. It was my first time there, the night was filled with great conversation and lots of laughs. It's never a dull moment with my girl Renee, she keeps me in tears from laughing so hard. It was exactly what I needed too.

After I met up with Rashad back in October, we started back having sex. I know, I should have left well enough alone, but what can I say–– that man turns me out sexually! However, I did decide to go into things with a different mindset. You see, I am no longer in love with Rashad. It's amazing how going 3+ months with absolutely no contact with a person can change your heart. This go round he is dealing with "old Gia." Let's not forget how great I can be at separating my emotions from sex. It's funny because old Gia would do anything for Rashad. However, I will never forget how hurt I was due to his actions. So now it's just about the sex and nothing more.

I'm learning that Rashad isn't completely over my telling the girls about our relationship, even though he said he understood why I did it. I say this because we keep having conversations about why I shared and how it made him feel. I don't know where it's all coming from now that everyone knows about our relationship.

**November 2015**
Rashad: You opened my eyes to a lot of shit
Gia: As did you. Thanks
Rashad: You were wrong for running your mouth to them & I was wrong for trusting that you wouldn't.
Gia: Ok Rashad those are your feelings and I respect them. You were wrong for talking shit about me to the girls when I was ALWAYS there for you as a friend. I was a fool to ever believe that you would never do that but you did.

Rashad: I was a fool to believe you wouldn't go put me out there is where the problem came from.

Gia: Okay…. We both know you are never gonna own your role in any of this. But I will say this to you, I was wrong for the things I did to you. However, I may be a lot of things but a liar isn't one of them. You can talk about me to Alanna all you want. I don't care what you think of me anymore. This is some childish shit!

Rashad: Wooow… Did Alanna call you?
Gia: Nope. Call me for what?
Rashad: I told her that I talk to you and I asked her why she said something to you about Angie.

Gia: Alanna wasn't the one who told me about Angie. Did you forget that you were who told me about you and Angie when we had one of our fall-outs? You don't remember sending me a text saying that Alanna is your BFF and that you promised her that after Angie you wouldn't mess with anymore of her friends and that's the only reason you and I couldn't have more? One thing about me I don't forget shit that's been told to me. You are mad because you "thought" she told your business but you ain't see shit wrong with the crew telling you mine. IJS…

Rashad: She hasn't told me any of your business! Where are you getting that from? I heard some things about issues that's been going on, but that's far from telling your business! I remember that conversation now that you mentioned it. Damnnn I don't know how I forgot that. She kept telling me that you (Gia) could never say that she (Alanna) told you anything about Angie and I! I forgot until now. I could have been cleared this shit up!

Gia: Yes, you could have! She may not have told my business. However, that doesn't negate the fact that Alanna along with Jasmine, Nia, and Ashley sided with you without knowing the entire truth. On top of that, for Alanna to defend Taylor whom she's barely known and has only hung out with a handful of times by saying "Taylor wouldn't put sugar in my tank" but call me, her good girlfriend, "crazy" for thinking it was Taylor without ever asking me any questions is not okay! They are supposed to be my good girlfriends and if either of them had questions, they should have come to me. Especially since the ONLY reason they now know anything about you and I is because I told them. I get why you defended Taylor because you were dating her. This is all so crazy to me and I will never understand why what you and I had is such a big deal to everyone.

Rashad: A lot of what you said isn't correct! I'm just going to leave it alone.

Gia: Okay, so am I!

A few days pass and Rashad is mad. I think it's funny. I tell him "don't be mad at me… You're the reason we're here. Remember you didn't appreciate me. You killed the nice, loving, supportive, do anything for you, Gia. That girl is gone!"

It's December 2015. I meet Alanna at her house to talk about all the back and forth between her, Rashad and I. Alanna felt it was necessary, you see, she had been put in the middle of something she had no idea she was a part of to begin with. But more importantly, we both decided our friendship was worth having a conversation. Alanna and I cleared the air and moved forward with our friendship as if nothing ever happened. It was great conversation, and very enlightening to say the least. This conversation meant a lot to me after everything I had been hearing. Honestly, I always felt as if Rashad was using his friendship with her as an excuse to keep us in a non-committed relationship, which, in hindsight, was all good because everything happens for a reason.

Later in the week I receive a text from Rashad: "Who's over your house? Wellll…"

The next morning I text back: "Oh shit.. I fell asleep.. Why didn't you ask me that when we first started texting?"

Rashad: "I was at a party."

Gia: Oh okay

Rashad: You're funny.

I call Rashad to see what he's talking about but he doesn't answer. So I text him back.

Gia: Oh, you couldn't answer the phone, but you can text? No, you're the funny one.

Rashad: What you doing?

Gia: I'm out

Rashad: Okay. Where are you at?

I don't respond to his text. I'm giving him the same treatment he gives to me.

Rashad and I continue to see each other here and there, but nothing on a regular basis. We are truly just in this thing now for the sex. It's now late December, Rashad calls and he brings up the past again. He still cannot get over me telling the girls about him and me. I can clearly tell he has been drinking. Whenever I want the honest to God truth from him, all I have to do is wait for him to get tipsy, that is when he will tell me how he's really feeling each and every time without fail. Only this time our conversation gets heated because I am not about to allow this man to speak to me any kind of way. I tell him how I am so over all the bullshit and he got me fucked up if he thinks I give two fucks about what anyone has been saying about me. I can careless if our friends are siding with him. I'm so over this shit, we are yelling at each other at this point. Then I hang up on him and he calls back with a much calmer tone. This time I hear him out and we end the conversation on a good note.

**January 1, 2016** (12:57am)
Rashad: Happy New Year Babe Rashad - Happy New Year Babe! Be Safe! 😮😮😮

Gia: Happy New Year!! You be safe 😮

A few minutes later my cell phone rings, it's Rashad. "Hey, you safe?"

"Yep, I'm good and I'm safe," I tell him. You be safe going to wherever it is you're headed."

It's a new year, Jasmine and I still aren't like we were but it's her birthday. So I send her a text wishing her a happy birthday. A few more months go by, I text her because both my daughters were graduating and they wanted Aunt Jasmine to be a part of their special day. Jasmine loves my girls so of course she made it out to both graduations. We never fully stopped talking, therefore we both decided to stop being so stubborn and met for happy hour to catch up. Jasmine and I had a great time, laughing and talking as if we never stopped talking for those few months.

Rashad and I continued seeing each other (sex only) off and on for months. It's July 3rd, I go see Rashad. Of course my visit is amazing because he rarely lets me down in the bedroom. I stay the night and he has me all over the bed; no position is off limits when it comes to him. Whatever he is feeling is where my ass is going to end up and I love that about him. I love his confidence inside and outside the bedroom. Though he tries to come across as a "bad ass" he is really a sweet man with a good heart.

The next morning I get up and go home like I always do. It's now July 4th, later that evening I see a picture of Rashad and a female at dinner on FB. Now, I'm not mad because we are nothing but friends who have sex at this point. However, I was taken aback because the comments were as if he is in a relationship with this female. Again, that's fine, but tell me. Allow me to decide if I want to continue having sex knowing he is now in a relationship. So I wait a few days and I call him because I want to know. Rashad knows well, therefore, he knew how much I hated having my options taken away. Now, Rashad tells me the lady in the picture is someone he's dating but they are not in anything serious. He is allowed to see other people and so is she but if or when that should change he will tell me. I half-ass believe him but for argument's sake, I simply say "okay."

Rashad and I somehow find ourselves having sex several more times over the next few months. By late November, both Rashad and I agree that we should just be friends and to this day; he and I never crossed that line again.

Rashad is a special man who will forever hold a special place in my heart. And as far as I'm concerned, even though the relationship didn't work out between us, it doesn't take away from the love, fun, and friendship that will bond him and I for a lifetime. You meet new people, make new memories, then you move on.

# 5

# Girl Talk
# ***Are The Dating Rules Different***

It is time for some more girl talk! So I ask the question: why are the rules for dating so different for men than they are for women? I get that women are known for being more emotional when it comes to dating and men are able to date multiple women without any emotion at all (or so they say). However, does that make it okay for the rules not to apply to them both? We all know that had Rashad's and my roles been reversed, and I was the one who was fucking every man from a dating site. I would be called all types of hoes for having slept with so many men. But more importantly, there is no way Rashad would have ever been okay with knowing I was out there fucking every Tom, Dick, and Harry. He would not have forgiven me and you can't tell me that he would not have had questions. Rashad would have felt some kind of way had I done to him what he did to me.

Most men would have wanted an explanation and an apology. I will never believe that he or any other man would have been okay with finding out that the female they have been intimate with and cared about has been out there just fucking. Why is this way of thinking still okay in this day and age? I'm confused as to why we still raise our sons and daughters with two different sets of rules and standards. Where is the respect? We have got to start teaching and showing our sons at a young age the importance of respecting women. We need to teach them that they too should have standards and it's not okay to give their body to any and every woman that is willing to have sex with them.

And yes, we need to be that direct. Because if we aren't, our young sons will grow up to be men that don't respect women; men that sleep around because they can; men that don't see the value in their woman or wife. They will grow up to be unfaithful womanizers with no remorse.

On the other hand, we raise our daughters to have standards, to respect themselves; telling them to not sleep around and that they should save themselves for marriage. Then they become women that don't believe it's okay to explore their sexuality, their sexual needs, and desires because all their lives they've been told that nice young ladies don't have multiple sex partners. This thought process is a part of the problem with women feeling free sexually. This is also the reason women aren't even comfortable taking a harmless pole exercise class, because they've been raised to believe that nice young ladies don't do such things. Complete foolishness I tell you!

I'm raising my two daughters to feel empowered and confident regardless of their size/skill level; to feel free with exploring their sexual desires, and to leave any inhibitions at the door. I'm teaching my daughters that they can have it all: career, family, house, and the husband of their dreams. hat it's okay to have mind-blowing sex, even before marriage but especially during. That it's okay to perform for their husbands. I want my daughters to feel comfortable doing whatever they desire while in the privacy of their bedroom with their partner or husband. Our young women need to know that it's okay to be a freak in the bed as long as they are always a lady in the streets. Far too often we shy away from having these direct conversations with our sons and daughters. We had better wake up or our daughter's only option for a husband is a man who only cares about himself and his needs. I know that's not the type of man I pray for when it comes to my daughters.

# 6

# The Cigar Lover

*So ladies, let's talk about the next man who enters into my life! I like to call him the "cigar lover"! This man will teach me a very important life lesson about men and honesty! The type of lessons I thought were behind me.*

It's the summer of 2014, I went to visit Jasmine at her house and she asked me if I knew this guy named Tony.

"Nope, his name doesn't sound familiar; who is he?" I said.

"His daughter dances on the same poms dance team as Jordan [Jasmine's daughter]," Jasmine explained. "That's how I met him, but I thought you knew him because according to his Facebook page, y'all went to college together."

Intrigued, I told Jasmine, "Pull up his page; let me see his pic."

We are on Facebook and I'm looking but I'm not sure I remember him. He kinda looked familiar, but not really. Tony is 5'9, brown-complexioned, and has beautiful light brown eyes. He is bald with a salt-n-pepper beard, and his style of dress is fly!

A week or so goes by and we're at Peyton's birthday brunch. I ask her to remind me of the guy's name she was telling me about before. It's Tony. "I'm going to send him a friend request to see if we graduated together, because I swear I don't remember," I tell her. "Oh, I found him. Just sent him a friend request and I will keep you posted."

A few days later, I received a call from Jasmine. "Girl, did you see Tony commented on your pic?" she asked, excitedly. "He said 'Hey Gia,'" she explained. "

I hadn't seen the comment. "Lol! Ok, he's been giving me a lot of emojis on a lot of my pics," I replied " I guess I'll tell him 'hey!'

"No, you gotta say more than that!" she said.

"Well, what should I say? You already know I'm not about to have a conversation over Facebook. I'm way too private for that. I'll just inbox him I'll call you back."

07/21
Gia: Hey, Tony thanks for the likes. How are you? I'm sending an IM because I don't like talking publicly on social media ☺

Tony: Ok cool it's all good. I'm just holding on. No problem I understand.

Gia: Oh, okay cool… What year did you come out?

Tony: I thought we came out together ('91). Was that your year?

Gia: Yeah…I don't know why I thought you were before me… It's the old age getting to me ☺

Tony: Lol! you know I changed my name after we graduated college. lol

Gia: OH, okay lol

Tony: It was for a good reason.

Gia: Oh I'm sure. Hey, did your daughter go to GP High School? I thought I saw a pic.

Tony: Yes, she went there last year but she's on her way to college in the fall.

Did your daughter go there?

Gia: Yep, my oldest but she came out in '08. That's good she's going away to school. My daughter went to HU.

07/22
Tony: My bad Gia, I crashed on you last night. Have a wonderful and blessed day!

Gia: It's fine. I'm pretty sure I did the same. Thanks and you do the same!

07/25

Tony: Guess what—I remember I had a CRUSH on you but I was dealing with someone back then. Lol. Don't kick my butt for saying that lol

Gia: Lol!! Was it just back then or do you have one now ☺

Tony: It was college, and I'll say I'm feeling you like shit... More than a crush. Are you married or in a relationship, if you don't mind me asking?

Gia: Not married... Are you in a relationship?

Tony: No, I have a friend. I'm not married. When I say friend, I mean she wants more, but I told her I'm not down with that in a good way. I know God has something in the works for me.

I like you Gia!

Gia: I date as well, but I'm not in a committed relationship. Maybe we can go out and get a drink.

Tony: Cool, yes sounds good to me. Here's my cell and my home number as well. Please feel free to call. Damn you made my night, no BS. (Cell) 202.555.5555 (home) 301.555.1111. I'm out of town this weekend.

Please pass your number if you can. If not, I understand.

Gia: Cool! Enjoy your trip. Here is my cell – 240.555.2222. Call me when you get back.

Tony: I'll be back Sunday. I'm going to call you Saturday. YES I'M BLUSHING FOR REAL

Gia: Too cute! You are funny ☺

Tony: I'm real. I just saved your number in my cell.

Gia: Lol... That's a good thing ☺

Tony: Yes... ☺☺☺☺☺ Can't wait to see you and hang out. I'm in the Maryland area.

Gia: Sounds good... I'm also in the Maryland area. So not far at all.

## Chapter 6: The Cigar Lover

Tony: My kids and ex-wife live near you. I'm here at the cigar lounge just smiling. Got my boys asking me "are you good slim?" I told them I'm good just made a POWER MOVE!

Gia: Lol... I've done the cigar lounge before. I didn't really know what I was doing but I had a great time.

It wasn't long before Tony and I were talking on a regular basis. He was cool, easy to talk to, with a little edge. Keep in mind, when Tony reached out to me I was still seeing Rashad. It was towards the end of him and I, but Rashad was still in the picture. As you know, Rashad and I were not in a committed relationship and free to date whomever; which he did a lot of. With that said, in the beginning I was nervous about dating them both; so I took things extremely slow with Tony. Up until this point in my life, I had never dated more than one guy in the same year, let alone within the same week. This was all new to me, but very exhilarating at the same time.

Even though I knew Tony from college, I had not seen him since we graduated. So it was as if we were starting over.

Just when you think you have the dynamics between love and relationships all figured out, life throws you a curveball and knocks you off your feet!

At age 46, I thought I had mastered this thing called love! Well, my idea of mastering love meant staying somewhat guarded. I am still unsure if this approach was fair to myself or any of the men I dated at this point. And my new friend Tony was no exception. After everything I was going through with Rashad, I was happy to have Tony to talk to and hang out with.

It wasn't long before Tony and I were meeting up for our first date. I remember our first date because I almost cancelled on him. It was during the week, and I rarely go out on a weeknight. I had already started talking myself out of going until I called Jasmine, and of course she talked me out of cancelling. After I hung up from Jasmine, I had a talk with myself. I said, "Ok Gia, you can do this girl. It's just a drink and some conversation. So go throw on a cute little maxi dress, touch up your makeup and get going!"

Tony was already at the restaurant, Proud Mary's, which was about a 30 minute ride from my house. Tony chose that restaurant because they have outside seating during the spring and summer months. He's a cigar lover, so it was the perfect place for him to enjoy his cigar and happy hour at the same time. Plus, it was a beautiful night; not too hot and there was a nice breeze blowing through the air. When I arrived I called Tony on his cell so he can direct me to where he is seated. He met me in the parking lot instead so we could walk over together.

Tony was wearing distressed jean shorts, a t-shirt, and some Timbs. My first thought was "DAMN! He's looking sexy as hell, he is just a little bow-legged. He is much cuter than I remember him being!" There is something very sexy about him, and that smile of his was so pleasant and welcoming. He made me feel at ease and less nervous about the date.

He had a spot on the grass area, where there was a bench and table for us to sit. It was an easy first date. We laughed, talked and caught up on life, family, and work. Tony kept asking if I was okay because he was smoking his cigar and I don't smoke at all. I reassured him that I was fine with him enjoying his cigar. He asked if I wanted dinner, but it was late and I had dinner prior to leaving my house. It was nice to sit back and enjoy the conversation. At the end of the night, Tony walked me to my car, gave me a hug, we said goodnight, and I went on home. 30 minutes later Tony called to see if I had made it home safely and that turned into another 30 minute conversation. From day one, Tony was very open and comfortable with letting me know how much he liked me. It has been a minute since I had someone so forthcoming about their feelings so soon. I welcomed all the attention but I wasn't going to let him in so easily.

At this point in my life, I had decided to do things differently than my previous relationship with Rashad. I moved faster than normal with Rashad, so now it's time for me to go back to the days when you actually took time out to get to know a person. You see, in my mind I was this badass who not only welcomed FWB type relationships, but also did them and did them well! That shit was all in my head, because in real life, I am just a girl who enjoys consistency and long-term dating. No, I do not require a title or commitment in the normal sense of the word, but I want to be courted. I do not want any man thinking they can ever just fuck me, because that type of relationship will never work out for me. Owning my truth is huge for me, and I'm sure Dr. Edwards will be excited to hear my news.

With that said, Tony and I took things slow. We talked a lot and went out on dates occasionally in the beginning. For one, I was still dating Rashad and had strong feelings for him. Plus, Tony was seeing other people as well. It was a great opportunity for us to build an amazing friendship, which we did. Tony and I could talk about any and everything, even though I was a little more private when it came to my personal life. I take great pride in the fact that I am able to provide dope conversation and I'm pretty. This makes for a win/win situation in my dating life. Men take to me because I am easy to talk to. They fall for me because I have a loving spirit and no matter what they tell me, I never ever judge. But more importantly, I provide serious support to the men I date; I am always going to be his biggest cheerleader! Men love women who allow them to feel free of judgement, and Tony was no different.

A few months go by, Tony and I have gone on several dates at this point. We are very comfortable being around one another and we enjoy each other's company. We are now a couple months in and still have not had our first kiss. It's kinda funny because Tony tells me all the time how he wants to kiss me. I tell him when the time is right he'll know and it will happen.

It's August and Tony's birthday month. This year his birthday is on a Monday, so I took him to dinner on Sunday to Matchbox, a restaurant located in DC. As soon as we walk into the restaurant, who do we see: my girlfriend Alanna and her husband having dinner. I say hello and proceed to introduce them to Tony. Alanna offers us a seat at their table which was sweet of her but Tony and I take a seat at the bar until our table is ready. This situation was a little strange for me because I had never introduced any guy I've dated to any of my girlfriends. But sometimes God has a way of just throwing you into uncomfortable situations as a part of your growth process. This was indeed one of those growing moments.

After sitting at the bar for 15 minutes our table is now ready and we are seated. The night is going well, the conversation is lit, we are laughing and having a good time! Tony ordered the Salmon Salad and I kept it simple with my regular Pepperoni Pizza. And of course we kept the drinks coming. As our dinner date comes to an end, I received a text from my daughter Alex asking if I would pick her up a salad from Chopt. This restaurant is only a few blocks away from where Tony and I are, so he rides with me to pick up the salad. He is sweet and up for whatever I ask of him. Before I take Tony home, we stop by my house to drop off the salad to Alex. This is his first time coming to my house, but keep in mind my daughters have yet to meet any man I've dated. Therefore, I asked Tony if he didn't mind waiting in the car while I ran her food into the house. Tony was very understanding and totally respected the fact that I wasn't ready to introduce him to my daughter.

I left my house and drove him home. Once we got to his house we sat in the car talking for what felt like forever, but it was only 30 minutes. As we finally said our goodbyes, Tony reached over to kiss me. I was smiling on the inside and thinking, "YASSS...he's not just a good kisser, he is an amazing kisser!"
'
The next day I called to wish him a happy birthday. The conversation was short and to the point. From there, we continued to

take things at a slow pace and we used this time to build what would become a very strong friendship.

Two weeks later, Tony calls to say he's taking me on a date. He won't tell me where, only that it is one of his favorite spots. I say okay, I'm down what time should I be ready? Tony tells me to be ready by 9pm. He picks me up and twenty minutes later we pull up to this bar/restaurant in Old Town Alexandria. I love its atmosphere and it is a nice crowd. We get ourselves a table and order some food and drinks. I see why this is one of his favorite places to come because the DJ is jamming and it is karaoke night. Tony and I are having a great time dancing, kissing, and laughing the night away! I am pleased he decided to share this part of his life with me.

As time went on, Tony and I got closer. He started the daily "good morning" phone calls and was texting me more regularly. Tony was starting to express his feelings for me more freely. I was torn, because even though at that time I did like him a lot, I still loved Rashad more. However, I was always very honest and upfront with Tony. I believe wholeheartedly that people should live in their truth! It has always been my belief that if I give trust and honesty, it will then be reciprocated. Right? It should be as simple as that. Well, I will later learn that is not the case at all.

It is fall of 2015, I'm having dinner and drinks with Cookie at Hop's in VA because I am mad at Rashad and it is over between us— again! I receive a text from Tony:

Tony: Hey, what's up?
Gia: Hey, Nothing just having dinner with Cookie.
Tony: What you doing after dinner?
Gia: I am going home.
Tony: Do you wanna come over?
Gia: I don't know because I'm not in a good mood.
Tony: What's wrong with you?
Gia: Rashad and I are over.

Tony: Oh, okay. Well call me when you leave and maybe we can talk.

Gia: Okay

I finish up dinner and conversation with Cookie and we say our goodbyes. I call Tony from the car because he always has a way of getting my mind off of Rashad. Tony answers and convinces me to come over his place to watch a movie. I agree and head to his house in Maryland. When I arrive, he is just so sweet and understanding. He doesn't ask me any questions, he just tells me it's going to be okay. It's funny because Tony also says to me "you and Rashad will get back together like y'all always do." I thought to myself "no he didn't just come for me on a sneak-tip." We go to his bedroom and attempt to watch a movie but I can't stop from being sad. On my ride to Tony's house I was crying in the car and had to pull myself together once I pulled up to his house. Needless to say, Tony being the amazing friend that he was, he didn't use my sadness as an opportunity to get me into bed. Nah, he did the exact opposite, Tony allowed me to cry and he held me until I cried myself to sleep.

I woke up the next morning still in his arms and he never mentioned Rashad or my needing to cry myself to sleep. He asked if I was okay and if I wanted breakfast. I wasn't able to stay for breakfast because I needed to get home and changed because I had clients that day. I don't know about y'all, but I don't know too many men who would allow a female he has feelings for to come over and cry about another man. I will always have mad respect for Tony as a friend; that was a bonding moment for the two of us.

A few weeks later, I am at Tony's house. It is a cold and rainy night but we are enjoying each other's company; we are having a good time watching my favorite TV show, *Law & Order*. But I just can't seem to get warm, it is so freaking cold in Tony's house and no matter what he does to make me comfortable, it's not working. I ask if he has any hot cocoa because maybe I just need something hot to drink. He goes to check but doesn't have any, so he offers me some hot tea. I am not feeling the idea of drinking any hot tea. Then he offers to drive up to the nearest 7-eleven to get me some hot cocoa. Awwww... Yes, that man put on his rain jacket and went out in the cold rainy weather to get me my hot cocoa. He is the sweetest thoughtful man and I love this about him because he always put my needs and wants first.

He returns to the house with cocoa in hand and I am happy! We get in bed and continue to watch back to back reruns of my show. As the evening goes on Tony starts kissing me and I am loving it because I love kissing, especially a man who knows how to kiss just as well as I do. To me, kissing is a great form of foreplay and seeing how we had not had sex yet, things were getting pretty steamy. Tony went from kissing my lips to kissing me down below. Tony is a talker, so he says "I wanna know whatcha taste like." So I let him have a taste, why not? He's an amazing kisser, so I can only imagine how good it's gonna feel when he puts his tongue down below.

Wow! As I imagined, his oral game was on point! Man, his ass had me making all types of noise, my ass was climbing the wall in the most amazing way. I love a man who can make me scream "wait, give me a minute" because that hasn't happened often.

Damn, I was not fully prepared for his oral game! Shit, and this is just foreplay...

My mind is racing and my thoughts are all over the place. I am a little nervous about going to the next level. Having multiple sex partners is new to me, but at the same time, I want to experience what it's like to have multiple partners. Honestly, I am a little late in the game—this is the single life all my girlfriends were living in their twenties, thirties and even to this day. I on the other hand had only been in long-term relationships until this point in my life. So here I am, 40-plus, and just experiencing all the things I should have been doing in my twenties. But hey, it is never too late for a new experience, right? So I put my fears aside, and for the first time in my adult life, I let go and lived in the moment!

It is November and I have to tell Tony that I'm going out of town with Rashad for his birthday. I was perfectly fine with telling him because I believe in complete honesty if asked a question. Now, I'm not out here volunteering information, but if I am asked, I will not lie to you. Therefore, when Tony asked what I was doing and if I had any plans the following weekend. I had to tell him the truth. For one, I am not in a monogamous relationship with anyone. So there is no reason for me to feel as though I need to lie to anyone. We are dating, yes, but we are both also aware of the fact that we are not only dating each other. Tony simply said "okay, well enjoy yourself." Okay, (I said) that went much better than I thought it would go. But trust me, that was not the last of that conversation.

I return from my mini vacation to Vegas and the following week is Black Friday. I am excited because if you know me, you know how much I love shopping all night on Black Friday, and this year is no different. I go out shopping with my daughter Peyton, we are both looking to purchase the 40" TV as gifts. We went to several Targets and just when we were about to give up at the last store, the manager tells us she has more 40" TV's in the back from people who had tickets but never picked them up. Yassss... Peyton and I are excited, we wait patiently for the manager to bring them out. Lord knows I don't need another TV in my house but I was buying this as a Christmas gift for Tony. I love Christmas and I love giving gifts to everyone. After Peyton and I get our TVs, we look around the store for more amazing sales. As we are walking near the back I see the motorized trucks for little girls and boys. They are so cute, so I call Rashad to ask if his daughter has one already. Rashad tells me she doesn't, so of course I purchase the truck for Rashad to give to his daughter for Christmas. I mean, in my eyes, every little girl should have a motorized car or truck to drive around in. The night of shopping comes to an end, and Peyton and I head home with all of our goodies.

Some time goes by and I'm starting to wonder if Tony isn't telling me the truth about his relationship with his other female friend. The reason I'm uncertain is because of her comments on his Facebook page. Man, I am telling you that social media will get a cheating man caught up. I ask him again if the two of them are supposed to be in a committed relationship and once again Tony tells me "no" they are dating but are free to date other people. Okay, I say and I take him at his word. Christmas comes and goes. New Year's Day comes and goes. Tony and I talk on the phone more than we see each other because I'm dating other people too.

We are now in the beginning of January and Tony finally comes to pick up his gift. He is shocked to see that I bought him a TV, but happy at the same time. We sit at my dining room table talking and catching up, and Tony mentions to me that he is moving at the end of the month. I ask him where and he says, "I'm not sure yet, but my lease is up and I'm not going to renew it. My sister and I are thinking about getting a house together." I say "okay" and leave it at that.

Then he said to me "ole girl asked me to move in with her."

"Wait...what did you just say?" I asked, taken aback. "I thought the two of you were just dating?"

"We are," he said.

"So why would you move in with someone you are not in a relationship with? That don't make sense to me, but okay.

"Nah, I'm not moving in with her, I'm just telling you that she asked me," he explained.

"Okay, Tony. If you say so."

He and I talk a little longer, then he gives me a quick kiss goodbye and heads on home.

A couple of weeks go by and I may have spoken to Tony twice because as you know, I've got a lot of stuff going on in my life right now with Rashad. Another week goes by before Tony and I speak again. This time he tells me that he and his sister found a place. I'm excited for him and tell him that if there is anything I can do to help, let me know. He says cool and that he may need to use my car. I say okay.

Today is moving day, and I call to see if Tony needs to use my car. He tells me he isn't sure yet. **Red Flag #1** Later that evening I get a call from Tony telling me how he is so pissed for not going with his sister when she found the house because it is so small and his room is even smaller. Tony goes on to say how this isn't going to work and how he is not going to be there long. Now that was **Red Flag #2**, but of course I want to give him the benefit of the doubt, because that is what friends do. So I let it go, even though my gut is telling me this nigga is lying to me. But hey, he is not my man and I got enough stuff going on in my life right now.

As time goes on, I notice that Tony has yet to invite me over to his new place, and that was out of the norm for him. So I ask him, "hey, are you sure you are living with your sister and not your other female friend?" Tony swears to me that he is not living with the other woman. Once again, my gut is telling me otherwise and once again, I let it go. We continue to talk and see each other, but nothing regularly because I don't trust that he is being honest with me. Tony is very vocal about his feelings for me. He has no problem telling me every-time we talk how much he loves me and wishes we could be together in a committed relationship. I see the love in his eyes every time he looks at me, but I don't know if he is the one for me. There have been so many times where he has been so inconsistent.

My cigar lover calls to tell me about his cigar event at a local cigar lounge in Waldorf, MD and he wants me to come show my support. I really do not like that place because it takes days to get that cigar smell out of my clothes, but I say "okay, I'll be there." It is a cold evening in March 2015, but I get dressed anyway. I put thought into what I wear because of all the smoke in that place. I make sure I wear clothes that can go straight into the washing machine. Okay, Gia just throw on a pair of jeans, a fitted top, a leather jacket, and your Chanel booties. Kept it simple, but cute! I decided to go to this event by myself. I don't plan on staying long, just need to show my support. I arrive, and seconds later I locate Tony and he takes me over to the other side of the lounge. Shortly after being there, he buys me a drink and while we are at the bar I run into my sister. She is there with her girlfriends. I introduce her and Tony.

My sister and her friends have a table on the other side, so I go sit with them because it's Tony's event and he needs to walk around and do his thing. I'm talking, having a good time, look up and who do I see over in the area where Tony has his table? The other chick he is also seeing. I think to myself "this nigga here!" I just shake my head and keep my cool because he is not my man, we are just dating. Of course Tony comes over to check on me and I say to him "seriously, you invited me to the same event as your other friend?

"Come on, Gia, it's not that deep," he said. "I told you she smokes cigars and she asked if she could come, so I said sure."

"Whatever Tony," I replied. "You got a lot of shit with you."

"Come on Gia, please don't be mad," he begged. "It's nothing with her. Come walk with me; I want you to have one of my t-shirts."

He walks me over to his table, introduces me to his friends, gets me a t-shirt, and continues to make small talk. I go back to the table with my sister. 30 minutes later, my sister and her friends are leaving to hit up another spot. They ask if I wanna go and I am happy to get out of all the smoke. I find Tony to let him know I'm leaving and he walks me to my car.

The next day, I call Tony because I have a real issue with him inviting both me and the other chick to the same event. He sticks with his point of view that it is not a big deal, and that I'm making it more than it is. I ask him again if there is more to his relationship than I know about, and again, Tony denies any type of commitment with her. I know his ass is lying, but I can't prove it and I don't care for real because I'm dealing with the ending of my relationship with Rashad. I just let it go for now.

Tony is still trying to convince me that we should be a couple, but I am not feeling it. I start to notice how, whenever I call him after 9 p.m., his phone is turned off. Now, I am not calling daily, but enough to notice there is a pattern. Here I go finding myself having yet another conversation with Tony about where he lives.

"Gia, it is not what you think babe. I promise you I do not live with Tracy," he says, trying to convince me.

"Tony, you must think I am booboo the fool. I know damn well you are living with that girl, but what I don't understand is why you continue to lie about it. If you are in a full blown relationship, say that shit. I won't be mad, I just don't want you lying to me and taking my options away," I tell him.

"I am telling you I don't live with her. Please believe me," he begs.

"Yeah, okay Tony." And yet again, I let it go for now.

I pull away from Tony for the most part because I am not dumb and I know he is living with Tracy. He continues to profess his love for me and continues to push for us to have a relationship, but I ain't having it. I put more and more space between him and me.

Up until this point, Tony and I had a somewhat active sex life. He and I did a great job at building a strong friendship first. It has always been important for me to get to know the men I choose to be intimate with. What I loved about Tony sexually was that not only did he have a high sex drive but he loved talking dirty to me. Plus, no matter how I challenge him sexually, he is always up for it. I remember this one time we were at his house chillin', and outta nowhere he says to me "let me taste you right now!''

I told him I was tired, but he was persistent. "Babe, please just let me taste you."

He knew all it took was for him to get those lips and that tongue anywhere near my sweetness, and it would be on. I finally say okay but only if you can go four rounds with me tonight. That brotha was all for it! Yes, he welcomes the challenge! I do not know what in the hell I was thinking, because he can last longer than any guy I've been with. At this point there is no turning back after talking all that trash I talked.

Tony throws me on the bed, undresses me, and pulls my ass to the edge of the bed; and putting my legs up high as he starts eating my kitty until I cum multiple times. Then he slides on the condom and makes his way into me, slow but steady. For the next few hours of dirty talking and love making we have gone three rounds and this nigga's dick is still hard! I am tired but I refuse to back down after all the trash I was talking. By the time we are done with round four, both of our old asses were tired as hell and outta damn breath. LOL! That indeed was a night for the books! I learned a valuable lesson that night too: never challenge his ass to anything more than two rounds.

Back to Tony living with Tracy and still trying to date me as if I don't know the game. After some weeks go by, I receive a call from Tony, he wants to come see me. So I say okay. When he arrives at my house he has flowers and a card. It is a sweet gesture! We go sit in the living room, we are talking about Rashad and how his girl put sugar in my gas tank. I catch him up on all the drama that I had been going through over the past few weeks. I ask him again about his living arrangements and promise him that I won't be mad if he just tells me the truth. Finally, he admits to living with Tracy! I am not at all shocked by the news because I knew in my gut that he was living with her. I tell him it is crazy that it took him five months to tell me the truth. He apologizes for lying to me. Then goes on to say how he didn't like the place his sister found for them and had no other option.

"There are always other options," I tell him. "I don't believe you ever planned to move with your sister. I believe that is just the story you came up with for me because you did not want me to end things between us."

He and I finish up our conversation but surprisingly I am not at all mad at him. I decide to maintain our friendship while keeping him at bay sexually.

We are moving into the week of Father's Day. Tony and I have a conversation about his plans, which by the way aren't any. I take him to dinner at the new restaurant on the water in Old Town Alexandria. Most of our dates were spent in Old Town; it's our favorite place to hangout. The night went well, we laughed and talked until it was time to leave. We end the night without any sex, just a little kissing.

A few months pass by and it's Tony's birthday. We aren't on speaking terms, but I still show up to his birthday party at DC Lounge with my face beat and hair pulled up into a messy bun, wearing jeans, a black flowy top, and a pair of peep toe leopard print pumps. I get Cookie to go with me, and she's looking super cute as well! I park my car at Cookie's house in the city and we Uber to the lounge. Music is loud but pumpin'. We see a lot of people we know, including our good friend Tim from high school. He is there taking pictures, and asks Cookie and I to pose for one. We're walking around and it isn't long before we run into Tony, lookin' all cute and shit. I ignore him and try to walk by without speaking but he grabs my arm and pulls me close to him.

"So you just gonna walk by me and not speak?" he asks.

# Chapter 6: The Cigar Lover

"Absolutely!" I exclaim.

"Why haven't you been taking my calls?" he inquires.

"Because I have nothing to say to you," I reply.

"You know I miss you!," he says, pulling me even closer as he whispers into my ear, "Damn, you look sexy as shit! Don't be mad at me," and then sticks his tongue in my ear and kisses me softly on the cheek. But I'm still playing hard to get. His friend walks up and Tony introduces us then goes on to tell me that he has a private section if Cookie and I wanna sit.

Cookie and I head over to the bar for a drink. We're laughing and having a good time dancing to the music, and 30 minutes later Tony sends me a text.

Tony: Hey, where you at?
Gia: At the bar
Tony: OK, come see me I'm in the back room.
Gia: OK, give me a minute

I finished up my drink and tell Cookie, "I'll be back. I'm going to go see Tony." She says OK and I head to the back of the club.

Tony is standing on the stairs, so I walk up and stand directly in front of him. He pulls me close and tells me he wants to come home with me once we leave the club. I am done playing hard to get. I'm drunk and horny, so I say okay. We talked for a few more minutes before I headed back over to the bar with Cookie. I have one last drink, then Cookie and I send for our Uber back to her house where my car is parked.

I am home long enough to hop in the shower before Tony arrives at my house. As soon as I answer, he grabbed me by my neck, and started to kiss me. Before you know it, he has me bent over up against the front door as he starts to hit it from behind doggy style! We make our way upstairs to my bedroom, get undressed and he has my ass across the bed. Then starts talking trash about me telling him how I don't want to see him anymore and he's not letting me go! The sex is intense, passionate, wild, and so good! He loves to grab me by my neck during sex, especially when he's kissing me and talking trash! This nigga hitting all the right spots; the sex is on one thousand! I'm still a little tipsy and my head is spinning like hell, but the sex is so good I don't want him to stop! It's times like this that I'm glad he does not know how to have a quickie! Damn, that was the best make-up sex I've had in a very long time! 45 minutes later, Tony takes a quick shower, kisses me goodnight, and then heads home.

Fast forward to 2016, and I'm back to withholding sex and just focusing on the friendship because Tony is still living with Tracy. Tony keeps telling me he's moving out, but I've heard it so many times before I just don't know what to believe anymore. He expresses his love to me all the time, and tells me he wants to marry me, but as far as I'm concerned it's just all talk as long as he is still living with Tracy! Tony tells me all the time how he'll leave her for me, all I need to do is say the word! I tell him all the time you can't leave her for me you have to leave her for yourself; and until you do, we have nothing to talk about! Don't get me wrong I have feelings for him, but I refuse to settle!

More importantly, at this point I had met and started dating this photographer named Kevin. This guy Kevin is so different from both Tony and Rashad! I'm feeling torn, so I keep them both at bay.

I have a lot going on in my life right now. My youngest daughter is graduating from high school and trying to decide which college she wants to attend, and my oldest daughter is graduating from graduate school.

## Chapter 6: The Cigar Lover

In February 2016, Tony comes over to visit me. We are talking and he tells me he is moving out over spring break, plus he has to have surgery on his shoulder. He asks if I could be his ride to the hospital and I say of course, that's what friends are for. However, I later find out that his surgery is the same date as Alex's new student college visit! I inform Tony and I feel bad, but he later tells me his sister is able to be his ride. I feel better knowing I didn't leave him hanging.

Two weeks before his surgery and Tony stuck to his word and moved out! Shocked the hell out of me but I'm proud of him!

Ladies, even though Tony has been very vocal about his love for me and how much he wishes we could be a couple, let's not be fooled because I will soon learn how his words don't always match his actions. There are two sides to this man: the sweetest, caring, loving person, and the compulsive liar! Tony is great at giving you all of the above. Honestly, in his defense, I don't believe he lies to hurt me or the other ladies. I believe it is the exact opposite. I think he lies as much as he does because in his mind telling you the truth means hurting you. Therefore, he will tell you whatever he thinks you want or need to hear from him. Again, in his mind, telling you what you want to hear will make you happy. It doesn't make it okay, I'm just saying that's his thought process.

While in Cali I received a call from Tony letting me know his surgery went well and that his sister was driving him home. I later learned that was a lie. It turns out Tracy (the ex whose house he just moved out of) was who took him to the hospital.

Why all the lies? I swear no matter how honest and direct I am with these men, their asses just won't give that shit back to me! I have always been very open about my dating life, especially if asked!

My conversation with Tony wasn't long because I wasn't alone in the car and he wasn't alone in the car either. I got back that following Sunday but had a busy day ahead of me. I had to meet with clients, then later I went to Alanna's daughter's dance recital and that was a few hours long. Therefore, I didn't get a chance to call and check on Tony until Monday or Tuesday. The plan was for him to stay in my guest bedroom while he recovered, but that never happened.

When we finally spoke, Tony said he was recovering well but was still in some pain. The weekend is here and I'm getting my daughter ready for her prom. I haven't heard from Tony in days. Later that evening I received a call from him asking "why didn't you tell me about Alex's prom send off?"

"Well I didn't know you would want to be here for that," I explain.

"Of course I wanted to be there! My feelings are hurt," he says.

"I'm sorry. I should have given you the option to make that decision," I say. (Now I think to myself "why is he whispering") but I don't say anything and let it go.

Monday comes around and Tony has posted pictures of himself from the weekend cigar event. This brother thinks he's so slick by posting multiple pictures of himself with a group of females and a couple of him with individual females. What he fails to realize is that I am not new to this "hide the chick you're fuckin' in plain sight so that no one is the wiser" game. I'm giving him the side-eye as I'm looking at all the pictures he has posted! What men also fail to realize is that there is something about the body language between two people who are having sex. It's a dead giveaway every time.

I hit up Tony via text; that was a mistake because I was calling him out on his shit. So of course he ducks me for the next two days. By Wednesday he finally gives me a call, talking to me about how it's not what I think and that he's not seeing any of the females in the pictures from the weekend cigar event. I don't believe him, I know this man very well and he's lying right now! But I play along just to see how far he's willing to go with his lies. He comes over after work after he wasn't able to convince me over the phone that he and the female in the picture were just friends. We're upstairs in my bedroom talking.

During the conversation he finally admitted to seeing the other woman. But he tells me it's nothing serious and that she's the one he met at the cigar lounge a few weeks prior. (I remember the event he's referring to because he came over to my house afterwards and was telling me how he saw this female there and how he thought it was me. He proceeded to show me a picture of her. I said to him the only thing she and I have in common is our complexion because she doesn't look anything like me. Also that was the same night I told Tony that he and I can't be in a committed relationship. I shared with him how I felt it was best that he went off and at least had sex with other women. Keep in mind he's just about to move out of Tracy's house. He told me just how much he loved me, all I needed to do was say the word. Instead I broke his heart by telling him how I don't see myself living with anyone and that I wasn't ready for a commitment type relationship. Tony stood in my kitchen with tears in his eyes and asked if I was sure this was what I wanted. With a straight face, I said yes.

After Tony helps me remember the night they met, I get more and more irritated. He tries to calm my nerves with a kiss while reassuring me that she's nothing but a friend. This man is one of the best kissers I have had the pleasure of kissing. His kisses get me wet each and every time. Damn! Then he puts his hand between my legs to feel my wetness. He plays with my kitty until all I want is to fuck the shit out of him. I am taking off his clothes at this point, no need in wasting time; let's get to this angry makeup sex is what I was thinking. After pulling down his pants, I get on my knees and give him the best head until I have him screaming and cumming at the same damn time!

Oh, but it doesn't stop there. This man is the only man I know who can cum and still have a hard ass dick afterwards that's ready to go again. Tony pulls me up from my knees, bends me over the bed, pulls down my pants and enters me from behind. He's being aggressive because he's mad with me for not wanting him the way he has always wanted me. He says to me "why are you doing this to me? Why can't I leave you alone? You know you are my weakness, that's why you keep fucking with my head. You didn't want me but you don't want anyone else to have me. Why? You know how much I fucking love you. Oh, shit you feel so good, c'mon and fuck this dick."

The next thing I know, he got me on all fours with my ass in the air. Minutes later he flips me over, he is on top with his one hand around my neck looking me deep into my eyes while he continues to talk dirty to me because he knows I love it when he grabs me by the neck and talks dirty. That shit alone could make me cum!

The following day Tony calls to ask if he can come over Friday night to talk. He wants to come clean about his relationship with Tori (the female from the pictures). This is his way of doing damage control, but I say "sure" and we hang up. It's 11ish Friday night and Tony is just getting to my house. I can tell this conversation isn't about to go well. He starts off by saying that he has been seeing Tori for a few weeks. Then he goes on to make this my fault by reminding me that I told him to go date other people. "If you hadn't pushed me away, we wouldn't be here having this conversation," he said.

"Oh, so now it's my fault that you're fuckin that girl? REALLY?" I said.

"I'm not saying it's your fault, Gia!" he exclaimed. "I'm saying I came to you, told you how much I loved you and wanted to be with only you, and what did you say?"

"I said you needed to go fuck some other women and then come back to me because you just moved out of Tracy's house. I am not about to be some rebound chick. Plus I don't see myself living with anyone right now," I replied.

"Exactly, Gia! So what was I supposed to do with that information? Even after I met Tori, I still came to you expressing my love and how much I wanted a relationship with you, but you wasn't having it," he said. "So don't give me attitude when you pushed me away. You handed me over to her."

"I don't want to hear that shit," I retorted. "I told you to go 'fuck' other women, not go start a full blown relationship with just one!"

"I am not in a relationship with her, Gia, it is still very new."

"Have you had sex with her yet?" I asked.

"Gia, do you really want to know the answer to that question."

"Absolutely!" I said.

"Yes, we have had sex."

"Damn, so you fuckin' her already?" I replied. "I thought you said you have only been seeing her for a few weeks. So when did the sex start?"

"It does not matter, we had sex."

"Are you fucking kidding me right now?" I had to remind myself of how I have been out the dating game for a minute and that hooking up sooner rather than later is a thing.

I start yelling and cussing his ass out because I'm in disbelief. Tony grabs me and just holds me tight because at this point I'm crying. He tries to calm me down by reassuring me that it is nothing serious with her. "She's cool and I like hanging out with her, but I don't love her. I love you and I wanted you, so stop making this about me."

He tries to kiss me but I'm not feeling it. I tried to put it all behind me and accept it for what it was. I try to remind myself that I didn't want a committed relationship with him, so how can I be mad. However, that thought process didn't last very long. I know between midnight and 5:30 a.m. we had some serious make-up sex. I could not get the thoughts of him with her out of my head. Therefore, we argued then had sex and I'm telling you this went on all night long.

Finally, Tony said, "I'm not doing this with you, Gia. I am tired and clearly you don't believe me. I'm going home so I can get some sleep."

Days later, I am on the phone with Tony and he tells me that he isn't coming over because he has to pick his son up from dance. I am confused because what does you picking up your son have to do with you coming over. Tony stopped responding and stopped answering his phone. I am fuming at this point but what can I do, he is not answering his phone.

Hours pass and I try to go to sleep, but I cannot shake this gut feeling I have. So I get up and take a ride. Because of Instagram, I know where she lives (people should really stop living their lives on social media). It was in that moment I decided to go catch him because without proof, he was just going to continue to lie. I decided to take Alex's car because it is dark and not as noticeable as mine. I typed the name of her community in my GPS and made my way to catch Tony. I literally drove for what seemed like forever but was about 45 minutes at 11pm on a Wednesday. It did not matter the time because my adrenaline was on one hundred.

I finally get to this community and it is like a damn Disney resort. Seriously, that is how huge it was. I think to myself "girl, you done drove your ass out to no man's land and now whatcha gonna do?" Lol… Okay, I need to locate the townhomes and go from there. I go around this big circle and the townhomes are down at the end of the street. Great, there are only three sets of them. The first set sits off by themselves and the other two face one another. Now, I gotta take a quick look at the picture in order to figure out which set is hers, because this is a big community and I am not about to drive around for an hour. I figure it out and drive around the front of the set of two and boom, there was Tony's truck. "This lying ass motherfucker…" is what I thought to myself. I call him while I am parked behind his truck, but of course, he doesn't answer.

I decide to leave him a note on his truck, but it starts raining outside. Now what am I going to do because he will never own being here without proof. I look around the inside of Alex's car for something to write on and I see this plastic sandwich bag in the backseat. I grab the baggy and then wrote my note, which read **You lying piece of shit, you've been caught!** Now to ensure that my note was still legible by morning, I put it inside the baggy. Then I pull off, but as I am driving, I realize I forgot to take a picture of his car. So I turn around and go take a picture of his tag, then I waited until I got back home and texted it to him. No caption was needed. Naturally, the next morning at around 6ish my phone is ringing off the hook. It is Tony but I keep sending him to voicemail. It must have been around 8ish before I finally answered the phone.

"Gia, listen, let me explain because it is not what you think," he began. "I am not going to lie, I was at her house last night but I did not stay the night. I just went over because she wanted to talk; it is nothing at all what you are thinking."

"You are nothing but a lying piece of shit and I do not have time for you, your games, or your lies," I said. "I only did that drive-by to prove to you that your ass is not slick and you will never be able to outsmart me. I keep telling you I am not your average female, I think like a dude and I really need to thank my ex for teaching me how to read men!"

"Gia, I promise you babe it is not what you think, she is just a friend."

"I do not believe nothing that comes out of your mouth."

"I just pulled to my job, I will call you later so that we can talk," he said.

"Don't bother!" I yelled

I know he has been lying about his relationship with Tori, so I reached out to her. Just as I thought, Tony was not being truthful with me. Tori informed me that she was indeed dating him and was under the impression that they were a couple. But more importantly, she had no idea I even existed. She seemed to be hurt by this information but like most women, she did not end things with him, at least not at that moment. It wasn't until she realized that he wasn't going to be honest nor faithful to either of us that she ended things between them. By the beginning of June, their relationship was over. At that point I was no longer seeing Tony, so it didn't matter to me one way or the other.

I had just spent years building what I thought was a solid friendship with Tony. The fact that he felt it necessary to lie about seeing someone new was disappointing and hurtful. But being the person that I am, I eventually forgave him.

Not only did I forgive Tony but I became good friends with his now-ex, Tori! You see, this is the outcome when you don't blame the other woman for a decision your man made. Turns out that Tori is cool and a joy to talk to. She and I built a friendship outside of Tony.

It's late night June 2016 and I am home in bed when I receive a phone call from Tony. He goes on to say how I was right about everything. However, I have no idea what he is talking about, nothing he is saying makes any sense to me. But against my better judgment, I allow him to come over and talk. This man has a way of driving me crazy and loving me at the same time. I don't know if I should stay or run for my life when it comes to Tony.

I decided to stay and work it out on some level, because I do love him. Tony and I spend the summer working on our relationship and rebuilding the trust. Everything was going great between us; we were communicating, going on dates, laughing, and enjoying this next phase. Although things are looking up for Tony and I, there is still something holding me back from fully committing to this man. It's a strong gut feeling that just won't go away, no matter how hard I fight the feeling. I don't know what it is honestly. Tony has been great and our sex life couldn't be any better. For the first time since Tori, I am actually happy being with him. I love seeing his face and hearing his voice. I love our long talks about life, business, our dreams, and goals. It is just like old times and I cannot get enough of it. So why do I have this annoying gut feeling that something isn't right? Tony has not done anything to make me question his loyalty to me, so I put the bad thoughts aside. I promised him that I would give us a chance, and that's what I plan to do.

Summer 2016 is coming to an end and it's almost time for me to take my daughter Alex off to college. I am both excited and nervous because she has decided to go off to the west coast for school. Though she had just spent the last four years away at boarding school, it is not the same because her high school was only a drive away from home. Now my baby will be many miles away, and I'm not ready. The only thing that is keeping it together for me is the fact that Peyton and Michael are coming with me to set her up. Don't think I could get through it without their support.

I would be remiss not to mention how loving and supportive Tony has been throughout this process. Tony was one of the first men I introduced her to in all of her 18 years of age. Yes, I was that mom who didn't introduce any man to either of my daughters until they were 26 and 18. At this point, it was Tony and the photographer. Both men loved themselves some Alex and were supportive. I am very grateful to have that level of support.

Since this is Alex's freshman year, we decided to stay five extra days to ensure she was completely set up in her dorm. With everything going well between Tony and I, he stays at my house while I'm gone.

And not because I need him to house sit for me, because I have an amazing security system protecting my home. No, he stayed because I'm trying to figure out if I want a full blown relationship with him. Plus, if I am honest, I can't say with certainty that I am ready to fully walk away from my other friend. But nonetheless, I felt sad leaving him behind because we left for Cali on his birthday. But we talk, text, and FaceTime the entire time I'm there. My last day in Cali I have a mini breakdown over leaving Alex. I mean I am crying uncontrollably, so I call Tony because I just need someone to help soothe my nerves; and he does just that for me!

We take the redeye back home and arrive at BWI airport at 5:30 the following morning. I call Tony when we land; he's excited to hear my voice, tells me how much he missed me. I am looking forward to seeing him because I can't stop crying over leaving my baby back in Cali. Tony and I talk throughout the day. By the end of the day he tells me he's going to the Harbor to smoke, and that's fine because that is what he does on Wednesday evenings. I needed to use his truck for something so we agree that I would come and switch cars with him. Well, at the last minute my plans changed, so I decided not to go meet him to do the switch. Later that evening, I receive a call from Tony saying that he isn't feeling well and there is something going on with his stomach. I go off because he hasn't seen me in a week, but more importantly, I am hurting right now. My child is in Cali and this man is faking sick. WTH??

I am thinking to myself how this shit cannot be happening to me right now, oh but it is! And shit just got real!

That night was just the beginning of Tony going MIA. I finally ask him if he is seeing someone else because his behavior is not adding up, but of course he denies seeing anyone. However, I know this man; therefore, I know better. It's now September and the holiday comes and all I get is a phone call from Tony, who by the way is still trying to convince me that he loves me and nothing is what I'm thinking. I say "whatever, I am not doing this shit with you again"! Another week or so goes by; I am at home working on a project for a client and a text comes through from one of my girlfriends.

Friend: Hey Gia! I see Tony has himself a new boo.

Gia: Wait, what? I don't know anything about a new boo.

Friend: Yes, she's been posting pictures of the two of them and tagging him. Hold tight, I'm going to screenshot it for you.

Right there in plain sight are pictures of them, along with memes she has tagged him in. So I send the pictures directly to Tony because if you know me, you know I am very direct. Of course he does not respond that night because he needs time to come up with his lie.

At this point I am so over all the bullshit with this man. I know what I bring to the table. I know I don't deserve this drama from a man that I am not even fully committed to and tell him so. For the next month he tries to go back and forth with me explaining himself but I am not buying it.

Oh, but it gets better! Tony and I are still friends on IG so I can see his posts. I see he's been posting pictures of himself, his son, and another little boy I don't recognize. I am assuming he is the other woman's son. But everything is not always what it seems.

Two weeks later, Tony and I are on somewhat speaking terms. He tells me about his friend's 50th birthday party because he is trying to get me back in his good graces. I could care less about his friend's birthday party until the pictures are posted on the Gram! Oh, here we go again with Tony trying to hide the woman he is fuckin' in plain sight. And I have seen this woman before, back in September. Though he took pictures with several women one-on-one that night. There is something about the body language between two people who are intimate. I have a keen sense for this type of body language. I ask him about her, but he tells me I am tripping because he isn't in a relationship with either of the women. I let it go because I do not care enough to argue with him over it.

Tony continues to try and win me back, but he is not consistent and I refuse to settle. Plus during the process of him "winning me back" I learned that he started dating that woman back in the summer of 2016 which is during the time we were supposed to be working things out.

This man is relentless when it comes to me, he will do whatever it takes to hold on to some part of me. And on some level, I am not ready to completely let go because here I go entertaining him again; but this time it is on my terms. I won't give him my heart again, I do not trust him like that, but the sex with him is pretty damn good. So I am willing and open to a FWB type relationship with him, which is different for us because we were never FWBs, we were dating and there were feelings involved.

I think I got this though… Until the week of Thanksgiving 2016, a week that I will NEVER forget! The weekend is here and I am feeling good. I did some Black Friday shopping with my daughter. Tony calls me on Saturday to check on me because he wants to make plans to see me. I'm talking to Tony off and on all day; he lets me know that he is at the mall with his daughter. I tell him he had better not be lying to me because there is no need for it. We are not a couple, so don't lie to me, I tell him. He promises me he is not lying, then goes on to ask what time we are getting together later that evening. I say, "I'll let you know because I have a few errands to run. I will call you when I am on my way back home."

I call Cookie because she and I were supposed to meet for drinks. But neither of us wanted to be in the house, so we decided on drinks at Chevy's in VA. Cookie asked if I would pick her up so we could ride together. I get Cookie around 7pm and we head on over to the restaurant. Cookie and I like to sit over in the bar area near the window, and thankfully there was an available table. Cookie's seat is facing the front of the restaurant and I am seated directly across from her facing the bar. We order a couple of margaritas and freshly made guacamole. It's nice to get out of the house, and though Cookie and I talk daily, we can never have too much girl talk. These days it seems as though I always have something going on in my life. We are laughing, talking, having ourselves a good time, and order our second round of drinks. And out of nowhere Cookie has this surprised look on her face. It was as if she had seen a ghost! I say "what's wrong?" Cookie gives me the head-nod and the eyes that are telling me I need to look. I turn around and it was as if I had seen a ghost.

There walking towards the bar is Tony with an unknown female. He is clearly surprised to see me but not as nearly as surprised as I was to see him and with a female. The female is walking in front of him.

"Hey, how is it going?" Tony said, sheepishly.

"I thought you were at the mall with your daughter?" I replied.
"I was but that was earlier," he said, unconvincingly.

"Oh, okay," I said, not believing a word coming out of his lying ass mouth.

The female continued ahead of him and takes a seat at the bar closest to where we are sitting. After speaking to me, Tony walks over to her and tells her to move further down to the other end of the bar.

My blood is boiling, I can't believe what I am seeing. No this dude not out here on a damn date when I just spoke to his ass less than two hours ago. At this point I am livid, I can't even finish my drink. Cookie is trying to calm me down but there's nothing she can say to me at this point. I tell her I'm ready to go. We ask for our check but before we leave I need to go over there and find out what in the hell is going on!

Cookie asks me what I am going to say. "I don't know but I'm going over there."

"Ok, but remember we are in VA," Cookie warned, "so just don't get us locked up."

"I won't! Oh, and I can ask him for my money for the blazer he had me pickup for him."

We pay our check and walk over to the bar where they were sitting. I say to Tony "hey, since you are here can I get my money for the blazer."

"Sure!" he says, and goes in his pocket, pulls out the money, and hands it to me.

"So what's this all about?" I asked directly. "I thought we had plans tonight and why did you lie about being with your daughter?"

"I didn't lie, and we still have plans later," he said.

"No the hell we don't," I replied, as I walked off.

Cookie asks me if I'm okay, but I am far from it. I am so angry because it is always the same bullshit with him. We are outside the restaurant and I just can't let it go. I tell Cookie, I am going back in. "To say what?" Cookie asked.

"I don't know, but I can't let this go, he got me messed up."

Cookie knows at this point there is no stopping me, so we walk back into the restaurant. I walk up to Tony and say to him "we need to talk."

"Not now Gia!" he says.

Yes now, and you got me twisted if you think you're gonna show off for this little groupie."

"Gia, don't do this please, this is not the time or place. We will talk later. I am not doing this with you right now. Please before you make a scene," he pleaded.

"I don't give two fucks about you or making a scene."

"Okay, Gia but we're not doing this right now," he said.

"Come on Gia, let's go," Cookie said.

That chick is sitting there with this smirk on her face. I am so pissed, I swear it took everything in me not to smack that smirk off her damn face. I thought to myself "bitch you had better be glad you're not dealing with 20 year old Gia!" as we walked out of the restaurant.

The restaurant is attached to a small mall. As we enter into the mall, we are approached by these three young girls with a baby inside a stroller. They ask Cookie and I if we can help them catch the metro back home because they don't have any money. As I'm looking to see if I have any cash, Cookie is asking them a million and one questions about why they have no money and why they are out with the baby; didn't they know they'd need to get back home? I am telling Cookie that it really isn't that deep. Right in the middle of talking to the young girls, out walks Tony and the chick. Cookie and I leave the group of girls mid-sentence.

Tony and I end up at the customer service counter where you validate your parking. I say to him again, "Tony, let me talk to you."

"Gia, I am not having this conversation here," he says.

"Tony just talk to her!" Cookie says.

He turns around grabs me by my denim shirt with his two hands and tries to make me walk with him. "You want to talk, come over here," he says, with his hands still on my shirt.

"Hell no!" I yell. "I'm not going anywhere with you, and get your hands off of me!"

"I'm telling you Gia, you're about to piss me off."

"I don't give a fuck about pissing you off," I say.

"Come on!" He says to the female.

"No! You need to stay right here and let them talk!" Cookie says to the female in a very firm voice. So the female stands over to the side near Cookie and does not say one word.

We are all now standing in the center of the mall. YESSS...the center of the freaking mall. Tony and I are going at it! He is trying to intimidate me, but that shit don't work on me because I am equally pissed off. At this point, we are up in each other's face and Cookie is on standby. My anger is at a thousand, and I feel no fear.

"Go ahead Gia," Tony says, "you're really pissing me off and I'm telling you, you don't know this side of me."

"Fuck you and trust, you don't know this side of me either!" I yelled. "You don't scare me! You out here showing off for that groupie bitch!"

"Watch your mouth, Gia!" he shouted.

"Fuck you and that bitch too!" I screamed.

I know he wanted to smack me, but instead he gives me a hard smush on the side of my face. Cookie jumps in between us. "Don't you touch her! You can't put your hands on her!" Cookie shouted at Tony as she grabbed his hands, refusing to let go.

I lean around Cookie and swing on him. Cookie is still standing between us and still keeping us apart with her body.

"It's okay Cookie!" I say. "Is that all you got, Tony? You're nothing but a punk! I am not scared of you and you better not put your fucking hands on me again!"

"Gia, I swear I am over this shit!" he screamed.

"No, I am fucking done! Never call or contact me ever again," I yelled.

"Let me go Cookie, I'm good, I am not going to hit her!" Tony said. "This is some fucked up shit you just did!"

"I just did?! You've lost your damn mind if you think I'm going to let you put this on me."

"Whatever Gia, I'm gone!"

"Go the fuck on, Tony!"

I look around and that chick was nowhere to be found. Her ass rolled out in the middle of our fight. At first her ass was acting like she was the shit with that little smirk on her face and trying to say little slick shit out her mouth! I have no respect for a female who stands by and watches the man she's on a date with going at it with another female but doesn't at any point try to break shit up. Nah, instead her ass just left. Honestly, it was probably for the best that she left.

Normally, I don't get mad at the other woman because you never know what that man is telling her or has told her. But this chick tried it with me instead of staying in her side-chick place. She is the type of female who would experience what she just experienced with this man she has only been seeing a few months and still keep seeing him.

Cookie and I start walking to the car when she notices that my earring is missing. We go back over to the center of the mall to look for it because they were expensive.. Thankfully, we found it on the floor. As we leave the mall my cell phone rings and it's Tony. I answer.

"Hello!"

"You are a miserable bitch!" he spat.

"Fuck you! I will be whatever you want me to be, you no good lying ass dog and stop calling me! I am fucking done and I don't give a damn about what you feel," I screamed before hanging up on him..

For the next two hours Tony called me, and each time I sent his ass straight to voicemail. Cookie and I get to my car, she's asking if I'm okay. "I'm fine," I say, "but I have not seen that Gia in 20 years! Girl, I promised myself that I would never let any man take me out of character like that ever again! I didn't shed not one tear and I felt no fear! It is a scary feeling, no lie!"

We get to Cookie's house, I go inside for a drink and to unwind. "Gia, I am still in shock!" she says. "Girl, I can't believe Tony."

My phone rings and it's Tony! Again, I send him to voicemail.

"Why is he still calling you? He and the girl must have met up there or otherwise he wouldn't still be calling you. Do you think she will continue to date him?" she asked.

"Yes," I said. "He is not going to let this go because he got caught in another damn lie. Plus, you saw how pissed he was but of course he will find reasons to make this my fault without ever owning his shit. I am not accepting any more calls from him. As angry as I am right now, I cannot do this shit with him anymore.

I've seen her before on his IG Page. He was with her at his friend's 50th birthday party. I never forget a face. See that is the type of slick shit he does. He posted pictures of him with her along with other females. His ass stay hiding his women in plain sight, like I'm dumb," I said.

"Wow! Gia, I just keep thinking about how shocked he was when he walked into that restaurant and saw us sitting there. our back was to him, but if you could have seen him, he took a deep breath. It was so funny in the moment. Tony knew he was wrong."

"Yeah, he was but it's all good," I said. "He is about to see a side of me he has never seen before. I can show him much better than I could ever tell him."

I finish up my drink and head on home.

# 7

# Girl Talk
# ***So You've Been Cheated On...
# What's Next?***

Ladies, let's talk about this thing called "cheating". I think it's safe to say that we have all experienced this at some point in our life. Cheating has got to be one of the harshest realities in life, but is necessary for us to grow and learn those life lessons. How we deal with being cheated on is what will shape us as individuals. This task may vary from person to person, because no two relationships are the same. How a married couple deals with infidelity will probably be completely different from the way a boyfriend/girlfriend couple deals with cheating. In a marriage there's more to lose and to consider, but as boyfriend/girlfriend, you may feel you are not that invested. One thing is for certain, two things are for sure: regardless of which type of relationship you are in, the feelings of betrayal and devastation are real. You are angry and hurt; you do not understand how or why this has happened to you. But before you confront your partner, stop and take some time to calm down and think things through, because trying to have a conversation while angry will get you nowhere fast.

I'm sure you have questions that you want answers to, and that's fine, but you will not get them if you approach your partner out of anger. This is when you call on your best friend or that one person you can talk to about any and everything. You need that unbiased but yet listening ear, you need to feel comfortable telling them everything. I know some people like to keep stuff inside so that they can deal with it in their own way, on their own time. However, it is just not healthy keeping something so devastating locked inside.

As private as I am, even I have to get that stuff out of my head or I'll be up all night because I don't know how to turn my brain off. If you don't have that friend you can talk to, I always say give it to God. Either way, what you do not want to do is start blaming yourself for the reason your partner cheated. We tend to look at ourselves for answers simply because we have made up in our minds that they only cheated because of something we did not do or did wrong. When in actuality, they are the one that did the cheating not you. So whatever you do, don't take on the injustice that was done to you by your partner because you did not cheat on yourself.

However, I get wanting to ask yourself what role you may have played in this. Honestly, I ask myself that very question at the end of every relationship. It's okay to think about previous conversations between the two of you, because knowing if he ever came to you expressing his unhappiness is important information. It doesn't negate the fact that your partner cheated, but it does help put things in perspective. Take the time to process all the facts before you approach your partner with your questions. Now that you've accepted that this is either not your fault, and/or that you played a role, it's time to talk things out with your partner. He needs to know how his actions have affected your life and your relationship. Lay it all on the table; don't leave anything up for interpretation. If he really loves and cares about you, he will be humble and apologetic. He will want to fight for your relationship.

He will promise you that this will never happen again, and may even try to tell you why/how it happened. Nevertheless, do not allow any of this information to stop you from remaining strong throughout this process. At this point, you need to figure out how you are going to handle the situation. By now you should have all the cards on the table, and the only thing you are trying to figure out: just how bad was it? Can you forgive him for cheating? This answer tends to vary based on the severity of the situation. Like was it a one-night stand, was it a long-term affair, was he emotionally attached? As far as I am concerned, all of the above will factor in my decision. I may be willing to forgive a one-night stand because men are able to detach themselves from the act itself but, if he is/was emotionally connected to the other woman, that is a whole other beast in my eyes.

However, once you have gotten your answer—whether it's yes or no—you must stand by your decision to either stay or to never take him back. If staying and forgiving your man is your decision, you must be sure you mean it. You do not want to forgive just because you are afraid to be alone or for superficial reasons; because believe it or not, the truth will come out later and will only damage the relationship further.

Also, a lot of women's initial reaction is to get mad at the other woman. What kind of thot would go there with a man that's taken? But we truly have to be objective and consider all sides. You don't know what kind of lies or untruths he has been feeding her as well. For all we know, she could think that's her man too. The issue and the solution to that issue lie between you and your partner. All the anger you feel towards that woman is truly misplaced and directed in the wrong path. Whatever rope or footing that this woman has in your relationship, your significant other gave to them. It's important to understand that and let the magnitude of that resonate with you so that you can weigh how that makes you feel about your partner and how much respect they have for you. Based on that analysis, you can decide if it's worth staying and building back the respect or trust you had before (or in some cases, never had) in the relationship.

Sometimes, when respect has left the relationship, it can make you feel less than and create issues with self-esteem. That is definitely when it is time to hit the door, when your self-worth starts coming into question. No one should have that power over you, but sometimes in situations like cheating, you feel so helpless it can make you feel powerless. Whatever regaining that power looks like for you, you need to do that. It could be leaving or creating some different rules in the relationship to make you feel like a mutual part of the relationship. Do not be afraid to make clear cut boundaries if that is what it takes for you to be comfortable again. Now, if you have to put a GPS tracker on him, make him check in every two minutes, or stalk his social media before you brush your teeth in the morning, then maybe you would be better off leaving than to go through that mental anguish. It is unhealthy to stay in a relationship that has you checking up on your man every second of the day.

I am no relationship therapist but I have been cheated on and I know firsthand the devastation you feel after finding out about your partner's infidelity. It is one of those pains that I would not wish on anyone. I have forgiven and I have not forgiven, but I made those decisions based on the facts and what I needed in my life at that time. I believe wholeheartedly that every couple needs to do what is best for them and their relationship. For me, I can say with certainty that if my man were to cheat on me where I am in my life today, there would be no forgiving.

Communication is so important to me and I make it very easy for my partners to come to me. If you find yourself wanting to be with another person, then you should end the relationship you are currently in first. I'm sure people are reading this and saying "well it just happened" I still love my partner. Cheating does not "just happen;" it is a decision. Therefore, you always have time to think about what you are about to do before doing it. Please understand, this is just my personal take on this very touchy matter. However, if forgiving is what you want to do. You have to go into this knowing that you can NEVER throw it back in his face, because a part of forgiving means not reliving the event.

## *A Wife's Point of View on Cheating*

My friend Pam and I had a very intense conversation about cheating, marriage, and relationships:

"Gia, let me speak as a wife. I will NEVER blame another woman for sleeping with my husband. I don't care if she knew about me or not. He took vows before God with me. He promised to love and honor me. He was supposed to protect our union. So if he makes a conscious choice (because that's what cheating is), to be with another woman, I cannot and will not blame nobody but him. As women we have to stop giving our husbands a pass but hold the other woman in contempt. The other woman did not vow to honor our union, that was my husband. Never lose sight of the fact that the commitment is between you and your husband. I understand that not every wife feels the same or as strongly as I do about this topic and that's okay too."

### *As I stated before, CHEATING IS A CHOICE!*

# 8

# The Cigar Lover II

The next morning I awake and though I am disappointed about what took place the night before, I am thankful God woke me up. After everything I experienced yesterday with Tony, I somehow still managed to get a decent night's sleep. But more importantly, I am surprisingly at peace. I do not feel anger, hurt, or pain, just disappointment. Before going to bed last night I prayed about my relationship with Tony and how to move forward as far as he was concerned.

It's Sunday, so I got up and went to church because I need to hear the Word and I also need continued prayer and a little more clarity from God because I cannot wrap my head around what just took place between Tony and I. Life has a funny way of throwing you into the fire without any warning.

Although I know for a fact that Tony would never do anything to purposely hurt me because that's not his character, I still cannot and will not pretend as if yesterday's events never happened.

I also cannot pretend as if I am innocent in all of this. I am aware that I should have waited until he and I were in private before having that conversation with him. I allowed my anger and jealousy to take me out of character. Now I am struggling with all of this because the bond between Tony and I that I thought was so strong and unbreakable has now been broken.

So how do we get past it? Can we get past it? Those are the questions rolling through my head right now. Plus, along with those unknowns, can I even forgive him? I still have yet to cry and I refuse to allow this to keep me down! Nope, after church I have errands to run as I do every Sunday. Therefore, I proceed with my day.

By late morning, both Cookie and Tori reached out to me to see how I was doing. It was sweet of them both! It is times like these when you appreciate your friends and the friendships y'all have built! I let the ladies know that I'm fine. They wanted to know if I have spoken to Tony. I hadn't and he hadn't tried to call or text me since last night.

I must have spoken too soon or talked him up because an hour later I received a text from Tony. It was just some bullshit ass message. No real apology because he needed to choose his words wisely just in case I decided to share his text with the chick who ran off at the mall.

**Nov 27, 2016**

Tony: I am not going through this BS ever again!

Tony: You do not matter in my life anymore!

I do not respond to either of Tony's texts.

**Nov 30, 2016**

Tony: Ok I am reaching out to apologize about Saturday. No matter what was said or what happened, I was wrong. I really lost myself and I apologize for that.

Again, I do not respond to Tony's text. So a few hours later he sends me another text apologizing.

Tony: I wanna apologize for my past actions. Maybe we just are not as compatible as we thought. If I hurt you or your feelings, please forgive me. I was wrong for putting my hands on you at all. I am as much at fault as you are. Gia, you didn't deserve any of this; the lies or the cheating. I gotta man up to what I have done to you. Please forgive me!

Listen, in the past, I would have responded to Tony's texts by now and we would be back on good terms. He has never seen this side of me, and I am positive that he is in shock by my silence. I have had all I can take from this man. Seeing him at the mall with another woman on top of the fact that I just had words with a different woman days before. At this point it does not matter to me how many times he apologizes, I still will not forgive him.

Those texts were followed by daily phone calls to my cell and my office. I either pushed his phone calls to voicemail or ignored them.

I then informed my two girlfriends not to tell me anything about what is going on with him. I do not want to see any pictures of him, not even if he is with another female. As far as I am concerned, Tony no longer exists to me.

Sometimes you have to show them better than you can tell them. Therefore for the next five months, I received weekly phone calls from Tony to my cell and office; sometimes once; sometimes twice a week. In addition, for 5 months straight I ignored every single one of his calls. Yes, I sent his ass straight to voicemail each and every time I was near my phone when he called me. That level of betrayal at that mall was the straw that broke the camel's back. Until that one Saturday afternoon when I had just finished my work day and was laying across my bed when my phone rung. It was Tony. I honestly contemplated for a minute or two, but decided to answer.

"Hello!"

"Hey, how are you?" Tony asked.

"I'm good. What's up, Tony?"

"You've been on my mind and I just wanted to see that you were good. How have things been going with you and your illness?"

"Everything is good and I am doing well," I replied. "Thank you for asking"

"Okay, I am glad you are doing well. I will talk to you soon," he said.

"Okay, bye!"

After we hung up I thought to myself "that was awkward." Two days later another call from Tony, then another, and before you knew it he was back calling me on a regular basis. So much so that I had to remind him that we cannot just pretend the fight never happened, and until we discuss it we cannot go back to our normal conversations. That is just weird and it does not work for me. Tony agrees and we decided to meet at his job in his office. When I got there he was acting as if nothing had changed between us. We had a long conversation over who was wrong/right in that situation. The conversation took place for maybe an hour. Ultimately, we both decided to agree to disagree. Tony goes to walk me to my car but as we hit the door to his office, he grabs and pushes me up against the wall, then proceeds to kiss me. Now, remember he is an amazing kisser, so naturally I kissed him back. Tony grabs me by my neck and has his tongue all in my mouth. It turns me on whenever he grabs me by my neck and takes control. Before I knew it my pants were down and I was bent over the chair and we were having sex right in his office. After we got ourselves together, he walked me to my car and I went home as if nothing ever happened.

He and I tried to go back to where we were, but the damage had been done. I don't trust him and that will probably never change. I had to be honest with myself, which meant I was no longer interested in playing along with his silly games. Playing games is all he's capable of, he is not the man you take home to mama. Not because he is an awful person but because since becoming social media popular, he is only interested in having sex with women. He is that guy who looks good on social media but in real life, Tony is selfish. He loves you as long as there is something in it for him. He is that guy who will start acting funny out of nowhere, which always, without fail means, Tony either met someone new or somebody came back into his life. He is famous for recycling his women; if you fucked him once you can pretty much get the dick whenever you want it. This dude has no standards, all it takes is pussy, your own place and you are back in! Such bullshit!

I have learned over the past year that Tony picks his women based on their need to have a man. He has the innate ability to spot a needy female from a mile away. He does not typically go for the "pretty girls" with standards. Nah that would require him to present himself as a real man; be accountable and not play childish games. This "new" Tony tells the women he meets that, "I don't know how to date." That is another one of his untruths to get himself out of taking these women out. Tony and I use to go on dates all the time but when you are out here living shady, you will say and do whatever it takes to get what you want.

I realized a long time ago that Tony and I would never work out because I hold him accountable for his actions. I am also the pretty girl with standards who has her shit together. Those just are not the qualities this man is looking for in his women.

It is sad whenever you have to fallback from someone you care about. However, there comes a time in your life when you realize that certain people/relationships/friendships just are not good for your soul! And at this point in my life, that someone happens to be Tony. He is that person you find yourself always forgiving but in real life, you know he is not sorry for what he has done or the pain he has caused you. Tony cares about Tony and only pretends to care about you for as long as there is a need of you.

This saddens me because we started out as such amazing friends. To think that the bond we built could so easily be broken by random females and untruths is crazy to me. I am never sad over the loss of sex from any man because sex is easily replaceable if that is all you are looking for. But a friendship is not something you accept from any and every one. It requires the two parties to mesh then build and grow upon this unbreakable force. However, when a grown man cares more about how many women he can be with, himself, and his popularity on social media more than he does your friendship, the outcome will always be the same: the ending of your friendship. I can never be who he needs or who he wants. More importantly, I will never try because I will never put the need of a man over my own. Therefore, at this point, Tony and I cannot remain lovers. Trust me, it is not from a lack of him trying because he still tries on a regular basis. I know that if I were to change my mind I could call him whenever I want and he will come. I also know that if I seriously wanted a committed relationship with him, he would say okay. Now, none of that means he would be faithful... Lol... I will say this, he and I are in a good place. We are friends who talk every now and then but nothing more. I will continue to wish the best for him because aside from his selfish ways, there is a very loving and kind soul deep down. It saddens me somewhat that our relationship has come to this because when Tony and I are together, it is nothing but fun! However, sometimes having fun and good times with someone just is not enough to sustain a relationship. So for now, I have decided to hold onto those memories of us and move on.

# 9

# The Photographer

*Now Ladies, this next man who enters my life will teach me a very important life lesson about trust and friendship! I call him "The Photographer aka My Peace."*

After dealing with the breakup from Rashad and learning that, Tony had moved in with Tracy, my life was crazy to say the least! Just when I least expect it, this incredibly sweet man enters my life! This man has such a peaceful spirit about him. He is not like any man I have ever dated before.

His name is Kevin. Well, Kevin came into my life when I was in a dark chaotic place. He brought an overwhelming amount of peace and calm into my otherwise crazy life. As I stated before, Kevin was completely different from every other guy I had dated in the past.

Kevin is a photographer. We met through my BFF Cookie while putting together my look-book for Rashad. I needed some photo editing done for a few of my pictures and Cookie told me about Kevin's work, so she reached out to him for me. After the introduction, Kevin and I started communicating via text. I liked his price and his work, so I went with him as my photo editor. At this point, Rashad and I were no longer seeing each other at all but I loved my pictures and decided to go through with the look-book. I sent Kevin detailed information on what I needed to have done to my photos. He seemed to be very nice and knowledgeable when it came to photo editing. I gave him my timeline and after doing some of the editing, a few of the pictures still needed more work. Therefore, I offered to come over to sit and show him exactly what I needed.

Kevin agreed to let me come over and sit with him while he made edits. After a few back and forth conversations via text, he and I finally agreed on a date and time. Well at that point I had no idea this was not the norm and he usually did not allow clients to come help him.

It's a cold Saturday evening in mid-January 2015, I'm wearing jeans with chocolate brown suede over-the-knee boots and a red fitted coat. I get to the photography studio which is located in DC and Kevin comes to the door. He's tall—6'2"ish—thin built, with a dark complexion and beautiful skin. He has a dimple in his chin, a low fade haircut, and a mustache and goatee. His style was kinda eclectic which took me by surprise. We go upstairs to his office and I take a seat at his desk, he opens up the file with all my photos. Right away, he makes me feel very comfortable. I can tell he is knowledgeable when it comes to his craft.

He pulls up the first photo; it's a pic of me in a red lace dress. In this picture, I am not wearing a bra and my nipples are on one thousand. Kevin got my skin looking tan and glossy. He starts the conversation, "this is my favorite picture of you."

"Oh, really? It is one of my favorites as well," I respond. "I love how you have me looking all tan with my light brown eyes popping."

"Yeah, and I made your blonde hair look a little more golden," he added.
"Yes, I noticed that too. In that particular photo, I was wearing a blonde wig. What other edits did you make to this picture?" I asked.

"I copied the right breast and pasted it in place of the left breast," he explained.

# Chapter 9: The Photographer

"Really? WOW! That is amazing," I exclaimed. "Hold up, is it because my boobs are not as perky as they used to be?" He didn't want to say it but I already knew my breasts were not looking all that perky in that picture. Lol.

"Well, this side was just a little more perky than the other one," he said with a smile.

"Okay, that is just amazing how you were able to do that because had you not told me, I would have never known."

"You are not supposed to know," he said.

"I guess you got a point there," I said.

"Let's move on to the next picture so I can show you the tan line on my thighs that you say you don't see."

"I really don't see what you see," he replied.

"Seriously, you don't see the line on my thighs? It's right there," I said, pointing to the computer screen highlighting my very clear tan line. I don't think Kevin was seeing what I saw, but he still did some editing to appease me.

Kevin is very laid back in a shy kind of way. He appears to be a lot younger than I am, but very mature at the same time. He is cool and easy to talk to. It is getting late, so we finish up for the evening and Kevin walks me out.

For the next week, Kevin and I continued talking via text and we set up another editing session at his place for the following weekend. I am on a time crunch because I am planning a LookBook Party for April. Therefore, I need to finish the photo editing so I have time to design my book and then send it off for printing.

We are now in February, Kevin and I have plans for me to come to finish our last editing sessions. I am looking forward to this meeting for many reasons. Not only will I have the finished product to send off to the printing company, but I also get to see Kevin. He has been calling and texting me, and surprisingly, I enjoy talking to him. I say "surprisingly" because he is younger than I am. I have dated younger before, but they were never almost 11 years younger.

It is Saturday evening; I arrive at Kevin's studio, pull up, and park in what is quickly becoming my usual spot across the street under the big tree. Kevin opens the door and we head upstairs to his office.

"How are you?" Kevin asked.

"I am good," I replied. "How is your day going?"

"Busy, I had to do some editing for this other client. Let me pull up your pictures so you can show me what else you need me to edit," he said as he opened the file.

"What do you think about adding some smoke to the two pictures with the cigarettes?" I asked.

"Yeah, we can add some smoke," he replied. "Let me show you the difference between these two."

"Okay. Oooh I really like the way the pictures look with the added smoke. It really looks as if I lit that cigarette myself and I don't even smoke!"

"You don't smoke anything?" he asked.

"Nope, nothing."

"Never?" He prodded.

I laughed. "Well, I tried weed once when I was 16 years old."

"Wow! Okay" he said.

"Why are you so surprised?" I asked. "Do you smoke?"

"I used to, but not anymore because my job does random testing," he explained. "But I liked smoking more than I do drinking."

"Why is that?" I inquired.

"Smoking kept me feeling very chill all the time," he replied.
Kevin has this way of getting me to talk. This dude even got me sharing personal things.

"What are you doing when you leave here?" he asked.

"I'm going to Barnes and Noble to pick up a book they are holding for me. Well, the book is actually for my daughter," I said.

"Which one do you have to go to?"

"The one on F Street because it was the only one who had it," I said.

"Did you check the store up the street from here?" he asked. I hadn't. "You should go see if they have it and save yourself a trip from going downtown."

"Yeah that is true, maybe I will."

"What grade is your daughter in and what school does she attend?" he asked.

"She is at a boarding school," I replied.

"Oh, really? I went to boarding school too, but the one I attended was an all-boys boarding school."

"Oh, wow that is so cool," I said.

"Is she your only child?"

"No, she is my youngest. I also have a 24-year-old daughter," I replied. "How about you, do you have any kids?"

"Yes, I have three," he said.

"Okay, that is cool," I replied. "I used to want a son, but God knew what he was doing when he gave me two daughters."

Kevin and I finish the final edits and he surprises me with a free video of my pictures. He put music to the background and set it up so that the pictures will continue to play on repeat.

"Kevin, this is the sweetest thing!" I exclaimed. "Thank you!"

"You're welcome! I thought it would be nice for you to have something playing in the background while your friends are over for the look book party," he said. "I just need to put it on a CD, but it will be available for you to pick up before your party."

This man has this overwhelming calmness about him; I swear his spirit is like no man I've ever encountered. The funny part is that I can tell he is feeling me. I picked up on it the first time we met. However, I am so unsure when it comes to him because I am not trying to get involved with another man right now. So I do my best to keep him at bay. But this brother is not making it easy for me. He is very consistent with his calls and texts. Kevin is making sure I know he is interested, but in a reserved kind of way.

# Chapter 9: The Photographer

For the next few months, Kevin and I talk on a regular basis but we don't go on our first date until June 2015. Listen, our date almost did not happen because a few days before I hurt my knee working out with my daughter Alex. I woke up that Saturday morning to a swollen knee and ended up at urgent care later that evening. I called Kevin to let him know that I was unsure if I could make dinner due to my injury. He was understanding and concerned for my well-being.

After leaving my urgent care appointment with a knee brace and crutches, I called Kevin to give him an update.

"Hey! I am just leaving urgent care and I have a knee brace and crutches, but I don't want to cancel dinner" I told him.

"Hey, are you sure? Because we can do this another night," he said.

"Yep, I'm sure," I replied. "I just cannot go any place that will require me to do a lot of walking. So just pick a place and I will meet you there."

"Okay, cool. Well why don't you meet me at Brookland's Finest," he said. "I will text you the address."

"Okay, I will see you soon."

I get to the restaurant; I am driving my daughter Alex's car. I am having a hard time parking, I hate DC street parking and having this brace on half of my leg is not helping. Kevin comes out to park the car for me. I hop my way into the restaurant where Kevin had us seated at the bar. It is a cute little restaurant; it looks like a house on the outside. I order a drink, my usual (Malibu & Pineapple Juice) not really hungry. Kevin orders the pork chops with vegetables, his food looks delicious. We sit there for about an hour talking. After dinner I gave him a ride home because he lives walking distance from the restaurant. Kevin and I pull up to his house but we sit in the car for another hour or so talking about everything from kids, our past, to past sexual experiences. You name it, we talked about it. I like him, he is a really genuine guy.

I know I say this a lot, but it has honestly been a very long time since I have met a man with such a calming soul. Do not get me wrong because both Rashad and Tony were nice men, they just did not have Kevin's calming spirit. After our talk we ended the night with a hug and I went home.

**June 30, 2015**
I call Kevin because we have a movie date scheduled. "Hey, are we still good for the 9:40 movie?" I asked.

"Sure," he replied.

Kevin and I enjoyed our first movie date. It was about to storm, so we did not hang around talking afterwards. However, he did call me to ensure that I made it home safely.

For the next couple of weeks, Kevin does a lot of texting and calling. Although, he sometimes came across as if he was nervous around me. Keep in mind, I am more than 10 years older than him. So I asked him straight up because I am a firm believer if there is something you want to know, the best way to get an answer is to ask the question.

During our next conversation, I asked Kevin "do I make you nervous?"

"No, you don't make me nervous," he responded. "Why do you ask?"

"Okay, I wanted to know because you seem so shy around me still. Not only that, but you spend a lot of time texting and calling. I'm just trying to figure out if you are trying to date me or just text me." We both laugh.

"Is that right," he said.

"Absolutely. However, I did not mean date 'only me' because I am good with you continuing to date whomever you want."

"Do you want to date me?" he asked.

"I want to get to know you, and we are already dating. We are friends who go out on dates but nothing serious," I replied.

He laughed and then said to me, "Cool, so we dating.

"What we have right now is a friendship with some form of dating," I corrected him.

I agree," he said.

"How many other women are you dating? And please be honest."

"I guess two," he replied. How many men are you dating?"

"I'm seeing one," I told him.

"Okay."

We finish up our conversation and call it a night. The next morning I awake to a text from Kevin. He must have sent it in the wee hours. "You up?" it read. So I texted him back.

Gia: Morning! I was knocked out when you sent your text.

Kevin: Morning, I figured that.

Gia: Are you at work?
Kevin: Yes, are you?

Gia: Yes but traffic was god awful because of whatever is going on at the Navy Yard. I was on my way to drop my Godson off to camp but had to bring him to work with me because they have his camp on lockdown.

Kevin: Oh wow, that is crazy.

Gia; I know. Well, I have a meeting, so I will talk to you later.

Kevin: Cool.

It is now July 3rd and Kevin is with his family for the weekend. He calls to see how my day is going and what I'm up to. Our conversation is short because it is late.

On July 4th, I receive a text from Kevin.

Kevin: Hey babe!

Gia: Hey! How is your trip going? Are you having fun?

Kevin: It's cool. Do you miss me yet?

Gia: Lol...Of course

Kevin: Not believing that but okay.

Gia: What? I do not say anything I do not mean. I thought you knew that by now. Are you missing ME yet is the real question?

Some time goes by and no response from Kevin. I am thinking to myself "well damn" then I send another text.

Gia: Hello, do you need to think about if you miss me or not?

A few minutes later he responds.

Kevin: No, I don't need to think about it at all. Sorry I was eating when you sent your text.

Gia; Okay, enjoy the rest of your trip and I will see you when you return.

Kevin: Okay, and I do miss you. ☺

Later that evening I meet up with my girlfriend Renee for dinner in Bethesda, Md. She and I decide to spend our 4th having dinner at Woodmont Grill since we were both kid free. It is never a dull moment when spending time with Renee; she is my funny friend who keeps me laughing all the time. After dinner we decided to ride down to Georgetown to see which stores were open and just walk around. To our surprise not one single store was open, only bars and restaurants. It was okay because we still had an amazing fun time hanging out. After we hung out in Georgetown we called it a night.

I get home and I receive a text from Kevin ,and for the next two hours we text our entire conversation.

Kevin: Wyd

Gia: Just got home. Look at you texting me right when I was thinking about you.

Kevin: What were you thinking?

Gia: Just wondering what you were doing and if you were someplace watching the fireworks.

Kevin: Yes, I'm still at the cookout and watching the fireworks, but I am sleepy.

Gia: Why are you so sleepy, it is still early. What would you be doing if you were home?

Kevin: You! Lol... Sike

I don't respond right away, so this is the next text I receive from him.

Kevin: Speechless?

Gia: Lmao! Do not say "sike." If you are going to say it/think it, you gotta own it. So really? You think you would be doing me? Oh, and NEVER speechless, sweetie!

Kevin: I could be doing you but you may not be ready for that.

Gia: Who knows, but what is there to be ready for? If it is meant to happen, it will happen. I am always ready, if it is what I want.

Kevin: Lol... I like your response @ NEVER speechless.

Gia: Are you sure you're ready to cross that line? Once you come over, there is no turning back. Lol

Kevin: I been ready.

Gia; Is that right? I would have never known. You act so shy around me and you still have yet to try and kiss me.

Kevin: Lol. You wanted me to kiss you?

Gia: I want you to feel comfortable doing you. If kissing me is what you want, how would I know if you don't try? You already know I am not into planning sex or kisses for that matter.

Kevin: Oh, it just happens.

Gia: It should! But honestly, I love that you did not try getting me into bed right away. Especially since, I would have never gone for that. Lol

Kevin: I am too laid back sometimes.

Gia: I like that about you. Hey, but when the moment is right and I am horny. We're having sex.

Kevin; Lol… You are funny.

Gia: All jokes aside. I really do like that you do not come at me like it is all about sex. It is what I like most about you. I like the respect you have shown me.

Kevin: Well, I am horny just thinking about you. Lol

Gia: That's a good thing. I would be disappointed if you weren't. I am about to get ready for bed. I will talk to you later.

Kevin: Goodnight.

The next morning I receive a call from Kevin. "Hey babe!' he said.

"Hey, how are you? When are you coming back?" I asked.

"I'm back in town; I am on my way to my house now," he said.

"Okay, call me later."

I love my new relationship with Kevin. He and I talk every day; either on the phone or over text. We do not allow a day to go by without talking at least twice a day. I can appreciate a man who is consistent. But more importantly, I appreciate the fact that Kevin does not play the dating games. It is so crazy because, you would think since he is the younger of them, he would be the one playing the games. But it is the total opposite. He's still very shy around me, but I can tell that there is so much more to his personality than he is showing me.

It's the week of July 7th and Kevin is scheduled to go out of town for work. He asks to see me before he leaves. I am actually looking forward to seeing him at his place, because he and I have been going out on dates but we are several months into this dating thing and have yet to have sex. So, this visit should be interesting.

It is now the day before Kevin leaves. He calls me.

"Hey babe! What you doing?" he said.

"Taking Alex to SAT prep class," I replied. "What's up?"

"Are you still coming to see me tonight?" he asked.

"Yes, but I have a major headache, can we meet up around 10?"

"Sure," he said.

"Okay, I will call you when I am on my way."

At 10:30 pm I call Kevin to find out where we're going so I can be there by 11 pm because I changed the time back by an hour. He doesn't answer, so I call back and still no answer. So I text him.

# Chapter 9: The Photographer

Gia: You're not answering your phone and I have no idea where we're meeting. I am not leaving my house until I hear from you. If I don't hear from you by 11pm, I am going to assume you're asleep.

At 10:44pm I receive a text from Kevin.

Kevin: Hey, where you want to meet?

Gia: We were supposed to meet at 11pm. I don't know what is open. You're obviously busy, so have a safe and fun trip. I will talk to you when you get back.

Kevin; Huh? You said 11 pm.

Gia: Yes, I said lets meet at ll. I called you at 10:30 so that I could meet you at 11 but you did not answer.

Kevin: Do you want to see me?

Gia: Yes, I wanted to see you before you left but now it is late. Where is it for us to go this late?

Kevin: I can come to you.

Gia: No, there is nothing open. I will come to you. I will call you when I get close.

Kevin: Okay.

I finally get to Kevin's house and at this point it's almost midnight. We decided to just watch a movie instead of going out. Kevin put on the movie and we're chillin' on the sofa in the living room. He pours me a glass of wine. We're talking and watching the movie until Kevin starts kissing me, caressing and kissing my breasts before going down. Damn, he's got me wanting to climb the wall the way he is eating the kitty-kat. His skills took me by surprise because he seemed so shy up until this point, but there is nothing shy in the way he has me calling out his name. After making me cum from our oral escapades, Kevin pulls out a condom from his pocket. We have now made our way onto the other sofa. I love that he is not trying to take me to the bedroom. I'm so over the typical bedroom sex.

Kevin pulls me close while we're kissing. Seconds later, he is naked and I am sitting on top. I ride him for a solid twenty minutes before he flips me over and inserts himself into me doggie style. Kevin grabs me by my hair then grabs my shoulders as he pulls me into him harder and harder. Damn, he is pounding the shit out of my ass from behind; I don't want him to stop. What an amazing feeling! Thirty minutes later and, whew lawd, we have finally gotten the first time jitters out the way. Boy oh boy, am I looking forward to what is to come with Kevin!

The next morning, July 8, 2015, Kevin leaves for his business trip. He calls me prior to leaving for his flight just to hear my voice, he says, so we have a very brief conversation.

"Good morning," Kevin said.

"Morning honey, how are you feeling?" I replied.

"I'm feeling good and you?"

"Tired as hell but other than that, I am good. Are you ready for your trip?" I asked.

"Yes, I am about to head out to the airport now. I will call you from the airport," he replied.

Later in the evening, I receive a text from Kevin.

Kevin: Hey babe.

Gia: Hey, I was just thinking about you. I hope you guys get off okay, with all the rain.

Kevin: I checked, and my flight is still leaving on time. This morning, I could still smell your scent on me. I didn't want to wash it off.

Gia: Really?

Kevin: Yes

Gia: Wow!

Two hours later, my cell phone rings and it is Kevin. "Hey babe, I'm on my flight," he told me. "I forgot to ask if you had a good time last night."

"Yes I did. Glad I came over, but the next time I wanna actually watch the entire movie," I said jokingly.

"Oops, my bad," he said.
"It's cool. We can have movie night when you return," I told him. "Have fun! Bye!"

"Okay babe, bye!"

**July 13, 2015**

Kevin: Hey babe, I just landed.

Gia: Yay, I missed you! I know you had fun!

Kevin: I did and I missed you too. What are you doing?

Gia: I am washing clothes; call me when you get home.

Kevin: Okay.

**July 16, 2015**

I left work early because I cannot be late for my appointment with Dr. Edwards. I arrive a little earlier than my appointment because street parking in the city can be crazy. After driving around for ten minutes I finally found parking and head into Dr. Edwards' office.

"Hi Dr. Edwards!"

"Hello Ms. Williams, how are you?" he replied.

"I'm good," I said  as I take a seat in my normal comfy armchair. "How are you, Dr. Edwards?"

"I am doing well. Ms. Williams, when you were here last, we talked a little bit about how you were handling the ending of the relationship between you and Rashad. You were very upset over how he handled things. Especially the way he handled you telling him about the sugar being put in your car. How are you feeling now? Have you spoken to Rashad since we last met?" he inquired.

"I am still very hurt by the way Rashad handled things, but in a sense, it is probably best that things happened the way they did," I said. "Oh, and no, I have not spoken to him. I refuse to call him and after our last argument, I am sure I won't be hearing from him either."

"Are you really okay with the two of you not speaking, or are you just saying that you are ok with not speaking to him?" he asked.

"I am really okay with where Rashad and I are right now. The fact that he never offered to help pay for the damages done to my car, sealed the deal for me. Plus, deep down, I knew a long time ago, that he and I would never be more."

Chapter 9: The Photographer

"Really? Why do you say that, now?"

"Well, because of how we met, and who our friends were. I knew it would never work out for Rashad and me," I explained.

"Honestly, Ms. Williams, I was really rooting for the two of you."

I smirk, shrug my shoulders and say, "Well, it is never gonna happen, Dr. Edwards."

"Let us talk a little about your relationship with the new guy, the photographer. Remind me of his name again?"

"His name is Kevin, and what would you like for us to talk about?"

"Tell me how are things going between the two of you?"

"Kevin is just a really sweet guy. He is so different from both Rashad and Tony," I explained. "I was not sure at first if I wanted to date him, because as I mentioned before, he is not my type. However, I like that he took the time to get to know me and date me. From day one, it was never about the sex with him, and on some level, I believe that is what turned me on. I appreciate the friendship Kevin and I have developed because of it, he and I are able to talk about any and everything. Can I just tell you Dr. Edwards, how refreshing it is."

"It is good to see you moving on with your life," he said. "I know you were taking things slow with Kevin, so how is that going?"

"It is going well. I have not taken things this slow in a long time and probably because when Kevin and I met, I was in the middle of my relationship with Rashad ending, and trying to figure out where my relationship with Tony was going, if that makes sense. Kevin and I are in a good place. We have taken our dating to the next level since my last visit."

"What does that mean, exactly?" He inquired.

"Really, Dr. Edwards?" I said smiling. "It means we had sex." We both laugh our behinds off!

"Okay, my only concern is for you," he said.

"I know, but I am good," I assured him. "I am truly loving this new Gia! We have talked about this before, how dating and having sex with multiple men was all new to me. Even though I love the consistency relationships bring, whether committed or not, I now know that I can still get that with dating more than one guy. It is exhilarating, and I don't feel the need to justify my actions to anyone.'

"You are absolutely correct. You do not have to justify your actions to anyone at all."

"Thank you, Dr. Edwards. But more importantly, we both already know that I am never going to share my relationship with anyone anyway. I mean, I have not had enough therapy to get me to open up and start sharing my personal business with others. Baby steps, Dr. Edwards, baby steps," I said as we both laughed.

"Okay, our time is up. We will pick back up at your next appointment. Same day and time?" Dr. Edwards asked.

"Yes," I confirmed.

Kevin and I are on a consistent roll, and I love it. The two of us are seeing each other more and more. He is still very laid back, but in a good way. I like the fact that Kevin initiates seeing me more, but I do wish that he was a little more aggressive when it comes to sex. I am learning through therapy how not to be so controlling. Therefore, I am trying not to take the lead on everything that happens between the two of us. This has been somewhat of a challenge for me, especially because not only am I a control freak, but I have a high sex drive too!

Later that evening, I received a text from Kevin.

Kevin: Hey babe! What's up?

Gia: Nothing much, what's up with you?

Kevin: You.

Gia: Really.

Kevin: I wanna see you.

Gia: I'm sure I can make that happen then.

Kevin: Make it happen.

Gia: When would you like to see me?

Kevin: This weekend.

Gia: Okay, but don't forget, I have packing to do. So, I can't be out too late. Just let me know when and where to be.

Kevin and I met up over the weekend for a quick dinner and drinks. It was good to see him. It is nice to have a conversation without an argument occurring. His spirit is beyond calming, which makes for a very relaxing evening whenever we are together. You would think that at this point I would be all over this man for a commitment, but I'm not. I am still so uncertain of what I want, or who I want. So that I am not leading him on, I make sure to keep the lines of communication open. Plus, with Kevin being ten years younger, I notice that he is still doing the party scene, and not just for work. I have come to realize that, on some level, the drinking and partying somewhat bothers me, but they're not on a "deal breaker" type level...yet. Aside from that, Kevin is pretty much the perfect guy in an imperfect kind of way. Therefore, I am going to continue dating him and see where this new relationship of ours takes us. I am going with the flow...for now. Lol!

**July 29, 2015**

I am getting dressed to go to the Jill Scott outdoor concert with my girlfriends. I, along with a couple of other ladies, am meeting Jasmine at her office because she has free garage parking. Ashley and I park our cars and ride with Jasmine. Of course we ran into some crazy traffic because it's rush hour on a weekday and the concert is way out in Virginia, but Ashley and I are not worried because Jasmine knew the back roads. So not only did we make it on time, but with time to spare. All the other ladies arrived, and we found the perfect spot on the grass. It is a beautiful night for an outdoor concert. It is about 8 of us on the lawn with our pop-up tent, lawn chairs, blankets, food, and wine. We are ready for Jilly from Philly!

While at the concert I receive a text from Kevin.

Kevin: Hey babe, what you doing?

Gia: Hey, I am at the Jill Scott concert.

Kevin: Oh, I didn't know you were going to her concert.

Gia: I am pretty sure I told you but that just goes to show how much you pay attention. ☺

Kevin: Okay, if you say so. Enjoy the show.

Gia: Thanks.

**August 1, 2015**

Kevin calls. "Hello," I answer.

"What's up babe?" he asks.

"Nothing much, I am on my way to dinner. What's up witcha? Do you want to meet for a drink later tonight?"

"Sure, what time?"

"It'll be around 10:00 or 11:00 because Cookie is coming over after dinner to help me do some unpacking," I said.

"Okay, I was thinking about getting a room tonight in the city so I can just chill out," he mentioned.

"Let me know and I will come by."

"Okay."

A few hours later Kevin sends me a text.

Kevin: Hey babe, I got a room at Hotel Monaco.

Gia: Okay, what is the address?

Kevin: 700 F Street, NW near the Verizon Center. Are you still coming?

Gia: Yes, I will be there but not until later. Do they have parking?

Kevin: I am not sure but you can valet park and charge it to my room. I am in room 108.

Gia: Okay, I will call you when I am on my way. I will be there by 11:00 pm, is that too late?

Kevin: No, not at all.

I arrive wearing my boyfriend distressed jeans, a white graphic tee, my high-heel black suede clogs, with a cute blazer. Kevin meets me outside at the valet booth. He greets me with a hug and kiss, and then the two of us walk a couple of blocks to one of the local bars to have a drink. I am enjoying his company because I have had one crazy day. Kevin and I talk and laugh while listening to the music at the bar. This was my first time at this particular bar, but Kevin knows about all the cool spots in the city. The two of us hang out for about an hour or so before we head back to the hotel room. In our minds, we planned this to be just a chill night, a time to relax and enjoy each other's company.

However, we decided to take a nice hot steamy shower together. Kevin starts to give me little soft kisses on my neck, moving down to my breasts. He is not a big kisser, but there are certain body parts of which that brother does an amazing job at kissing. The hot water hits my skin, dripping down my face. Kevin is taking his time with me as he moves down my body, skillfully kissing every part of me. I close my eyes and lean my head back underneath the water, allowing my long curly hair to feel the hot steamy water. He gently lifts my left leg, placing it on the tub as he starts to eat me so damn good. As I moan louder and louder, I say "stop," but really mean "don't stop." I grab ahold of his head, as I push his face into my wet throbbing kitty. I wanted to be sure he felt me grinding, while he was eating my kitty. Whew chile! I need more showers like this one.

We finally wash up, so that we can chill for the rest of the evening. We get in the bed and find a movie, but that chill shit didn't last long. Kevin pulls me close for a goodnight hug. Oh, but I know that hug, and I am here for it. I am ready for part two. Ten minutes into watching the movie, the TV was now watching Kevin and me. Oh, and it was well worth giving up my chill night. I rode his dick until I made him scream, "Oh baby, oh baby, I'm about to cum! Baby please, oh shit baby, I'm cumming!"

Yesss…now that is how you end an impromptu date night. That is how you keep them wanting more of you, and more of your time. A strong friendship, good conversation, along with amazing sex will keep him thinking about you no matter who else he is seeing.

The next morning is Saturday. I get up early, shower, and head out because I have to work. I kiss Kevin on the forehead before leaving. He offers to walk me out, but I say to him "No, stay and get some more rest. I will be fine and I will call you later."

Kevin and I try to talk just about every day if not every other day via text or phone. He is really good about sending me "good morning, babe" texts. We make time in between our busy schedules to date and to talk because it is important to us both.

The upcoming week is going to be crazy for me because I have work, therapy, plus I have to get Alex, my youngest daughter ready for her Miami trip. She is growing up too fast, I still cannot believe she is about to go on a "girls trip" with her girlfriends, along with a couple of the moms. I am having a hard time wrapping my head around the fact that the girls are in high school. It is about 8 of them and they have been friends since kindergarten. A couple days later I get Alex off and I am back at home and in the bed when I get a text from Kevin at 1:40 in the morning.

Kevin: Hey babe, where are you?

Gia: Home... Where are you?

Kevin: I'm out but I am getting ready to go home.

Gia: Oh okay.

Kevin: You always up.

Gia: I am about to go to sleep. I just got home not too long ago.

Kevin: Where did you go?

Gia: I went to drop Alex off because she is going to Miami tomorrow.

Kevin: Oh sweet, I should come visit.

Gia: You can visit me tomorrow, it is late and I am sleepy, but text me to let me know you made it home safe and sound.

Kevin: Okay, I will.

In the midst of my crazy week, I have therapy. This time I focus most of my conversation on my relationship with Kevin. I want to figure out why I won't allow myself to walk away from Tony completely so that I can enter into a more committed relationship with Kevin. I say it is because he loves to party, but is that the real reason, or am I just hiding behind that as an excuse? That is the million dollar question I keep asking myself, because it is not like I have had a conversation with Kevin about how his partying ways bother me. So I ask myself, is it fair to Kevin that I am, in a sense, holding something against him that he is not even aware of? I don't know, but these are all the questions going through my mind; all the questions I need Dr. Edwards to help me figure out before I do something to push him away.

Have you ever met someone who makes being with them seem so effortless? That is what Kevin does for me. I say this, I know this to be factual, but yet and still, I will not share this information with the one person who should hear it, and that is Kevin.

Dr. Edwards leaves me with a few things to think about and to work on for my next therapy session. I do not like when he assigns me homework, but I know it is needed in order to get to the root of my issues.

In the upcoming weeks, Kevin has to travel for work. We make plans to go out before he leaves for his trip. Kevin and I decide on a movie date. both work two jobs, so as you can imagine our schedules don't always make it easy for us to see each other as much as we would like to, but we make it work. In order for us to continue working at this dating thing, I suggested a standard movie night during the week. This is needed because seeing each other only on the weekends or when our schedules permit is not cutting it. Since Kevin teaches class on Wednesday nights, we decided to make Tuesday night our standard movie date night. Plus, what is better than five dollar Tuesday at all Regal Cinemas. Now, I have never been a big movie lover because I am always thinking of other things I could be doing with my time during those two hours. Therefore, making this suggestion is what I call "growth" for me, and it speaks volumes when it comes to how important Kevin has become to me.

It's Thursday, so I'm at my therapy session and I share with Dr. Edwards how I am making progress with Kevin. Hell, I even put movie date night in place, now, tell me that isn't progress. Lol! I also share with Dr. Edwards how much I appreciate the fact that even though Kevin and I have an active sex life, we have more date nights without the involvement of sex. This type of relationship makes my heart smile, even though I love having sex. I want to do things a little differently with him from the way I have been doing them with Rashad and Tony. In due time, I will add more sex into our relationship.

Dr. Edwards is pleased with my decision to move things away from it becoming a primarily sexual relationship. Dr. Edwards is big on men stepping up to the plate and being held accountable, because that is what real men are supposed to do. Dr. Edwards tell me all the time "It doesn't matter how guarded you are, a real man will not allow you to push him away."

Dr. Edwards is right, because no matter what I do to keep Kevin at bay, he will not give up on me. He will give me some time, but he never gives me attitude—even when I know he feels some kind of way about me still seeing Tony here and there. Kevin will simply say to me "I don't want to know." I respect this man so much more than he will ever know.

The weekend is here and I am up early on this Saturday morning preparing myself for clients. After working all morning and most of the afternoon, I shower and get dressed so that I can go get Alex from school because she and I have a lunch date planned. I love spending quality time with her; I have to get it in while I can before you know it she will be off to college. Some would argue that I should already be used to her being away since she attends boarding school, but I would have to argue that is not the same at all. While I am out, Kevin calls to say he would like to see me, but not tonight because he is working. We decide on Sunday.

I wake up early Sunday morning and get my day started. I get Alex to SAT Prep, and then we go grocery shopping to get snacks for her dorm room. I receive a phone call from Kevin asking if I can spend the night with him. "On a work night?" I say jokingly.

"I am a little hesitant, but I have no clue why because I am grown and so are my daughters for the most part. I think to myself, there I go being all weird again for no real reason. So I break down and tell Kevin that I will stay the night with him. I am actually looking forward to our hotel stay. I am exhausted and looking forward to a quiet evening with him.

I arrived at the hotel shortly after Kevin. We walk out to grab dinner before heading back to the room. Kevin and I spend a relaxing evening talking and watching TV before going to bed. I love when we spend quality time together; it is my absolute favorite thing to do. As much as I love sex, I love spending quality time equally as much. The next morning, I am awakened to the touch of Kevin caressing my breasts. I love the way he caresses my body, he knows all the right places to touch and kiss. It isn't long before he is playing with the kitty. At this point I am wet and feeling tingly inside. Enough of the foreplay, I want to feel him inside me. This morning we got it in, he gave me some good-good in the bed and the shower. I swear morning sex is the best; it has a way of putting you in the best damn mood.

For the next couple of months, Kevin continues to be his normal consistent self. We continue with our weekly Tuesday movie dates along with daily conversations. Life is good with Kevin, and I am trying not to allow the fact that I am still seeing Tony from time to time change things between Kevin and me. It is not easy because we know how good I am at fucking up a good thing.

It is my birthday week; my actual birthday falls on a Monday this year. Kevin and I decided to just keep our regular Tuesday movie date instead of going out on my actual birthday because my daughters always take me to dinner on that day. However, he calls me first thing in the morning on my birthday.

"Happy Birthday, babe!" he exclaimed.

"Thank you, babe!"

"Are you going to work?" he asked.

"Yep, because the girls are taking me to dinner. Plus Alex's school is closer to my office. So Peyton is picking me up and then we are picking up Alex," I explained.

"Cool! Enjoy your day babe and I will call you later."

"Okay, and thank you!"

It's Tuesday so I pick the movie and time then text it to Kevin as I do every Tuesday. Tonight I picked a late movie so that Kevin and I could have dinner first. We sometimes would have dinner before or after our movie dates. I met Kevin at the restaurant and he greeted me with a kiss and another happy birthday wish. He is such a sweet man.

After the movie Kevin walks me to my car like always and then hands me a gift box. I wasn't expecting a birthday gift from him; yes we are dating, but not exclusively. I open the box and it's a really nice gold watch. "Awwww...I love it!" I say to Kevin, and then I give him a big hug and kiss. He is so thoughtful!

Over the next couple of weeks we went to see several really good movies—*Crimson Peak, Steve Jobs,* and *The Intern* just to name a few.

The holidays roll around and I am out doing some Christmas shopping with my girlfriend Britney. She and I have this Christmas tradition where we spend a full day of shopping, going from store to store and from mall to mall. This year I wanted to get Kevin something, but I was unsure of what to get. I knew it was not going to be any shoes because he is a lot like myself and already has plenty of shoes. Britney and I head into Nordstrom's men's department. She is trying to help me find something special for Kevin while shopping for her man too. Finally I come across this super cute leather bomber jacket. It's that really nice soft leather and it has a sweat hood attached. I know it may not sound like it is cute but trust me this jacket is bad. I show it to Britney, she loves it and then I check out the price. I look at Britney and say,"Ohhh, look at this price. No wonder it is so freaking cute!" We both start laughing before she asks if I am going to buy it for him. I contemplate for a brief moment, but I love it and I want him to have it. I don't give it to him until after Christmas on one of our dates. I hand him the bag with his gifts in it at the end of dinner right before I got in my car to leave. I prefer if my friends open their gifts in the comfort of their homes and not in front of me. This is just another one of my weird idiosyncrasies. Kevin calls me when he gets home and he loves the leather jacket along with his other gifts. He was totally surprised and that made me happy!

New Year's Eve is approaching but Kevin has to work an event and I am completely okay with not seeing him, because I am not into spending the holidays with men I am not in a committed relationship with. Plus, I have not introduced him to my daughters yet. I am trying to do better at letting down my guard when it pertains to certain things within my personal life. I am what one would call "a work in progress."

**January 1, 2016**
I receive a call from Kevin. "Hey babe! Happy New Year!"

"Hey honey! Happy New Year to you too!" I replied. "How was your event last night?"

"It went well."

"That's good. What time did you get home?" I asked.

"I don't even remember, because after I was done working I hung out some and went to another bar," he said.      "What did you end up doing?"

"Nothing but Alex had a little get together here at the house. Some of her girlfriends are still here."

Kevin and I continue our conversation for another twenty minutes before getting off the phone.

Right before Kevin's call, I received a text from Rashad and an hour or so after Kevin's call, I received a call from Tony. All wishing me a Happy New Year! This is my life… Lol

Right now I am mainly just dealing with Kevin and Tony. Rashad and I are just cool for the most part. Even though I really like Kevin, it bothers me how much he parties. I cannot lie; it is the one thing holding me back from wanting more with him. Outside of that, he is the perfect guy in his own imperfect way. Nonetheless, Kevin continues to be consistent when it comes to our relationship. He has a weekly commitment on Thursdays and it is near my house, so he usually comes over on Thursday nights to visit with me while killing time too. I always enjoy seeing him because he is so laid-back and we rarely get into arguments. Spending time with him is so refreshing.

It's March 2016 and Kevin is over for one of his Thursday night visits. We're talking and I share with him that I am going to LA in a couple of weeks to take Alex on her "new accepted students visit." It is myself, Peyton, and Kevin standing at the kitchen island in my home. So I get this bright idea to ask Kevin if he wants to come along because Alex has to stay on campus. Plus I hate driving in cities I am unfamiliar with because I am simply the worst when it comes to directions. I am that person who gets lost while using a GPS system. Lol.

Kevin seems to be open to the idea of traveling with me to LA. Peyton asks him to please go and help me because she worries about me driving by myself in LA. We all laughed. Kevin asks me about dates, so I give all the details and he gets out his phone and looks up flights. He is not able to leave out on the same day that Alex and I are, but will come the following day. Just like that, Kevin purchased his airline tickets and is coming to LA with me. This will be our first official trip together. I am excited to spend time with him while Alex is at her overnight visit. I booked an extra hotel room for Kevin because the last night there Alex will be with us.

A few weeks pass and it is time for our trip. This is a very busy time for me because I scheduled a photo shoot for my new company right before I leave. Cookie is my photographer but we use Kevin's studio to do the shoot. It is not as simple as having all the ladies show up and take pictures, nope, there is so much I have to do in order to have them picture ready. It is the day of the shoot and we get to the studio located in DC at 8:00 in the morning. We go upstairs to the back dressing room of the studio to set up. Peyton is the makeup artist for this shoot, so she gets started on makeup. Kevin is not there to help out with the shoot he was supposed to just be there because we're using his space. However, Cookie had somewhere she needed to be by a certain time, but we weren't done shooting. Thank God Kevin is an amazing photographer and the man I'm sleeping with because he was able to finish the photoshoot for me. Okay, great, that is out the way. Now I just need to pick my photos and provide them to the lady developing my website, but at least that part is complete.

The following weekend Alex has a photoshoot scheduled with Kevin to take her senior pictures. Peyton is there as the makeup artist and big sister. Kevin decided he wanted to take some of her photos outside, so we drive to a location not too far from the studio in DC. After we finish up there we head back to the studio where Kevin continues with Alex's photoshoot.

Days later, Alex and I leave for LA. We arrive to pick up the rental car, check into our hotel and then hit the streets of LA because it is both our first time here. Alex has a list of places and restaurants she wants to try. So she and I check out a few on our own but we wait for Kevin to arrive before we go to the beach and to the mall. The next day Kevin calls, it is early in the morning he is at the airport. He lets me know that he will take an Uber to the hotel so I don't need to come pick him up. Those are the little thoughtful things I love about him. Sometimes it is just the little things that matter. By the time Kevin gets to the hotel, Alex and I are up and dressed.

The three of us hit those LA streets until it is time for us to drop Alex off to the campus for her overnight stay. Actually on the first day of her visit, the university planned a dinner for the parents. So Kevin dropped both Alex and I off to campus. It was good for him to have time to go and do his own thing. Later that night Kevin came back to pick me up, then he and I hung out for a few hours before going back to our hotel room. I was looking forward to some one-on-one spent with Kevin, because he and I had not had sex in over two months. The thing about our relationship is that it is not based around sex. Kevin and I may not have had sex in over two months, but he and I spent a lot of time together during that two month timeframe. He could be having sex with someone else. I wouldn't know and I really don't care.

I asked him once if he is sleeping with anyone else and he said "no," so all I can do is take him at his word.

Now we are back at our room and we are both tired. We take a shower and get ready for bed. Tired or not we are not about to let this moment pass us by. Kevin gets into bed and starts giving me soft kisses on my lips, then my breasts. As he moves his way down my body, he is kissing my stomach and then he starts to eat my kitty. I close my eyes and enjoy the feeling he's providing me with in that moment. I cannot help but to grab his head and grind. I swear this man can eat some pussy. DAMN! I am moaning louder and louder before I cum in his mouth. Kevin then slips on the condom and takes me on another round of screaming his name until I have cum for the second time. If this is what I get for waiting two months to have sex with him...itch, I am going to start going every two months because that dick was on point tonight. We wake up and have a little morning sex before we start our day.

Everything is wonderful, we just had a night and morning filled with amazing sex and now it is time to see LA. Kevin and I go get breakfast then we go pick up Alex from her overnight visit at the university. The three of us spend the day hanging out. Our first stop was Venice Beach; we walked the boardwalk, took pictures, and then stopped at this restaurant for lunch. Kevin orders us a pitcher of frozen margaritas but I can't hang the way I used to so I only have one glass. Well, technically, I only had half a glass because Alex finished my glass. After we left the beach we went to the mall. By this time I could tell that my controlling ways were starting to get to Kevin. But more importantly, he is very stuck in his ways and that was starting to get on my nerves. Needless to say, we both have some issues and were getting on each other's nerves. Lol...

The difference between Kevin and me is that I deal with my issues head on but he harbors his. Kevin is clearly annoyed with me at this point but while at the mall I see these sneakers that I love. I debate whether or not to buy them, because I hate spending a hundred dollars on sneakers that I end up never wearing. Kevin asks me if I want them, and I say yes. So even though he is not feeling me at the moment he still buys me my sneakers. The three of us continued hanging out and making sure to hit all the places Alex wanted to visit. Kevin isn't talking much because he is in his feelings because I'm controlling. I never said I was not controlling, it is the one thing I am always upfront about. However, I have come a long way, because at least now I am able to compromise and I know how to let things go.

Kevin just is not there yet and by the next day he and I are barely speaking. Alex says to me, "Both of you are wrong and both of you are stuck in your ways. Mom, you cannot be mad at Kevin because he thinks you're controlling and he shouldn't be mad at you because you have always been controlling. Y'all need to figure it out because this is silly how you all are barely speaking."

This coming from my then 18-year-old daughter but she is correct in everything she's saying. So I try and make a conscious effort to put everything I am feeling behind us. Later that night I go down to his hotel room and try to initiate make-up sex, but this joker is acting like he is too tired and just needs to take a nap. So I leave it alone, and the next day we leave to come back home. It is strange, because clearly he and I are still in this weird space. I do not like it, so I continue to break the ice between us. Kevin parked at the airport, so Alex and I rode back home with him. He dropped us off, gave me a quick kiss on the lips and then drove off.

A few days go by but Kevin and I are not talking as often as we were. There is something still bothering him about our trip. After a few weeks of the cold shoulder, I call Kevin because we need to talk about this before it goes any further. Of course, Kevin being Kevin, all he says is that "we're cool." That is his favorite thing to say whenever he really is not "cool." I try and let it go because I cannot make this man talk to me. Plus I am still dealing with Tony, so I don't have time to baby Kevin. Weeks goes by without me seeing Kevin and we are only texting here and there. Finally, I reach back out to him in a text.

Gia: Hey, I noticed the change in you since our return from LA. If you are not able to get over whatever you're feeling from that trip, you need to tell me.

Kevin: I'm good. We're good.

Gia: No we are not good. We barely speak and we haven't seen much of each other. I don't know about you but I cannot operate this way. If this is not something you can get past, then we can end it all–– the friendship and the relationship—because I am not about to deal with no half-ass shit with you.

Kevin does not respond. "Okay," I say to myself, "I guess I have my answer." Two days later I finally receive a text from him.

Kevin: Good morning babe!

"Here he go again thinking everything is cool because he gave me space," I think to myself. I do not respond right away because now I am annoyed. So after some time has passed, I receive another text rom Kevin.

Kevin: So you not speaking?

Gia: Hey, how are you? We need to talk.

Kevin: Okay.

Somehow Kevin and I manage to work through our issues, but we are still not seeing each other as much and I am not seeing Tony either because I pushed him away too. I seem to be very good at pushing men away.

# Chapter 9: The Photographer

I go into my next therapy session with that very same thought process. I let Dr. Edwards know that things are not all that great with my love life. I cannot seem to keep it together. I like both Kevin and Tony but I am not sure I want to commit to either. Kevin parties too much and Tony lies too much. They are both nice in their own way, but mainly I am not sure if Kevin and I can really get past my controlling ways. I mean, I do know how to compromise. So it is not like I cannot fix the problem, it is more about do I want to invest any more time into fixing the issues between Kevin and me.

What I love about going to therapy is how great Dr. Edwards is at listening. Yes that is his job, but I also love how he never makes me feel like I am being judged for all the crazy shit I am sharing with him. Anyway, Dr. Edwards tries to help me come up with a game plan moving forward with both men. We shall see how this works out because right now I am going through major drama with Tony, which makes the things I am dealing with Kevin about look like a walk in the park.

A couple of months pass; Kevin and I are back talking on a somewhat regular basis. He comes over to see me, it's a Saturday night. Peyton and Michael are home, so we are all trying to figure out what we want to do. We decide to go grab dinner at Outback and one of Peyton's girlfriends is meeting us there. Dinner is good and the conversation is great! Peyton's girlfriend is going through a breakup so Kevin is giving her some advice. I love when a man can handle himself in any conversation with any group of people. Kevin pays for dinner and we head back to my house. Kevin and I have some amazing sex in the shower before going to bed.

The summer is fastly approaching, and I am on the phone with Kevin and somehow he and I get on the subject of Ocean City. Well to my surprise Kevin tells me that he has never been there. I am in shock because it is only two hours away and he has traveled all over the world but has never gone to Ocean City. So I say to Kevin, "that is unheard of and we need to fix that." He responds "okay."

191

The following week I call Kevin to find out when his next free weekend is because he works most weekends and he tells me he is free the following Saturday which happens to be July 9th. This also happens to be Peyton's birthday but he is in luck because Peyton has plans with Michael and their friends.

I rearrange my Saturday work schedule to accommodate Kevin's rare Saturday off so that we can go to Ocean City for the day. Kevin gets to my house around 11 am. We decided that he would drive, but after a good 45 minutes into the drive I could clearly see that Kevin was tired because he hung out the night before. So we pull over to the next gas stop to get drinks and I take over driving from there. We finally arrive in Ocean City and as soon as we are walking in we hear this voice say. "Hey Kevin!" I swear everywhere we go he knows someone. Kevin goes to give the woman  a hug and introduce us before saying "good seeing you." We walk the boardwalk for a while and  have a few drinks. Then we take a taxi to the outside water bar and there is where we ended our night. Kevin and I had so much fun! I am so happy I got to be the first person to take him someplace he hasn't been. Even though it was just Ocean City because as I stated before "it's the little things that matters most." He and I will always have that, no matter how many times he revisits Ocean City. He will always be reminded that his first time was with me and that is what makes our Ocean City trip so special.

Kevin will always be that man who brings peace and calm into my life. Even when he and I go weeks without seeing each other. Over the next few months I don't spend as much time with Kevin but I always make it a point to talk to him either by text or phone.

We are now in the Fall of 2016 and Kevin and I are still good. We have this uncanny connection that just cannot be broken.

I love the fall; it is the most beautiful time of the year. Plus my birthday month falls under the fall season. This year on my actual birthday I am having a rooftop happy hour at this hotel near my job. I was expecting a nice group of family and friends coming. My close friends from work, my cousins, Cookie, Jasmine, Peyton, Michael, and of course Kevin all were there. Kevin never disappoints, he is always there when I need him most. That is the unbreakable bond I speak of whenever I mention his name to anyone. This is why I so fondly refer to him as "my peace!"

Christmas is right around the corner and everyone knows that is my favorite holiday. I love curling up on the sofa for two months straight watching Christmas movies. Anyone who does not know this about me along with the fact that I love milk and the movie *Grease*, are not real friends of mine. Lol.

All jokes aside, I truly love this holiday. There is just something so magical about it for me. This Christmas Kevin and I decided not to exchange gifts. Well, I decided something different because I wanted to do something special for him. When I took Alex to college back in August, Kevin gave me his credit card to buy her a refrigerator and other things needed. Before Alex left he bought her a pair of sneakers just because he is sweet like that. Kevin is not that guy who does things in order to get something back in return; he does things from the kindness of his heart. Everything about him is so genuine and rare for someone his age. He is way more mature than the men I have been dating. Our conversations are more intense and more stimulating. Yes, I love a man who knows how to fuck me good, but there is nothing like a man who is capable of fucking my mind! And Kevin is that man! He knows how to stimulate your mind and he is selfless. What more could you ask for, and still I find ways to push him away every chance I get.

Yay! Christmas is finally here and I cannot wait to give Kevin his gift. He is going to be so shocked because we are not exchanging gifts this year. I call him to let him know I need to see him because I have something for him. I just want to meet him to give him his gift and because we work right next to one another, I have him meet me in front of my building after work one evening. We hug, give a quick kiss on the lips, I hand him his gift and Kevin says to me "You know you did not need to get me anything."

"I know!" I said. We make a little small talk before saying goodbye.

Later that evening I receive a call from Kevin.

"Are you serious!" he exclaimed. "I cannot believe you bought me this!"

"What are you talking about? It is just a watch," I said.

"Yes, but it is an Apple watch," he said. "I can't believe you did this for me! I love it! Thank you so much!"

"You're welcome! I'm glad you love it. I thought it would be a nice surprise seeing how you recently switched over to the iPhone. Plus, you are always so good to me so I wanted to do something special for you. Something you wouldn't expect."

"Again, thank you!" he said.

"You're so very welcome!"

**January 1, 2017**

Kevin: Happy New Year babe!

Gia: Happy New Year 😲

Kevin: What you doing? Are you still watching Christmas movies?

Gia: Lol...Yes, how did you know?

Kevin: That is all you watch this time of year.

Gia: That is so very true my friend. How was last night, did you work?

Kevin: Yep and it was cool.

Gia: What plans do you have for today?

Kevin: Just chill and get caught up on my shows.

Gia: Okay, call me later.

I am back at my therapy session with Dr. Edwards. Today I want to talk about this weird space I am in with Kevin and our relationship. How do you make something make sense to someone on the outside when you yourself do not quite understand the dynamics between you two?

"At this point in our relationship, I am not certain what we are to each other anymore. I know I am not ready to commit but I also know that I am not ready to walk away," I explained to Dr. Edwards. "So where does that leave us, you ask? Somewhere in the middle." We both laugh.

"Seriously, I am so confused when it comes to this man. I know it is not fair of me to hold on to him, but I feel that we both are holding on to each other. I am sure he is fuckin' other women, even though he tells me otherwise. And do not try and defend him Dr. Edwards," I said half-jokingly. "I think I will continue to go with the flow and see where our relationship takes us."

The weekend is here, and tonight is Jasmine's birthday happy hour at Ruth's Chris Steak House in Crystal City. I am looking forward to laughing it up with my girls. It is always a fun time whenever we get together. I walk in wearing my blue fur coat, jeans, a cream-colored one-piece top, and some pumps. Everyone is there for the most part, but we are still waiting on one or two more ladies to show up. Good food, good fun and pomegranate martinis—what more could a girl ask for!

After I leave dinner, I call Kevin to see if he would like to meet me at my house. He is out and about, but says sure and that he'll call me when he is on his way. I go home shower and get ready for Kevin to come over. It is not long before I receive a call saying he is on his way. Two hours later Kevin pulls up to my house, he showers and is telling me about his day. I am mad tipsy and horny as hell, but I am trying not to be my normal aggressive self. However, that does not last long because I quickly say to him "Come get in the bed, I'm horny and ready to have sex." Kevin laughs and says "Okay!" I start giving him some head because the fastest way to get a man's dick hard is by giving him some good ass head! He loves when I give him head and I love watching his eyes roll back and his toes curl up. But I do not let him cum. Nope, I get on top and I ride him reverse cowgirl style because I want my ass all up in his view. I say to him "Smack that ass like it belongs to you!" It had been a minute since we last had sex, but damn that was well worth the wait.

It's March 2017, and I am on my way to dinner downtown for my girlfriend Nia's birthday. It is a small crowd tonight—only about 7 or 8 of us—but we still have a good time. The food and drinks are amazing. However, while I am at dinner I get a text from Rashad. Now at this point, Rashad and I are legit just fuckin', but not on a consistent basis like before. I use him for dick only, and nothing more. He wants me to meet him at his house, and of course I am down for a fuck session. Especially now because Kevin and I are in this weird place and I am still not speaking to Tony after our big fight. At least with Rashad I know I will never be disappointed sexually.

But before I go meet Rashad, the girls and I walk down to this other restaurant for drinks. We stay there for about an hour; it was nice because they also had music playing. I receive another text from Rashad asking what time I am leaving dinner. I inform him that we are finishing up as we speak. I am having mixed emotions about meeting Rashad, mainly because I hurt my knee again and I am in some serious pain. Hey, but this is the life of a single woman when there is good dick available—you don't say no just because you're in a little bit (or in my case, a lot) of pain. Nope, you pop that pain pill and keep it moving. And off to Rashad's house I go! Lol.

By the time I get to Rashad's house my knee is throbbing, so I have to be strategic with my sexual positions tonight. With that said, there will be no riding because my knees most definitely cannot take that type of friction. I am at Rashad's house, and he is the man that loves foreplay (specifically, head) to get him ready. It is crazy because as much as I love having sex, I have never been one who loved giving head. Rashad is the only reason I do it as much as I do now, and he is the only one of the three who got it on a regular basis. He is also the only man I have ever given head to and swallowed with. I would never tell him because I do not want him thinking he's special. I let Rashad know about my hurt knee so he is gentle with me; there isn't any flipping me all around like he normally would do. Tonight my legs are up high in the sky and I am in some serious knee pain but we still manage to get a good ole' 45 minutes in before falling to sleep. I get up the next morning and go on home.

The next day, out of nowhere, I get a text from Kevin.

Kevin: Hey, what's up?

Gia: Nothing…

Kevin: What you doing?

Gia: Nothing…

I'm sure he  can sense my coldness from my one-word responses, so he calls me. "Hello! You alright?" he asked.

"Yep, I am good," I told him.

"What's up with your responses?" he prodded.

"I don't know what you mean; I am giving you the same cold treatment you've been giving me," I retorted.

"Gia, I don't know what you're talking about."

"Okay, Kevin, if you say so."

"Why do you always try and make something out of nothing?" he asked.

"That's right, Kevin, I am just making this shit up in my head. But tell me this—when was the last time we saw each other?"

"I don't know..."

"My point exactly!" I exclaimed. "It's all good Kevin; I am going to always meet you right wherever you are. So if you want to go MIA, so be it; I will go MIA with you. I am not about to play games with you. I don't even know who you are anymore. I am assuming you're seeing someone otherwise your behavior does not make any sense."

"Gia, there you go, you always think it is about another woman," he retorted. "I have been working a lot and just chilling. I am not seeing anyone, and I am not having sex with anyone."

"Okay, Kevin; if you say so."

"I will give you a call tomorrow," he said defeatedly.

"Okay, Kevin. Bye."

For the next few months, I see Kevin maybe once, but we have been talking and texting.

It is now Father's Day, so I give Kevin a call.
"Hey! Happy Father's Day!"

"Thank you!" he replied.

"How are you?" I inquired.

"I'm good."

"So what are you going to do today?" I continued.

"Nothing."

"What, you don't have plans with your kids?"

"Nah, I am just chillin' in the house right now," he said.

"Okay, well do you want to go get dinner?" I asked.

"Sure!"

"Okay, I am going to get dressed and come to your house. I will call you when I am on my way."

I get to Kevin's house and I take him to this nice restaurant off Wisconsin Ave NW in DC. Kevin has never been here before, which is shocking. We have a great time with food and drinks. After dinner we go back to Kevin's place, sit in the car and talk for a few minutes, kiss, and say goodbye. Kevin jokingly mentioned sex, but I was not taking the lead this time. If he wants to have sex he is going to have to ask me for it, because I am not about to make it easy for him.

Honestly, I do not know how Kevin and I got to this weird place we are in right now. Yes, he has been reaching out more but I am just not feeling his vibe right now, so I keep him at bay. Again, I know that I am not ready to completely end things with him but I also feel like he needs to figure some things out—or maybe it is me who needs to figure out what I want. I am sure Kevin is not going to continue to sit around and wait for me to say I want more. He is not that man who is going to make the first move toward a commitment. However, I know if I go to him and say I want more, he would give me more. I am just torn right now.

**August 3, 2017**

Kevin and I seem to be on  good speaking terms for now. So I ask if he would like to go with me to take Alex back to school, and promise him he won't have to drive me around.

Kevin: How long you gone for and how much are the flights?

Gia: I am coming back on Monday. Tickets are $340 plus hotel.

Kevin: I am not sure.

Gia: Are you at least thinking about it?

Kevin: Yes.

Gia: Okay, I am going to get my tickets this weekend but by Monday at the very latest.

Kevin: Okay.

A few days later I text Kevin -
Gia - Morning honey!
Kevin - Morning babe!

Later that evening I shoot Kevin another text because he is leaving town for work.

Gia - Hey, did you get to Miami okay? Call me later.
Kevin - In the air now.
Gia - Okay 😲

A few days go by and we have been speaking regularly. But it's now August 8th and I need to know if Kevin is going to Cali with me or not. So I send him a text.

Gia: Hey, are you coming to Cali with me?
Kevin: I really wish I could maybe later in the year. I don't have the leave right now.
Gia: Okay! I am not happy but I understand.
Kevin. Thanks babe!

**August 12, 2017**

I am revamping my website, so I schedule a photoshoot with Kevin at his studio in D.C. Prior to the shoot, Kevin has been acting strange; either not responding to my text messages or responding late. I ask if he is seeing anyone because it isn't like him not to respond to me or not answer the phone when I call. Kevin tells me "No, and there you go thinking it is about another female." I say okay and let it go, but my gut is telling me otherwise. We are at the studio; Kevin is doing what he does and looking so freakin' cute. I just love watching him shoot. I especially love it when he turns his baseball cap to the back and gets real low. I swear watching him work turns me on! At the end of the shoot Kevin and I are talking. I thank him for doing the shoot and give him a couple of wet kisses before packing up to leave.

**August 16, 2017**

It's late in the evening, around 9 pm, but I have been thinking about Kevin so I give him a call.

He doesn't answer, so I send him a text because I am pretty sure he sent me to voicemail.

Gia: I am pretty sure you pushed me to voicemail but okay.

Kevin: I am at the bar and you wouldn't hear me.

Gia: Okay.

Kevin: What you doing? I want to see you. I want to have sex.

Gia: Oh really! You would pick tonight of all nights to ask for sex.

Kevin: Are you busy?

Gia: Not really, just helping Alex pack. Call me when you leave the bar, so I know you're on your way.

Kevin: Okay.

It's hard to believe it is fall already. Where does the time go and why won't it just keep still. I have so much going on with my schedule, it is crazy. The next few months are going to be super busy. I am in the process of starting a new show and I have so many birthdays coming up. First on the list is Angie's, and this year she is having a rooftop party. It's different because we all are wearing headphones, with different music playing. It is my first time here, but I am feeling the vibe and we all have a good time.

It is a cool September afternoon and I am pulling up to my therapy session. I finally find parking and am now in Dr. Edwards' office.

# Chapter 9: The Photographer

Today I am sharing with him how distant Kevin has been acting towards me lately.

"Kevin and I talk, but mostly via text, which is unusual for us. I continue to ask him if he is seeing anyone special or in general, and he continues to tell me that he isn't. But his actions do not match his words. We have only been talking via text. So I said to him 'Let's just end all communication between us, since you don't seem to have time anymore.' He says that that's not what he wants, but I don't know what else to do. Honestly, I am going to push back by not responding to him when he reaches out to me. I am not here for convenience; you know I am not that girl."

I go on to say to Dr. Edwards, "Have you ever met someone and the potential for a great relationship is there, but you won't or can't let go of whatever it is you are fighting against within? That is me with Kevin, I know he is an amazing soul but I am just not ready. I often wonder if my pushing Kevin away had anything to do with my relationship with Tony. I also saw the potential in Tony as well. However, I am a firm believer that you cannot date someone's potential. You have to meet them where they are, in their walk at that moment. So for now, Kevin is still very much so into the club scene and I am too old for that lifestyle. Maybe Kevin should date someone closer to his age who also likes going to the clubs still. I don't know, but I do know Kevin and I need to figure out why we are both afraid of letting go."

The next birthday up is mine! I decided to go to the rooftop again since my birthday falls on a weekday. Kevin won't be able to make it because he is out of town for work. It is cool because I am also planning brunch on Sunday. Kevin gets back in town on Saturday and said he will be at brunch on Sunday. However, the morning of my brunch, I receive a call from Kevin saying he has to go pick up his son and won't make it to brunch. I say "okay" because I understand that your children come first.

For the next few weeks Kevin and I talk a little more and he is calling a little more, but it is still not at all on the same level as before. I don't feed into it anymore because I have a lot going on with my new show. Therefore, I need to focus my time and energy on building my brand and my business.

In one of my conversations with Kevin, he mentioned how he was thinking about taking a break from teaching. I thought it was a great idea only because he works so much. To my surprise, in a recent conversation with Kevin he tells me he has a new class starting. I swear he is a workaholic! A few days later I go on Facebook to catch up and to kill time. I have not been on for months. I am on my timeline and there are some picture of Kevin and a female. It appears she tagged him in the pictures. So I click on his page and there are several pictures of the two of them, and I am pissed. Kevin is a photographer therefore he posts pictures with women all the time and they have never bothered me. However, there is something different about the body language between these two in these pictures.

I send Kevin a text, because if you have questions, the best person to give you the answer is the source.

Gia: Hey! Are you dating someone? I know we haven't been talking daily and I am hardly ever on FB. So maybe I missed something or a conversation. I don't know…

NOTHING. Not one word from Kevin. I call him and he tells me he is on the metro and will call me back. I allow a couple of hours to pass and still NOTHING; no return call. I send Kevin a text because I already know he is not going to answer my call.

Gia: I thought we were friends. I would never allow you to find out I was in a relationship through social media! I guess I have more respect for you than you have for me.

Chapter 9: The Photographer

Kevin: Stop it!

Gia: Do not say "stop it" to me like I am your child or as if I said something wrong. You "stop it." I am entitled to think it is shady that you did not tell me!

Kevin: It is not shady, Gia

Gia: Okay Kevin! You are entitled to feel however you feel. Clearly you and I do not see eye-to-eye on this. And you just answered my question. So take care and I wish you well.

Kevin: You and I will talk.

I stop responding to Kevin's texts. The next morning I wake up to a text from Kevin.

Kevin: Good morning.

Gia: Morning.

Kevin: What you doing?

Gia: Getting ready for work. What are you doing?

Kevin: Getting something to eat. I am going out to VA to do some modeling stuff I am trying to get into.

Gia: Cool and good luck!

Kevin: Thanks.

A few days go by and Kevin has yet to acknowledge my ending our friendship or him being in a new relationship. I guess we are pretending it isn't real and that I will stop asking and it will just go away? It won't! I want to hear him say he is dating someone. So I text him.

Gia: Gm Kevin, so what we are not about to do is pretend I did not see those pics on FB or that you have yet to have a conversation with me. But it is what it is at this point. I think it was wrong of you allowing me to find out over FB. I am sure you gave no thought to how I would take seeing that. You and I clearly do not have the same level of respect for one another. Oh, and I have decided to unfollow you for a while. I do not want to see pics that she has tagged you in every time I go on FB.

Kevin: You do not see pics. You trippin. I said we will talk.

Gia: I know you did. I am not trippin, Kevin. I am not mad either!

Kevin: So, what is the problem?

Gia: It is because of how I found out! That is the problem.

Kevin: Nothing on my page says she is my girlfriend. I have had many pics with women; why does this one bother you?

Gia: I am not dumb, Kevin, I can tell the difference between a "hanging out" pic and a pic with someone you are dating! The body language is completely different.

Of course Kevin stops responding. Oh, but he calls me later that evening when he got off work. He still won't admit to dating, but tells me we are going to talk. He asks if I could just give him some time because he is packing and trying to move. I say okay.

A week turned into several weeks. It is clear Kevin is doing his best to avoid me at all costs. I take a step back; listen, the damage has been done at this point. If it were nothing, he would have said that instead of avoiding the question. I am not calling or texting him but he has sent me a couple of random "gm" texts. I am not feeling him or his texts. If he cannot have a conversation with me, I have nothing to say to him. I am deserving of at least a conversation. Hell, we have been dating for almost three years!

Weeks pass and more pictures surface on FB because she apparently likes to tag him in every picture. Maybe this is her way of letting other women know they are together. I don't understand this concept but I am a super private person, so different strokes for different folks.

Now I am angry, and there is clearly something more between them. There is no way he is only running into her every time he goes to the club. I am pissed off, but do I want to call or text him? I decide to send him a text.

Gia: Kevin, I no longer want to have a conversation with you. I am over this shit, and I have nothing more to say to you. We are no longer friends. I do not want to have anything else to do with you. Don't call me or reach out to me, and I won't call or reach out to you! I am done!

Minutes later Kevin calls and says, "Hey, can we talk? I can come over after work."

Kevin and I are now in my bedroom going back and forth over his new relationship.

"What is it that you want, Gia? Where is all of this coming from? You didn't want a relationship but now, all of a sudden, you want to be with me? This is crazy," he said. "If you want our friendship to be over, that is on you, but it is not what I want."

"Kevin, you are dead wrong about me and my wants. I never said I did not want you or our relationship. I said I was not ready for a commitment and that still has not changed. I always thought that when the time was right you would be there, but I guess I was wrong. So you were with her all these months, while you were still seeing me, kissing me, calling me and at no point, did it dawn on you to tell me about her? I am so confused and angry."

"That is not true," he said. She and I didn't start dating until late August and one day she came to me and said she only wanted to date me. I said, 'okay.'"

"Oh, so just like that you were in a relationship but still didn't see the need to tell me, and
you are going to sit here and try to make me believe you didn't think I would care?" I asked furiously.

At this point I am yelling, but he is just as calm. One thing leads to another, and we were having some wild ass break-up sex on and off the bed! DAMN! I need a cigarette and I don't even smoke! ☺ Needless to say, Kevin and I are still having break-up sex once or sometimes twice a week.

The Christmas holiday is here and it is my favorite time of year! I am out at Walmart looking for a tree for my mom. I remember Kevin telling me he wasn't going to put up a tree this year, and of course that is not ok—it's Christmas! So I pick him up a little pre-lit tree. He sent me a picture once it was up. I also got him the Alexa for his new place.

The following week, I wake up to a "Good morning" text from Kevin, as I do most mornings actually. I texted him back.

Gia: Good morning, Kevin.

Kevin: What you doing?

Gia: Watching Christmas movies. Whatcha doing?

Kevin: OMG, you and your Christmas movies. Just got out the shower.

Gia: Oh, so you're naked 👀👀👀

Kevin: Yep

Gia: You are such a tease!

Kevin: Come get you some.

Gia: You offering me some when you are on your way to work? How about you make that offer when we don't have to rush.

Kevin: Lol!
Gia: I thought so because you're a tease, Kevin.

**January 1, 2018**

– Kevin: Happy New Year, Gia!

– Gia: Happy New Year, Kevin!

Kevin: What you doing?

Gia: Lying in bed.

Kevin: Oh okay, I'm about to make a stop near your house.

Gia: Okay, are you stopping by or are you not by yourself?

Kevin: Lol... I'll stop by. Do I need to stop at the store?

Gia: Lmao... I don't know.

Kevin: Pulling up.

Gia: Okay, park behind Peyton's car because Alex is about to leave with my car.

Kevin: Okay.

Kevin and I continue having our weekly break-up sex until one day we get into an argument because I realized that I am still bothered by his relationship and how he allowed me to find out. Sometimes you think you are over something but really you are just harboring it inside. That is where I was with this whole thing. Plus I am not down for being a side-piece for any man. It is one thing to date multiple people because you are free to do so, but it is something completely different when the other person is not fully available to you.

Listen, when or if I EVER decide to become a "kept" woman, it won't be just for some dick that is for sure. So Kevin and I decide we are done having break-up sex. I must admit that only lasted a couple of weeks. Damn, here I am going back on my word. All I am thinking about right now is how will I ever explain this to Dr. Edwards. I am more afraid of telling him about my affair with Kevin than I am about actually having the affair. Lawd, what am I going to do. How long can I go without going to therapy? But before I can talk to Dr. Edwards, I must talk to Kevin about how I am feeling and how I am not about to become a booty call. Kevin hates when I use the term "booty call" or "side-piece" because he swears he has NEVER treated me as such or EVER tried to make me feel like I was either.

**February 2018**

I have been hearing things about Kevin. I heard that he was engaged. I am livid, to say the least. It is funny because I have not seen him in over a week. This is very unusual for him and me.

So I decide to go straight to the source. I text him late one Saturday evening.

Chapter 9: The Photographer

Gia: Wow! I just heard you were about to get married. When were you planning on telling me? After the fact? SMDH… First you let me find out about the relationship on FB! Then you let me hear you are basically engaged through the grapevine! Clearly I mean nothing to you! And clearly there is no respect for me! I am not doing this! Take care, Kevin, and I wish you well with your six month rushed relationship!

On Sunday morning, I receive a response from Kevin.

Kevin: Good morning! Now who told you that?

Gia: Who told me does not matter, but clearly the word has gotten out.

Kevin: I have not told anyone anything.

Gia: Where are they getting it from then, Kevin?

Kevin: I don't know, but if I decide to do that, that is on me.

Gia: What? Okay, I am about to cuss you the fuck out! So I am going to stop this conversation before I say something I cannot take back! Clearly you do not give two fucks! Take care.

Kevin: I do care!

Gia: It's whatever! You're right… It is your decision and it is your life! I guess next I will be hearing that she is pregnant. Again, you don't give two fucks about me. So you are good with the way I keep finding out shit! SMH… Do you Kevin, but I am not about to be your little "booty call" until you get married! So now you can be faithful to the woman you are rushing to marry. Well that is if I am the only one you have been seeing. Who knows with you, you are not the man I thought you were. You want me to pretend as if none of this matters but I cannot do that. And I am not about to keep fuckin' some guy who

211

does not give a fuck about me! So there is absolutely nothing left between us. Now I know why I have not seen you in over a week.

Kevin: Gia, none of what you are saying is true. I do care about you! I am not ducking you and I am not engaged. You told me to tell you if I ever decided to do that. I promised you I would not let you hear anything else from social media or another person. So I don't know why you believe I am engaged when I am not.

Gia: Kevin, I just do not have anything else to say. We are not in a good place. I cannot keep going through this with you.

Kevin: Gia, what are you going through? I am telling you the truth. I would not let you hear from someone else. I am not engaged.

I just stop responding to Kevin. So for the next week or so, he's on top of his "good morning" texts, calls, and FaceTime. He finally convinces me that he is not engaged and promises me he will never allow me to find out anything like that from anyone other than himself. He and I have some amazing make-up/break-up sex! All is good with him, but I am still on the fence. Hey, but for now, the sex is good. I have decided to go with the flow and to take it one day at a time. I cannot allow my emotions to get the best of me. I have to keep Kevin at bay. I have to remain in control of what happens between us and what does not happen.

I know for a fact that Kevin is emotionally invested in his relationship with me. I know that he should probably figure that shit out before he even thinks about taking his relationship with her any further. I will never understand how someone who is not faithful during the dating phase of their relationship could possibly believe that they are ready for marriage. However, Kevin is that guy who would propose out of guilt. But, hey, that is just my opinion! All I know is that I cannot and will not allow whatever Kevin has going on to affect my life. I am in the middle of building a business; therefore, I need to stay focused on that and that alone. Sex with Kevin is just that: sex.

# 10

# Girl Talk
# ***Final Thoughts***

Ladies, let's get into this girl talk. Sometimes we lose sight when it comes to men. We confuse gifts, meals, and the word commitment as loyalty. We tend to make excuses when their WORDS don't match their ACTIONS! Don't forget that you were a BADASS before you met him. His LOVE and FINANCES mean NOTHING if his LOYALTY isn't coming with it! No exceptions!

That's real talk! If I can't have the total package, then leave me alone! I am at a point in my life where I know what I am not willing to settle for simply for the sake of having a man. I believe 100% that there are still a few good men left! I refuse to put pressure on myself and rush into a marriage with a man who isn't capable of being faithful or a man who showed me upfront during the dating phase that he is going to maintain relationships with other women outside of our relationship. At what point do we hold men accountable? It is one thing to openly date multiple people, but it is unnerving to think the man I love, who supposedly loves me, is out here having emotional and sexual relationships with other women.

I learned a long time ago that every relationship is going to teach you something. You will, without a doubt, walk away with some type of lesson learned. God has a way of placing you into situations for which you were ill-prepared, and making it so that you not only survive, but came out on top.

If I have said it once, I have said it a thousand times: we as women have got to do better at holding our men accountable for their actions. Thinking that because this man has chosen you to be "the one" is not enough when his actions are not matching his words. I understand that there is a shortage of men, and on any given day, there are twenty women to every one man. However, this should not mean that women should now settle for a half-ass somewhat faithful man.

Hell nah! The crazy part of all of this is that cheating has become the new faithful, and there are a lot of "faithful" men out here these days. Lying has become the new truth, and at that point, just throw the whole damn man away. What is even crazier is that women all around have accepted this thought process (well, except for throwing the whole man away part)! Lol.

So many people—men and women—are out here living their lives on social media, and most often things are rarely as wonderful as they appear. Ladies, please understand that no matter how much you tag your man, no matter how many hashtags you use to describe how "wonderful" your relationship is, no one is buying what you are selling! Listen ladies, if your relationship was as solid as you try so hard to portray it over social media, there would be no need to publicize it the way you do.

If you know you have a cheating man, but you have to convince yourself that tagging him and/or adding hashtags will make the other women he is cheating with jealous—It won't! No female who is cheating with your man or knows that your man cheats is going to look at your post and think to herself "damn I want what she has for myself!" NO female wants a cheating ass man, and if he is cheating on you, he will cheat on her too. She is not waiting on the sideline for him to leave you; she sees how he is treating you.

Therefore, if you are not going to hold these men accountable, at least stop living your life on social media because you are the one who will start looking insecure and willing to settle just for the sake of having a man. We all have forgiven a cheating man once or twice in our lifetime. However, at some point you have to learn your worth and learn to love yourself more than you love that cheating man. We as women also have to learn patience and know that it is okay to be single and dating. You do not have to settle on the first man who offers you that committed relationship. Ladies, stop rushing and moving so fast; it is okay to take the necessary time needed to actually get to know that man you are willing to give yourself to. Honestly, I am still amazed at how easily it is for men to get keys to your house, and if you're not giving keys you are still allowing them full access to your home within weeks of dating. Hearing how this has become the "new norm"" is mind-blowing to me. That is one thing I will NEVER be able to relate to because I am just not that girl! More power to those of you who are, but it will never be me!

Love is a beautiful thing, if shared with the right person. I believe there are still some good faithful men out there waiting for one of you beautiful ladies, but he will never find you if you are too busy laid up with a fuck boy!

Therefore, I challenge you to embrace whatever life lessons God is throwing your way! Trust and believe you will come out a much stronger woman because of them!

# 11

# The Photographer II

**April 2018**

It's a Friday night and Kevin calls to see where I am because he wants to come over. I tell him I'm on my way home and will meet him there. I had just left the gym, so he and I sit at my kitchen table. I missed him and was happy to see his sweet face. It had been almost two weeks since I last saw him and we never go a week without seeing each other in person. Remember, earlier in the week he was in Miami on travel for work.

An hour or so has gone by (where does the time go?), but I am enjoying catching up on his day. We talked about his birthday brunch he was doing with his family the next day. It was at that point that, for whatever reason, something told me to ask him about the other female he has been seeing. It's crazy, because I never ask about her; mainly, because she has been a non-factor to me. But this night was different. I had a gut feeling that Kevin was not being honest with me. Therefore, I asked the question. "Do you see yourself in something more with her?"

He beat around the bush by answering the question with a question (I hate that shit). "What do mean?" he asked.

I rephrased my question. "Do you plan on taking this relationship with her to a more committed level?"

"Umm, yeah," he said underneath his breath.

And at that very moment his phone rings. "This is her," he said.

"Speak of the devil," I thought to myself. "Okay, so answer it!" I urged him.

"I am not going to answer while I am here," he said.

"Okay! So why are you telling me that it is her calling?"

"I am going to have to go, though," he said.

"Okay, so go!"

At this point I am annoyed, so I say to him, "Kevin, I cannot do this anymore. I am done! I didn't sign up for this shit."

"Why are you done?" he asked.

"I do not understand how we got here, Kevin. You are the only man who has ever brought peace and calm into my life, and here we are, three years later, and I am dealing with this foolishness."

"Gia, I can still be the person who brings peace into your life!"

"No, Kevin, you can't. So figure out what you are doing, or I am done for real. I am not having sex with you anymore until you figure this shit out! I am not some side-piece!"

"I never said you were, and I have never treated you as such!" he said.

"You just did," I said. "If you are seriously trying to have some type of real relationship with her, why don't you try being faithful! I am not playing this game with you anymore!"

"Gia, are you serious right now?" he asked. "Are you saying you don't want to see me anymore?"

"What I am saying, is that I am not having sex with you anymore!"

"Are you serious?"

"Yes, I am done playing this game with you!" I shouted.

"I am not playing any type of game with you, Gia!"

Kevin pulls out a condom from his jacket pocket and tosses it across the table, then tells me "Well I guess we won't need this, huh!"

"Yep, you guessed right," I said.

"You can have it then" he said.

"I don't want your condom!"

"You said we aren't using it so I don't need it. So you can keep it, here."

"Kevin, stop playing with me. I do not want your condom, so stop trying to give it to me!"

"Why are you mad, Gia, when you never said you wanted anything more? Had you said something we would not be having this conversation!"

"I guess for the same reason you never said you wanted anything more, Kevin! I guess neither one of us were open or honest about our feelings!"

"Gia, don't you think that if you had told me about your feelings a year ago things would be different between us?" he asked.

"Maybe, but you and I both know I'm not the only one with feelings that weren't shared," I said.

We get up from the table so that I can walk him to the door. While at the door Kevin says to me, "Please don't be mad because nothing has changed!"

"If you see yourself in a committed relationship with her, then everything has changed," I replied.

"I gotta go, give me a hug," he said.

"No!"

"Why, if you're not mad?"

"I'm not mad, we're good!" I said.

"So give me a hug!" He grabs and pull me close to him for a hug and a quick peck on my forehead.

Five minutes later he calls. "Gia, why didn't you ever say anything about your feelings? How would I have known you wanted more if you never told me?" he asked. "Don't you know by telling me that would have worked in your favor? You don't think things would have been different for us?"

"Listen, I did not feel the need to rush into some type of committed relationship with you," I explained. "I was very secure in what we had; we were happy and in a good place, or so I thought."

"Well I am about to pull up to the house, but we will talk."

"Okay, Kevin! Enjoy your birthday tomorrow with your family!"

The next day is Saturday, April 7th and I get up to start my work day. Even though I am mad at Kevin I know I still need to wish him a happy birthday at some point today. Sometimes it is so hard to stay mad at him because he is so freakin' sweet!

I finish my work day at around 2:00 pm and go into my family room to relax before I get ready for the rest of my Saturday errands. I am sitting on my sofa and decide to go on IG to get caught up and kill some time.

OMG! The very first post I see is a picture of Kevin on one knee proposing to the other woman! For a brief moment my heart stops beating. I literally gasped for air as my phone dropped to the floor and tears filled my eyes! I am in such disbelief! I take a second to gather my thoughts and to get myself together because this shit cannot be happening to me! Whose fucking life am I living right now? This man was just at my house last night and never mentioned proposing to her! This shit cannot be happening. My stomach is in knots and the tears won't stop running down my face.

I pick up the phone and take another look before I call his ass up! But of course he does not answer the phone because I am sure he is celebrating. So I send him a nice little nasty text.

**April 7, 2018**

Gia: How could you do this to me?? Your ass proposed and put that shit on social media? Why would you let me find out this way? HAPPY FUCKIN' BIRTHDAY!

I allow a few minutes to pass before I realize that I am not done saying how I feel.

Gia: YOU SAT YOUR ASS AT MY TABLE LAST NIGHT AND DID NOT SAY ONE FUCKING WORD ABOUT PROPOSING! I HATE YOU!! NEVER SPEAK TO ME AGAIN!

Oh, and you better come clean and tell her the truth too!

Maybe an hour or so goes by before Kevin responds to the many texts I have now flooded his cell phone with.

Kevin: Huh? Come clean?? Didn't you ask me about her last night?

Gia: Yes and NEVER did your ass mention proposing to her. SO FUCK YOU! You let me find out about your engagement over social media! That's some fucked up shit, Kevin! But more importantly, you were going to have sex with me last night and then let me wake up to a picture of you on one knee? Who the fuck does that?

Kevin: No. Nothing was going to happen.

Gia: You are a fucking liar because why else did you pull out the condom, Kevin? Nothing happened because I just got back from the gym and because I had a gut feeling. Plus, it was not until I said I am not having sex with you anymore that you tossed the condom across the table and said "Since we aren't using this tonight, you can keep it!" I hate you and I have nothing more to say! You better tell her the truth!!

Kevin: About what? I'll keep it real with her.

Gia: I HATE YOU! STOP TEXTING ME! You promised that you would never do anything to hurt me! Since I mean so little to you, you cannot ask or tell me what to do about my fucking feelings. I don't owe any loyalty to you.

Kevin: Okay. I'm sorry.

Gia: This situation would not have been so bad had you told me yourself and had I not given you an opportunity last night. The crazy part is that I NEVER EVER ask about her. Once you finally admitted to seeing her months ago, I felt there was no need. But look at how God works! He knew what was about to go down, thus allowing me to open the door for you to tell me about the proposal! Oh, but yo ass still chose to ignore His signs. You still chose the cowardly way out!

Kevin: When you asked about her last night I should have said it. I should have told you.

Gia: You DAMN straight! There is no excuse because not only were you at my house for hours last night, but you talk to me every damn day via texts, phone and/or FaceTime. At no point did you say one word about proposing. Kevin we talked about everything last night including your birthday celebration. So you had plenty of opportunities. But you want me to believe that at no point could you find the words to tell me? Instead you allowed me to find out via social media! This shit is so fucked up!

Kevin: I'm sorry!

I stop texting him and call Cookie, but she doesn't answer, so I send her a text.

Gia: OMG, Kevin just proposed to that girl! I just saw a picture of him on one knee! I can't stop crying.

Thirty minutes later Cookie calls because she saw my missed called but hasn't read my text. She is happy but immediately she can hear from the sound of my voice that something's wrong.

"What's wrong, Gia?" she asked.

"Did you see my text?"

"No, I just saw the missed call. Let me see what it said."

Before I can tell her, she starts reading my text. "OMG! Gia, no, I can't believe Kevin did this," she said. "What was he thinking? I'm in shock. Why wouldn't he tell you?"

"I don't know!" I said. "All I know is that I went on IG and there was a picture of Kevin proposing to the girl!"

"No, are you serious? Nooo Kevin, why would he do this to you and not tell you! I'm so disappointed in him because I gave him way more credit than this," she said. "Out of the three of them, he is the one I liked the most and maybe because he's the one I know the best, or maybe it's because I'm actually friends with him! He's such a good guy; I'm just in shock right now."

"I know, Cookie, I feel the same way. The really fucked up part is that he was at my house last night!"

"No...Gia, you are lying…Did y'all have sex?"

"No, but not because he didn't want to; but because I wouldn't. It's crazy because I never ask about her and for some strange reason I did last night! Something on my spirit was telling me to ask about her and I guess this is why. So even though I opened that door for him, his ass never said one fucking word about proposing to her! I'm so hurt right now and of course he's not answering his phone."

"Oh my God…"

"But Cookie, the hurtful part isn't that he proposed to her! The hurtful part is that he didn't tell me and allowed me to find out over social media! I told him months ago when I realized he was seeing her to never let me find out anything else about their relationship over social media! And if he decided he wanted to take his relationship with her further, to tell me in person."

"I know you did, but he probably didn't know how to tell you or probably didn't want to hurt you," Cookie said.

"Allowing me to see this over social media was way more painful than it would have been hearing him say the words!"

"Oh my God... I am sorry you're hurting," she said. "I am on my way to your house right now. I can be there in 20 minutes!"

Once she arrives, she gives me a hug and I start crying all over again. We are both in shock because this is not Kevin's normal character. Cookie keeps repeating how in shock she is because he is such a nice guy. Then she goes on to say, "But this is what happens when you put someone on a pedestal. You have always referred to Kevin as your 'peace' and you have always maintained how different he is from the others. None of this is your fault, I am just saying you thought so highly of him and here we are looking at a picture of him proposing to another woman."

"Cookie, I would have bet any amount of money on him never hurting me! It goes to show that you never really know someone as well as you think. I will never fully be able to put into words how devastating it was seeing that picture. No one will ever understand the pain or the betrayal I am feeling right now."

"I know, but it is going to be okay. I am so mad with Kevin right now for doing this to you!" Cookie said.

Later that evening Kevin kept trying to call me, but I'm not taking his calls. I can't hear his voice right now and I do not want to hear what he has to say. I am too hurt and too pissed to talk to him right now, so I send him to voicemail. It is amazing how on the day of his engagement he was able to find time to call me. It is funny how once a man thinks he is about to get caught, he will do whatever it takes to prevent the other woman from talking. SMDH

He and I kept going back and forth over text because he is trying to make what he has done to me make sense, but he can't. Nothing he can say will make this craziness make sense to me. Kevin is trying to apologize; he wants me to know how he never meant to hurt me.

He and I continue texting because I still got shit to say.

Gia: Kevin, when your ass made the decision to go buy the ring, you should have told me then! But on some level, I understand your thought process, I do! Oh, because I know you thought about this shit, how could you not! You knew the moment I learned of an engagement I would end our relationship. So you chose to keep it from me. Being the typical man, you wanted to hold on to me for as long as you could. This was so selfish of you and so disappointing! This is not what you do to someone you care about! You obviously did not give two fucks about my feelings!

Kevin: Gia, that is not true. I do care! I'm sorry!

Gia: I don't want your "I'm sorry!"

# 12

# The Prayer

Lord Father God, I give all praise and glory to you on this day, as I do every day. But today Lord, I come with a heavy heart and very much so in need. I just saw something that has changed everything for me. I am asking that you remove anyone who doesn't do me any good. Lord, with tears in my eyes, I ask that you give me the strength to walk away from toxic people and/or toxic relationships. I am writing down this prayer to you and placing it on my prayer wall because something has got to give. Lord, I need some peace and clarity in my life, and I am willing and ready to do whatever it takes. I understand that I play a role in what's acceptable in my life. Lord, this is hard for me because as you know, I do not trust easily, but I opened my heart and allowed myself to trust all three men.

Understanding that no two were the same, and also realizing that I put a lot of trust and faith more so into Kevin versus Rashad and Tony. So here I am sitting in the floor of my prayer closet asking for your guidance, Lord. I don't understand how the one man I thought was sent to provide peace and calm in my life has turned out to be a fraud.

So, Lord I ask that you help me find a way to remove all the pain, hurt, and anger I am feeling towards the three men I let my guard down to be with. The three men whom I allowed into my personal space! Lord, you know me; therefore, you know that was not an easy task. Lord, I know there is a lesson in this somewhere. I also know that you will reveal it to me when the time is right. I know that this too shall pass, but Lord I am hurting right now! What's crazy is that I am more so angry with myself than I am with the men. I know that you don't make mistakes, therefore, each of them were supposed to be a part of my life! I know that they each served a purpose.

Lord, I know I am not supposed to question you or to ask "why me?" But sometimes it is so hard because I truly want to know "why me?" What have I done to be deserving of the type of dishonesty and lack of respect from these men! I know I am going to be ok because I am a very strong woman, with an even stronger faith. Oh, and Lord, I know you got me this time like every other time.

Lord, I thank you for your grace and mercy! I thank you for loving me unconditionally; but Lord I am asking if we can do things a little differently the next time you send a man into my life! Because Lord I don't want just ANY man and will patiently await the right man. I am not that female who just needs to be married for the sake of saying I have a husband. Nah that is not who I am or the woman I seek to become! Lord, you know and understand my heart, my needs and wants.

So, Lord, I pray that the next man who enters my life is a God-fearing man with values and morals. A loving, funny, faithful man who loves himself, is a great father (if he has kids), knows how to lead, is financially secure, sets goals, has dreams and ambitions, and puts family first. A man who will love my daughters as if they were his own, who knows how to be my best friend and my lover, but most importantly, a man who believes with all his being that through you, Lord, all things are possible! So, Lord, until we find THAT MAN, I'm good!

Now Lord, I also accept that there are things I need to do and work on in preparation. I respect the fact that you are not going to send me a man that I am not ready to receive. And Lord, in knowing this, is partially why I started therapy. And I say "partially" because therapy isn't just about getting prepared for a man. It is more about healing and growing through knowledge and understanding. Lord, I don't know what my future holds but I know that, with or without a man, I am  without a shadow of a doubt  covered; and that is really all that matters to me. I know I am not what is perceived as the "norm" (not the normal mom, friend, or lover) and never have been. But Lord, you already knew prior to my conception that I wouldn't be the "norm." Therefore, you continuously showed me through my daily life that I was made for this and that I am special. I was not born to be the "norm!" Nah, not at all! I was born to shake things up, to exceed beyond what was expected of me. To not be put in a box, because my untraditional ways would lead me to greater things. Things that wouldn't necessarily make sense to the outside world. So you made me perfectly flawed, and you continuously showered me with your love and mercy—flaws and all!

Lord I know today's prayer session has been longer than normal, and we've been sitting inside this closet together for well over an hour. But Lord, I needed this; I needed to feel the comfort of your love today more than ever! And though I cannot seem to stop crying as I pray and write to you, for some strange reason the tears bring me a sense of comfort in knowing I serve such an amazing and awesome God. I thank you, I love You, and I will continue to give all praise and glory to You. I cannot thank you enough for loving and guiding me.

All these things,  I pray to you in Jesus name! Amen!

# 13

# The Photographer III

It is early Sunday morning, April 8, 2018 and my phone rings. It is Kevin. I decided to take his call.

"Yeah, what you doing?" he asked after I answered the phone.

"I am in the bed. What's up, Kevin."

"I hope this isn't you texting her from a random number talking about how I was just having sex with you in February," he said in an accusatory tone.

"What? Wait, someone is texting your fiancé about you?" I asked.

"Yeah!"

"Well it's definitely not me. Let's be clear: If I were going to text her about us, it would not be from some random ass number. You both would know it was me because I would come with proof that you were with me! So do not call me about some bullshit."

"Well, I have no idea who it could be" Kevin said.

"It's whoever the fuck you were fuckin' back in February!" I screamed. "This is even more fucked up!"

"But that is what I am saying. I have no idea who it could be!"

"How hard can it be to narrow it down? How many people were you fuckin' back in February? Because I asked you if you were

231

sleeping with anyone other than the two of us, and according to you, she and I were the only two. So I am assuming that was a lie too? Why the fuck you lie?"

"I didn't lie; I swear this person is lying because I haven't slept with anyone else. Whoever she is, she told her that we met a year ago when I did her edits," he said.

"So, what; you just out here fuckin' everybody whose edits you work on? This shit is crazy and what did you really think would happen when you put your proposal all over social media knowing you're not living right? You can't play around with people's feelings. You just proposed to someone who has her personal contact information on social media. So whoever that female is, she is obviously pissed and feeling just as betrayed as I am feeling right now."

"I am so mad right now!" he said. "I am telling you I did not have sex with anyone else and if I find out who she is..."

"Why? You are mad at her because she told your fiancé y'all were fuckin'? Are you serious? So you are going to do what to her, Kevin? You cannot be mad at whoever she is for telling your now fiancé' that you were cheating on her. I am sure you'll find a way to talk yourself out of it. I am not sure how though,  because you guys are only 6 months into this relationship; or so you said. Who even knows if that part is true. Hey, but based on what I know, she will forgive you because you guys obviously care about what other people think, or you would not have posted your proposal all over social media. She will forgive you because that's what we do as women when we think we are so in love. We forgive cheating ass men; we make excuses for their actions. We as women tend to overlook the facts especially after we have convinced ourselves that that man is the one. This is the shit that happens when you rush into a relationship with someone you didn't take the time to get to know."

"I don't know if she will forgive me because this female keeps texting her telling her shit," he replied.

"Listen, I don't know what to tell you, but I'm dealing with my own pain from the outcome of this bullshit. So, I'm not about to be that normal listening ear you're use to me being. I'm still trying to deal with the betrayal I am feeling.

Kevin, again, this is what happens when you live your life on social media especially when you know damn well you are not living right. So do not come at me with this bullshit because if I wanted to hurt you for what you have just done to me, we both know I could blow your shit out of the water!"

"But why, Gia?" he asked. "Why would you want to do that? What would you gain from it? Okay, I gotta call you back."

We hang up.

It's Monday, April 9th, and I wake up to a text from Kevin.

Kevin: Good morning!

Gia: Good morning.

Kevin: Gia, I am sorry about everything.

Gia: Kevin, I honestly don't know what to say. I'm hurt and trying to make sense of it all.

Kevin: Wish I could've told you.

Gia: You could have, and you should have! You sat right in front of me and never said a word!

Kevin: Gia, I don't want to go back and forth.

Gia: No worries! I have no intention of going back and forth with you! I will leave you with this.: You had better THANK God that I love you, because I'm angry and feel betrayed. Let me tell you how that's never a good combination and usually there would be hell to pay!

Kevin: Thank you and I am sorry.

A few hours pass and I get another text from Kevin.

Kevin: WYD

Gia: Why are you doing this? What do you want from me, Kevin?

Kevin: I mean we were friends. Once again, I am sorry.

Gia: I am so fucking hurt right now! I can't believe you of all people did this shit. If you think proposing to her so soon knowing you've NEVER been faithful will make you feel better…. IT WON'T!!!

My phone rings; it's Kevin. I send him to voicemail.

I get another text from Kevin.

Kevin: Gia, I just called you. You sent me that text, but you won't answer the phone.

Gia: I don't want to talk to you, Kevin. You need to come clean with her before any more skeletons fall out of your closet. I am sure she will forgive you. Trust me, hearing this is not going to change anything. She will be mad for a minute, but she is not going to end the relationship. Therefore, it is best that you tell her about me as well; because that is not something you want her to find out later.

I am telling you from experience, if the other chick is on the phone giving your fiancé' play by play of your fuck session and she is still looking to you for answers, she is not going anywhere. If this is not a deal breaker for her and she is only 6 months into this relationship with you… Again, she is not going anywhere because clearly she wants a husband. Meanwhile you are out picking up breakfast for the two of you while she is back at home receiving texts from some random chick you fucked back in February. Further confirming the fact that she is not leaving. First, you guys just publicly got engaged over social media, and I am sure she does not want to tell everyone that her new fiancé was cheating on her the entire 6 months. That would be extremely embarrassing; you guys have not been engaged a full 24 hours. On top of that, here you are calling me first thing the morning after.

You knew that was not me texting her because why would I say we fucked once in February? You just wanted to have a reason to call me and for me to tell you everything is going to be okay. But it is not okay, and I am very hurt right now.

Kevin: I don't need this shit right now; I can't handle all of this drama. I swear I don't know who the other female is or why she's telling her that we had sex in February.

Gia: Just STOP IT, Kevin! I don't know what to tell you but I'm dealing with my own pain from the outcome of this bullshit. I can't do this with you! I don't want to hear about your issues with your now "fiancé!" So, I'm not about to be that normal listening ear you're use to me being. I'm still trying to deal with the betrayal I'm feeling. This is your drama, brought on by you, and you alone. This is what happens when men think they can have their cake and eat it too. There are repercussions to getting caught. You want me to care and listen to how this other woman is lying on you, but I believe there is always some truth behind that woman who comes forth with information. I do not understand why you feel it is okay to bring me into this mess.

Especially since I am dealing with my own mess caused by you and your new engagement. You are asking an awful lot of me right now.

Please know that I am not trying to blame you for everything that has happened between us, because I am able to accept my role in all that we have gone through. I accept the fact that I handed you right over to her by pushing you away, by not sharing my feelings, by not verbalizing my wants or needs, and by being unsure of wanting a commitment. However, none of that negates the fact that you did not tell me you were going to propose when you talk to me  every damn day. And none of that negates the fact that you are now engaged. I know you want to hold onto the emotional part of me! I have been down this road before with other men. It was a different scenario but the outcome was the same. Just like you, they wanted to hold onto some part of me. I am not doing this with you; it is not fair to me!

So no, you can't talk this over with me! I am done being your sounding board, your listening ear, the person you are able to talk to about any and everything. So stop It! Stop texting me and stop calling me! Trust, this is not easy for me. This breaks my heart and I am angry with you for putting us in this situation. I trusted you, Kevin! You went from being the only man that brought peace into my life to being no different from the other men!

Kevin: Gia, I can still be that to you. I can still be the peace and calm in your life, which does not have to change.

Gia: No you can't! You are engaged! You are no longer just dating her, Kevin!

For the next few days Kevin continues to reach out to me. If he said "I am sorry" once, he said it a thousand times. But not even a thousand "I'm sorries" will make the pain go away!

He tries to call but I am not feeling him today, so I send him a text. I have things to say and I don't give a shit if what I say hurts his feelings. I am done sugar coating shit for him.

Gia: Why are you moving so fast with her? Do you believe by proposing so soon it will make you feel less guilty?

Kevin: That's not what I'm doing.

Gia: Okay, but people don't cheat during the honeymoon phase or any phase, not when the love is real. So tell yourself whatever helps you sleep at night. I am sure you care about her. Hell, you may even love her on some level. But you are not in love with her or you wouldn't be calling me daily; and you damn well wouldn't be still engaging in sexual activity with me on a regular basis. But whatever, Kevin! It is no longer me who needs convincing.

Kevin: You're wrong Gia!

Gia: Okay Kevin, but no good will come from this marriage. When two people get married for the wrong reasons, that shit never lasts.

Kevin: I am not marrying her for the wrong reasons. We're good!

Gia: You're good, but you were trying to fuck me the night before you got engaged! You're good, but it's hurting you to see me hurt! And there is absolutely nothing abnormal about that shit?

Okay, Kevin! "Be good" and leave me alone! But trust me every time you are over there masturbating because she's barely fuckin' you, it will be my face you are envisioning! I will be the one you are thinking about! The way I ride you, the way I kiss you from head to toe, especially when I give you that good-good that makes– your eyes roll back and your toes curl up. Remember "you're good" when you cannot replace that feeling. Hell, I will even take it one step further because what we shared was never based on sex. It is so much more, we have the type of friendship that is not easily replaced, but if you want me to believe "you're good." I tell you what–prove it! If you really want me to believe you are happily in love, prove it by leaving me alone! Stop reaching out to me because nothing you say will make things better between us! Nothing you say will make the fact that you betrayed me any less painful! For many reasons but I will give you the short list:

1) You made a conscious decision to propose to her and not tell me!

2) You made a conscious decision to buy a ring and not tell me!

3) You made a conscious decision to come see me the night before and STILL NOT TELL ME!

Those are facts and you don't get to erase the facts in order to justify the means!

It blows my mind how people like you think you get to magically erase your past to justify the shady fucked up ass shit you've done! It does not work that way honey, and I am tired of giving out free passes! It is time I hold motherfuckers accountable! I know I said I wasn't angry, but I lied! I am fucking angry and rightfully so!

Kevin: Gia, how many times do I have to say I am sorry?

I stop responding. After a few days pass, I finally accept another one of his phone calls.

"What's up, Kevin," I said, answering the phone.

"You okay?" he asked.

"No! I'm not okay! So tell me Kevin, at what point were you planning on ending things with me? Was it going to be before or after the wedding? Did you really think I would keep seeing you as you continued to grow your relationship with her? Are you on drugs because that shit will never happen!"

"No, it is not like that, Gia."

"Okay, because as much as I love you and will miss you terribly let's be clear, I will ALWAYS love me more. So don't you ever ask me to settle just because you want to hold on to some part of me! I don't have to settle for being a side-piece, and I won't! You men got a lot of damn nerve. I swear you are un-fucking-believable."

"What are you talking about? You are not a side-piece so stop saying that! I never made you feel that way," he said.

"Yes you did, the moment you decided to get on one knee without so much as a warning. It's whatever Kevin, none of that matters now. We can no longer see each other! You cannot have us both!"

"Gia, what are you saying? I am telling you nothing has to change between us."

"Kevin, are you kidding me right now? Everything has changed! How many times do I need to say 'you are engaged?' I am sorry, but I can't do this! IT IS OVER!"

"Gia, what does that mean? Are you saying we can't be friends at all? GIA..."

# 14

# Gia

**M**y life! My terms! My journey! Let's talk. Over the past five years I managed to develop three amazing friendships, which took me on an unexpected whirlwind love fest. What an amazing journey it was. As a bonus, I got to experience some good times, lots of laughter, and some amazing sex. For the first time in my life, I experienced dating multiple men at the same time. I know this concept is nothing new, men and women alike have been dating this way for centuries! However, for me, this way of dating was new and exhilarating! Without a doubt, this was one of the most freeing experiences of my life. With that said, this thing called dating definitely has a few elements to it that made for a very humbling experience for me.

Not many women can honestly say they managed to meet not one but three amazing men within a five-year period. Each of these men brought something different into my life. As well as left me with some valuable life lessons.

Although none of the relationships worked out, again, how many women get to experience love three times over within a five year timeframe? This experience has taught me many things, one of which is that no two men are the same, which is what I loved most about dating them. Yes, you can love more than one person but the love for each will never be on the same level. "Loving" someone and being "in-love" with them are two completely different sets of emotions.

Therefore, my love for each was different, just as my experiences were between the three. Rashad was special to me for many different reasons. For one, I was not seeing anyone when I started dating him, and he was the first man for whom I let down my guard. However, my relationship with Rashad was by far the most difficult because he was my only FWB. His pride would never allow him to own his feelings for me. By "feelings" I don't mean he was "in love" with me; and though I "loved" him, I wasn't "in love" with him. However, we developed a mutual, loving respect for one another. It was hard for me to let go of him, but I did.

Then there was Tony, he started off as an amazing friend, and was so loving and open about his love for me. Which could have been a great thing for us if there were not two sides to this man. To this day, I wish I could ask for the "real" Tony to please stand up. I often wonder if he took me through so many changes because it took him so long to get me. Nonetheless, being with him was a mostly pleasurable experience.

Last, but definitely not least, is Kevin. I will never regret allowing this man into my life. The level of peace, calm, and joy he brought into my life was God sent. I do not regret much about my experiences these past five years, but I do regret pushing Kevin away.

With God working on me through my relationships, I was forced to learn so much about myself, my needs, and my wants. But most importantly, I learned a valuable lesson about deal breakers.

I have always prided myself on my directness and honesty. I was always upfront within my dating life. I never wanted anyone to ever have to wonder where I stood or what I was thinking.

Listen, I am not here to play the blame game because I am able to accept that I was not fully ready to receive their love at the time they were trying to give it. I accept that I am somewhat of a "runner" and

I pushed each of them away in some way, shape or form. This is especially true with Tony and Kevin; I basically handed them right over to the next female. Learning how to check and correct yourself for the role you played in the ending of any type of relationship is not easy It is what I call "growth!" However, let's be clear, just because I accept my role does not negate the fact that they each did things that were hurtful and caused me pain.

Initially, I walked away with a little regret and a few "why me" questions, but after much soul searching, I realize they were all a part of God's plan. God placed them in my life as lessons.

Even though, in my mind, I am this strong soldier with an unbreakable exterior and a heart of steel, in actuality, I am so much more than just that. No matter how tough and guarded I can be, I am also the same girl who is sensitive and loves hard. I had to learn how to balance the two, but that is what therapy is for. Therapy became a great healing tool! It is because of therapy that I am able to walk away in peace and without regret. Love is a beautiful thing, and I refuse to allow a few unsuccessful relationships deter me from ever wanting to experience love again.

However, I will never forget the friendship, love, or pain that came from those relationships. I am a firm believer that everything happens for a reason, and God makes no mistakes—not even when it comes to love or relationships! I will take these experiences and build from them!

I have grown so much! I will continue to be the strong, confident woman I was prior to the hurt. What doesn't kill you can only make you stronger, right?

Therefore, the strong woman that I am constantly evolving to become will do my best to never allow myself to become the woman who is willing to settle for another man who isn't able to be faithful. I will continuously do my best to never waver just for the sake of "having a man." As long as women continue to settle and not hold our men accountable for their actions, our men will continue to think it is ok for their words never to match their actions! So often we as women are afraid of being alone or starting over. It is not okay to cheat, and I am not giving any passes.

My advice to women is make his words match his actions, never fall in love with potential, don't lower your standards, know your worth, and believe ALL red flags—they are red for a reason.

My advice to men is do not seek a commitment you clearly are not ready for! Be honest with your woman regardless of if it is going to hurt her feelings. You see, hearing of your man's infidelities from an outside source is hella painful!

Trust, I'm aware that not all women are where I am in my walk, and more power to those women who are willing to settle, I, on the other hand, want more for my life! Dating multiple people is one thing. Oh, and just because we are only "dating" does not mean you don't have to be honest and upfront. I truly refuse to settle, and if that means remaining single for another five years, I'm good with that!

Listen, I am far from perfect, and I'm not looking for the perfect man because he doesn't exist! But I am ready for my imperfect man who is willing to love me, flaws and all! I don't believe my wanting an honest, healthy, loving, faithful relationship is asking for too much!

I am very protective of my time, my space, and my energy. I do not make getting close to me easy for anyone. So if I allow you into my world, my space, and my heart, do not mess that up because where I am today, I am not about second and third chances. As I enter  this next chapter of my life, I know with certainty what I bring to the table. Therefore, I do not have to settle.

Chapter 14: Gia

Sometimes the unknown is scary simply because you might get hurt. Take me for example: for the first time in years, I took a leap of faith within my personal life. Commitment is hard for me, not because I am incapable of being faithful, but because I put up all types of walls and roadblocks. However, had I not let down my guard, I would not have experienced those three relationships. Yes, I got hurt; but in the end, I do not regret the experience. Those experiences taught me that life can be hard, and commitment can be even harder, but sometimes you have to let go and just live in the moment.

Going through the ups and downs of those relationships, I discovered exactly who I am as a woman, mother, friend and lover.

Life isn't always easy, but you have to live to learn to love.

Therefore, until I meet the man that I am meant to spend a lifetime with, who is also God sent, I will continue to walk within my truth as a single woman. I will continue to demand respect, consistency, loyalty, communication, and honesty from any man wanting my time and/or my love. Most importantly, I will continue to be simply and unapologetically Gia ♥

# *About the Author*

LB Taylor the Author is more than just a writer; she is a mother, a daughter, a sister, a friend, a career woman, and an entrepreneur. A powerhouse in her own right, LB Taylor uses her life experiences to guide her podcast series "Love/Sex/and Lies....let's talk!" It was only a matter of time before she channeled her creativity to become an author that develops captivating stories with complex characters.

LB Taylor adds true authenticity to each character and storyline to create a powerful space that draws in each reader. Line by line, you are forced to see yourself in her character's life by reflecting on past experiences you may have endured. With her "coffee shop conversation vibe" she expertly weaves in her debut novel, LB Taylor is the friend in your head that you want to talk to again and again.

For more information about LB Taylor, visit www.lbtaylor.com

www.ingramcontent.com/pod-product-compliance
Lightning Source LLC
Chambersburg PA
CBHW070222030726
47505CB00006B/1778